JUST CAN'T GET ENOUGH

"So, this is how the night ends?"

"What were you expecting, Darius McRae?" Celina asked, her voice like a midnight tease.

Darius stood up and walked over to her. He didn't care if it was too soon. He had to taste her lips. "This," he said as he captured her mouth with his.

Darius's swift move caught her off guard. But what surprised her more than anything was the way she responded to his kiss, melting against him as she rose to her feet to fully lose herself in it. She parted her lips and welcomed his tongue into her mouth. It was as if his kiss had awakened every repressed desire she'd ever had. No one had ever made her knees quake or her heart shiver the way Darius had with one kiss.

JUST CAN'T
GET ENOUGH

CHERIS HODGES

Kensington Publishing Corp.
http://www.kensingtonbooks.com

DAFINA BOOKS are published by

Kensington Publishing Corp.
850 Third Avenue
New York, NY 10022

All Kensington Titles, Imprints, and Distributed Lines are available at special quantity discounts for bulk purchases for sales promotions, premiums, fund-raising, and educational or institutional use. Special book excerpts or customized printings can also be created to fit specific needs. For details, write or phone the office of the Kensington special sales manager: Kensington Publishing Corp., 850 Third Avenue, New York, NY 10022, attn: Special Sales Department, Phone: 1-800-221-2647.

Dafina and the Dafina logo Reg. U.S. Pat. & TM Off.

ISBN-13: 978-0-7582-1975-6
ISBN-10: 0-7582-1975-X

First mass market printing: August 2007

10 9 8 7 6 5 4 3 2 1

Printed in the United States of America

PROLOGUE

Elmore, South Carolina

Eight-year-old Celina Hart tried not to eavesdrop, but her parents were arguing so loud that she couldn't help it.

"Who is she Thomas?" Rena, Celina's mother, yelled. "It doesn't even matter because I'm sick of this!"

"Woman, just calm down. It's not what you think and I get sick of coming in this house every night defending myself to you."

Slowly, Celina crept from her bed and walked down the hall and stood outside the door of her parents' bedroom. Through the crack in the door, she watched her mother grab a big blue suitcase.

Thomas rolled his eyes. "You think you're gonna put me out of my own house?" he demanded with his arms folded across his chest.

Rena dropped the suitcase on the bed. "You can have this damned house, Thomas. This whole town looks at me like I'm some sort of fool because you're running around with that woman as if you're a single man without a family. How many women in church on the usher's board with me have been in your bed?"

Thomas shook his head. "Don't start this again. I made a mistake and you're holding on to it like a dog with a bone."

"You're my husband, Thomas, not my boyfriend. You made a commitment to me and our child. I want a divorce."

He laughed and watched as Rena began haphazardly stuffing her clothes into the suitcase. "Where are you going to go? You've never been farther than Columbia, South Carolina. What about Celina? What about all the friends she has here? You're going to just uproot her because you're mad at me?"

Rena stopped packing and glared at Thomas. "When's the last time you've been a real father to that girl? On the rare occasion when you *are* at home, you play with her like you're a damned eight-year-old."

"I'm encouraging her love for art. That little girl has talent. A lot more talent than—"

"Shut up!" Rena roared. "It's just easier for you to play with her than to be a father. It's better when I'm the bad guy, right? I'm the one who makes her clean up the paint, come inside when it gets dark or care for her when she falls in a ditch and cuts her arm. I can be unhappy without you and, as I've been doing, I can raise Celina without you."

"Then leave," he said, flatly. "I am who I am and that won't be changing no time soon." Thomas reached into his pocket and pulled out a cigar.

"Don't you dare light that thing in here," she snapped.

"You're leaving, so why does it matter?" He bit down on the end of the cigar as he felt his pockets for his lighter.

Rena shook her head and began sobbing. "You don't

even care if we leave, do you? I thought this would be your wake up call and you would love me like you vowed to do."

"I love you, Rena," Thomas said as he spat the cigar to the floor. "I can't excuse what I do. I've tried to do the devoted husband thing. I've spent my youth being a husband and a father and I guess I wasn't ready for all of this."

"Then you should've never married me. It's been ten years and now you decide after we've started our family to say this was a mistake? You go straight to hell, Thomas Hart!" Rena continued packing. "Celina and I are going to Chicago."

"Chicago? What are you going to do there? You're barely working here and you're going to be able to make a life for you and my little girl?" Thomas shook his head.

Celina's eyes grew wide from fear. She didn't want to leave Elmore and all of her friends. She'd just been awarded a first place ribbon for a picture that she drew in the Elmore Elementary School art competition.

Creeping down the hall, Celina silently prayed that she was in the middle of a nightmare. Chicago was a big scary place and she didn't want to go there. Elmore was her home and her parents couldn't get a divorce. Could they?

The next morning, Celina realized that the night before wasn't a nightmare. Her mother entered her room with red rimmed eyes and that suitcase. Celina tried to pretend that she was asleep, but Rena shook her shoulder until Celina opened her eyes.

"Mommy, it's Saturday. I want to sleep," Celina said.

"I know, but we're going on a trip," Rena said, smiling though her tears.

"I don't want to go."

Rena frowned. "Neither do I, but we have to leave."

Celina looked up at her mother with tears shining in her young eyes. "Did I do something wrong? I promise I won't get paint on the floor anymore. Please don't leave Daddy."

Rena wrapped her arms around Celina, hugging her tightly and rocking back and forth. "Sometimes, we have to do things that we don't always want to do."

"But, don't you love Daddy anymore?" Tears ran down her cheeks like rain.

Rena wiped her daughter's tears away with the edge of the sheet. "Sometimes, love is not enough."

Sniffing, Celina defiantly said, "I'm never going to fall in love!"

Rena pulled her daughter's covers back. "Don't say that. You have a bright future ahead of you and you don't know what's in store. Now, get out of the bed and help me get your things together."

"Are we going to at least tell Daddy good-bye?" Celina asked as she climbed out of the bed.

"Well, if your father gets here before we leave, then yes. Otherwise, we'll call him when we get to Chicago," Rena said.

Celina began gathering her favorite toys as her mother packed her clothes. Then she spied her water-color set that her father had given her a few weeks prior. She wrapped it in her Barbie pillow case and stuffed it in the bag with her dolls.

A few hours later, Celina and her mother were climbing into the family's Buick and headed down to the Elmore bus depot. As they drove, Celina looked for her father's beat-up Ford truck. She never saw it.

Rena parked the car and left the keys in the ignition. "Mommy," Celina said. "What are you going to do with the car?"

"Someone will tell your father where to find it, I'm

sure," Rena said as she lifted their suitcases from the backseat of the car. She handed Celina a couple of small bags for her to carry. "Keep your head up and come on," Rena said as she noticed people staring at her.

Celina heard a few women who were walking by say, "About time," or "He'd be the one getting on the bus."

That day, Celina was proud of her mother. She ignored it all and walked like a queen as she carried those bags. But even as an eight-year-old, she promised herself that she'd never find herself in this predicament because love wasn't enough.

CHAPTER 1

Paris, France, Twenty Years Later

The crisp smell of roasted coffee beans wafted through the air, tickling Celina Hart's nostrils. Mornings in Paris had become her favorite time of the day. As the sun cast a golden glow over the city, shopkeepers lazily swept their storefronts, preparing for the throngs of tourists who would flock to the outdoor cafés as soon as the noon sun rose high in the sky. Celina liked to blend in with the locals and rise early. Blending in wasn't easy, though. Her French was more than a little rough, since she'd only been speaking the language for a short time.

Celina was one of the few American artists who had been chosen to take part in the celebration of Hector Guimard. Her trendy work that hung in some of New York's most popular galleries and the mural she'd created in Harlem featuring Zora Neale Hurston had caught the eye of the right people. But Celina knew it was Bill Clinton that had gotten her to Paris. When the former president commissioned Celina to paint a portrait for his Harlem office, she had been fast tracked as a hot artist to watch. And the world was watching, much to the dismay of her mother, Rena Malcolm, who would've been content to have her daughter stay in one place and teach art.

Celina had tried it and it didn't work out for her. She had to move and see the world. That's just what her art allowed her to do.

Dressed in a pair of white capri pants and a pink tank top, Celina headed for what had become her favorite table at Café de la Paix. It sat on the end of the rows of tables, nearest to the road. She watched as the city began to come alive and Paris visitors spilled onto the streets seeking coffee before they began a day of sightseeing and a night of partying.

"Bonjour, mademoiselle," the slim waiter said as he set a steaming cup of café au lait in front of her. Every day for the last two months, the same raven-haired waiter had been serving her coffee and a chocolate croissant.

"Bonjour," she replied through her smile.

"Croissant?" He held an ivory plate out to her with a flaky piece of bread on it.

She shook her head no as she blew on the steaming cup and stifled a yawn. The waiter nodded and walked away. Celina reached into her brown saddlebag, retrieved her sketch pad and began drawing the landscape, its rolling hills and flat-top cafés. Some people drank coffee and read the newspaper, but she sipped java and drew. Since being in Paris, she'd been inspired. Celina was never one to draw landscapes, but how could she not commit Paris to paper? Though she was enjoying her work inside Castel Beranger, she hated that the morning was the only time she saw the outdoors. Her mural was nearly finished and there was talk of her creating ones in some other places around the city.

By the time she finished her sketch, the café was filled

with sleepy tourists speaking in broken French and sucking down black coffee.

Reluctantly, she put her pad away when she realized that another reason she had gotten up so early was to beat the rush at the American Express. She dropped her colorful money on the table to cover the cost of her coffee, then headed down the block. Her stomach rumbled as she sniffed the fragrance of bread wafting through the air. Paris was no place for a low-carbohydrate dieter and Celina was glad she didn't deal with fad diets. She kept her svelte figure by running three miles a day and maintaining a healthy obsession with martial arts. Her mother had suggested that she learn how to protect herself when she moved to New York. Celina enjoyed karate; it stimulated her creativity and kept her edgy. She hadn't been able to find a karate class since she'd been in Paris. Celina walked into the post office, known as the American Express, to pick up what she was sure was a letter from her mother and to cash in some more money.

"*Bonjour*, mademoiselle," the postal clerk said, smiling at Celina. She returned his greeting. The man opened her box and handed her a stack of mail.

"*Merci*," she said as she took the mail from his hands. Flipping through the letters that followed her from New York, she stopped when she spied a South Carolina postmark. The shaky handwriting on the front of the wrinkled white envelope was unmistakably Thomas's. Celina dumped her other mail in her bag and ripped her father's letter open.

Baby, I'm sick. The words stabbed her in the heart. She continued reading, fighting the tears welling up in her eyes.

I don't mean to dump all of this on you while you're in Paris, but I need you more than I've ever needed anyone before. It may not be fair for me to ask this of you, but I want to spend time

with you before it's too late. Your mother tells me you're quite the
artist and that you're spending the year in Paris.

I'm so proud of you and I wouldn't ask this of you if it wasn't
important.

Celina's breath caught in her chest and the tears fell
from her eyes. She couldn't remember the last time
she'd talked to him, since they hadn't been close after
her parents' divorce nearly twenty years ago. Celina had
only been eight at the time and she'd never quite forgiven him for letting them leave Elmore, South Carolina, all those years ago. His eye for other women had
led to the demise of his marriage.

While Celina was growing up, Thomas did his best to
be a good father, spending every holiday, summer vaca-
tion, and school break with his daughter. Rena had re-
married two years after she and Celina settled in Chicago.
John Malcolm had been a good stepfather, never trying
to take Thomas's place in her heart. It had happened
anyway. Thomas had taken on the role as a distant uncle
to Celina, but John was her father figure—the one who
did the heavy lifting, like doling out discipline and other
things that fathers were supposed to do.

Still, Thomas was family and she knew what she had to
do. Celina ran out of the American Express in search of
her boss, Monsieur DuPont.

Celina walked into Le Palais Garnier, the old opera
house where the Foundation's headquarters was housed.
Monsieur DuPont had set up an office in the basement
of the historic building. Dashing down the rickety stairs,
she frantically knocked on the man's door.

"Ah, Mademoiselle Hart, what can I do for you?" he
asked when he looked up and saw Celina standing in

front of his desk. "Your mural is shaping up very nicely. I love your style."

"I have to leave," she said, her voice shaky and barely above a whisper.

Monsieur DuPont offered Celina a seat when he noticed the paleness of her face.

"What's wrong?" he asked as he buzzed his assistant. "Did something happen stateside?"

Celina tried to form the words to tell the art director why she was throwing away one of the biggest opportunities of her career. "Um, my father is . . ." Her voice trailed off. Should she go home to her father? Where was he during the last twenty years of her life? When she'd been sick, it had been her mother and her stepfather, John, who'd cared for her and comforted her. Thomas had only been around when it suited him to be or when he'd been expected to be around. Why couldn't he have been a better husband? Then he and Rena would've still been together and she could've taken care of him.

Celina felt like a bitter twelve-year-old as those thoughts floated around her head. She didn't realize she still harbored resentment over her parents' divorce. She was a well-adjusted adult and she had no thoughts of her parents someday reconciling. But, like every other child of divorce, subconsciously she wanted mommy and daddy together.

"Your father is—?" Monsieur DuPont asked, then he spoke in French to his assistant, asking her to bring water in for Celina.

"Dying." The word spilled from her lips like a rancid sip of milk. "I have to be with him and I know . . ." Tears began spilling down her cheeks like a summer rainstorm.

"Mademoiselle, I understand. If you must leave, you

must. Your work here has been wonderful and you will be welcomed back in the future." Monsieur DuPont walked over to the chair where Celina sat sobbing. Her eyes looked like wet black diamonds as she looked up at him. He placed his hand on Celina's shoulder and stroked her gently. "Family is very important. I understand that you have to leave."

She nodded and, in the back of her mind, wondered how often she had taken her family for granted. Celina hadn't seen her father in two years and she hadn't made a huge effort to talk to him before she left the country. It was past time for her to go to South Carolina and spend time with him. She had to forgive Thomas and allow him into her life in a more significant way before it was too late. And if his letter was any indication, the clock was about to strike midnight.

CHAPTER 2

Everything seemed to move at light speed after Celina received her father's letter. Two days after she announced that she was leaving, she was in a rental car turning down Drivel Drive in Elmore, South Carolina, her birthplace.

Elmore was a quaint little town an hour away from the state capital. Other than the azalea bushes, there wasn't much going on in Elmore. Many of the people who lived in the town were retirees or lifers, folk who had never gone farther than Columbia.

The moment Celina's plane touched down in Columbia, she'd called Rena and told her about Thomas's letter. She heard her mother gasp over the phone when she told her that her father was dying.

"I'm glad you're going to him. I thought something was going on when he called and asked for your address," Rena had said. "He needs you and you need him."

Celina had agreed and, as she turned into her father's driveway, she realized that she did need him. She needed him to answer questions that had haunted her for twenty years. Why hadn't he fought for his family all those years ago? She parked the car behind Thomas's beat-up Ford pickup truck. A smile spread across her face as she remembered the days she and her neighborhood friends played on the bed of the truck. It had been her favorite hiding place when she and Darius McRae, her best friend at the time, played hide and seek. He'd always find her, though. Celina hadn't thought about Darius in years. The last time she'd talked to him was her sophomore year of high school. For no reason at all, the two had lost contact. The last she'd heard he was a hotshot lawyer in Washington, DC. *It's good he's living his dream too,* she thought, as she got out of the car. *We were lucky to get away from here.*

The first thing Celina noticed when she stepped off the asphalt driveway was the lush green grass. The lawn looked as if it had been cut with scissors; not a blade was overgrown. The azalea bushes were in bloom and the blossoms were so purple that Celina thought they had been painted. She wanted to capture the yard on canvas and hang it in the living room above the fireplace. At that moment, she realized that Thomas didn't have any of her work adorning his walls, while her mother and John had several of her prints, including a portrait she'd created for them on their tenth anniversary. Celina knocked on the front door, since she didn't have a key to her father's home. A few seconds passed before she knocked again. Worried and fearing the worst, she turned the knob, found the door unlocked, and walked into the house.

The state of the home where she spent the first eight years of her life took her breath away. The carpet was stained beyond recognition. It was no longer nutmeg brown; it just looked like plush dirt. The yellow paint on the walls had faded and the mantle above the fireplace was sagging and threatening to fall to the floor. "Daddy," Celina called out. "Daddy."

A frail Thomas Hart slowly ambled into the living room. He was wrapped in a flannel robe, despite the fact that it was over ninety degrees outside. Celina studied her father's face. His caramel skin looked ashen, his face gaunt, and his eyes, black like hers, had lost their sparkle. His hair was completely white and thinning across the top of his head.

Celina's bottom lip trembled as she looked at her father. This wasn't Thomas Hart, a man who had to fight women off with a stick. This man standing before her looked as if he'd given up on life and was waiting for death to take him away.

"Daddy, sit down." Celina cleared some of the clutter on the leather sofa. She ignored the rips along the arms of it. The years hadn't been kind to Thomas or the furniture that she had grown up playing on.

"I don't need to sit down. I need to walk around a little bit. I was in the bathroom when you were knocking on the door," Thomas said. "I guess you don't have a key, huh?"

Celina looked at him and shook her head. "What happened to the place? And who keeps up the yard for you?" The contrast between the inside and outside was remarkable.

"The young man next door," he said, as he finally sat down on the sofa. Thomas looked at Celina and smiled, though she thought his face was going to crack from the effort.

"I'm glad you're here. I didn't want to tear you away from Paris, but . . ."

"It's okay. I need to be here," Celina said. "This place

needs a good makeover. Do you pay the kid who takes care of the yard?"

Thomas shrugged his shoulders. "He never comes in, I just hear the lawn mower going."

Celina began picking up some of the old newspapers and magazines that cluttered the living room. "Well, I'm going to give him some token of thanks after I get this place looking livable again."

Thomas snorted and chuckled. "You are your mother's daughter."

Celina knew what he was saying should have been taken as a compliment, but his words enraged her. "And just what's that supposed to mean?" she spat out angrily.

"Watch your tone, baby girl, I'm still your father. And all I meant was your mother hated clutter and wanted everything in its place."

Celina closed her eyes and took a deep breath. "I'm sorry," she whispered. "Have you eaten anything today?"

Thomas shook his head "no." Celina took the armful of papers she had scooped up off the floor and sofa, then headed to the kitchen. Just as she suspected, there was no food in the refrigerator. "I need to go to the market," she called out as she stuffed the papers in the trash bag. "What do you want for dinner?"

"It doesn't matter," he said, then broke into a fit of coughing.

Celina decided that she was going to make something healthful. The way her father was bundled up, she knew that homemade soup was in order. But what was wrong with him? She hadn't asked him about his illness because she wasn't sure she wanted to know what was sapping the life from her father just yet. Celina tied the top of the trash bag together and headed out the door to deposit the rubbish in the can. She had to get to the farmer's market before it closed. The one thing she missed about living in the south was the fresh food that could be found right around the corner. The farmer's market had always been her favorite place. She could sample the fresh fruits before buying them and the meats were homegrown and free of the chemicals that were found in the food at the local supermarket. Celina was going to enjoy her time in Elmore and her time with her father.

Celina returned from the farmer's market with bags full of fresh cabbage, carrots, oranges, cucumbers, lettuce, chicken breasts, and sweet corn on the cob. She balanced the bags in her arms as she pulled the door open. She wasn't surprised that Thomas hadn't locked the door. In their neighborhood, everyone knew each other. But Celina was going to make sure all of the doors were locked from now on. She had been in the city long enough to distrust most people, including those she'd known for years.

She set the bags on the countertop, and then walked into the living room to check on Thomas. He was lying on the sofa with his eyes half-closed. He was so still that she began to panic. "Daddy," she said frantically.

His eyes fluttered open. "What, child?"

She released a cleansing sigh of relief. "I thought . . ."

"I'm not dead, yet," he said as he sat up and coughed several times in succession. Celina kneeled down beside him and stroked his back. "I'm okay."

Celina shook her head. "No, you're not. You said you needed me and I'm here to take care of you. That's what I'm going to do."

Thomas looked up at his daughter and their eyes

locked. There were so many years missing between them. Celina didn't know this man, who had been more like a favorite uncle who always gave the best presents. How were they going to make up for lost time when they didn't have much time left?

"I don't have much time, according to the doctors. I don't want to die alone, even though I may deserve to do just that." The sadness in his voice almost made Celina cry. How could she want to punish her father, when it seemed he was doing a good job of it himself?

"I'm going to fix you some homemade soup," Celina said. Looking at her father's thin frame, she wondered when he had last had a good meal.

Thomas was a proud man and obviously no one in the community knew what was going on. Elmore was the kind of place where people took care of each other and Celina knew many of the local churchwomen would have brought him hot meals every day. Thomas reached up and grabbed Celina's hand, holding it tightly. His bony fingers felt like sticks against hers.

"Celina, I've always loved you and your mother," he whispered. "I just didn't show it all the time. When she moved you two to Chicago, I thought it was best that I leave you all alone. I'd hurt your mother deeply and she needed a new start."

Celina nodded as she slid her hand from Thomas' grip. It sounded like a bad excuse to her. He still could've tried to have a more substantial relationship with her. She wasn't his wife; she was his daughter.

"I'd better cook," she said. Celina walked into the kitchen and looked at its tattered state, knowing that she had a lot of cleaning to do before she'd fix a meal. Mounds of dirty dishes sat in the sink and on the counter, covered by a thin layer of mold, and the bottoms of the cast-iron pots were coated with the residue of an unrecognizable goop that was once food. Celina grabbed the bags of food and placed them in the refrigerator. The only thing inside of it was an aging box of baking soda.

How has he been living like this? she thought sadly. Celina closed the door and began cleaning the mess. Everything about the kitchen was the same, but different. Celina remembered standing next to her mother, drying the dinner dishes. Thomas would always go outside and smoke a cigar after dinner. He'd tap on the window and blow round circles at Celina, who'd stand on her tiptoes to get a better look at her father. Rena would tap on the window and tell him to stop. She'd then turn to Celina and warn her about the dangers of smoking and tell her never to start.

Celina smiled as the memory played in her mind. Those had been the good old days and she wished that they had had more of them.

Once the kitchen was somewhat presentable, she began cooking. Celina chopped the fresh chicken breasts into bite-sized morsels and dropped them in a pot of simmering water. She dumped salt, pepper, and oregano into the pot. While the chicken simmered, making a thick broth, Celina prepared the vegetables, precisely chopping the fresh Vidalia onions, carrots, green peppers, and celery. She stirred the chicken, making sure it was done before she tossed the vegetables in. Celina lowered the heat on the soup, then fixed herself a plate of raw vegetables. She was definitely going to take some back to the city when she returned.

Once the soup was done, Celina fixed Thomas a bowlful and a glass of freshly squeezed orange juice. She carried the food to her father and set it on the coffee table where he could easily reach it. Thomas slowly sat up and smiled at his daughter.

"How's Rena?" Thomas asked, in between sipping the soup.

Celina nodded. "She's fine. Is the food okay?"

Thomas nodded approvingly. "You look and cook like her."

Celina stood up and walked over to the window. Hearing Thomas talk about Rena was somewhat bittersweet. If things had been different, Rena would have been there taking care of him. But his unfaithful ways had broken up the marriage. Watching the demise of her parents' marriage had scarred her on the notion of love and happily ever after. That's why it was so easy to walk away from Terrick in Chicago. Even though her ex-fiancé never gave her a reason to distrust him, she couldn't let go and let him love her. She definitely wasn't going to marry him, no matter how perfect everyone thought he was for her.

Terrick Johnson had been an artist as well, but for an advertising agency. He and Celina had a chance encounter when he'd signed up to take a course that she was teaching. Celina hadn't been the professor that he'd expected and she'd never expected to have a student like Terrick, who inspired her so much.

One evening, when she'd given the class a test, she'd been sitting at her desk watching and sketching his strong jawline, piercing brown eyes, and long dreadlocks. She'd been so engrossed in her work that she hadn't noticed him when he walked up to her desk.

"Is that supposed to be me?" he whispered.

Celina's face had flushed with embarrassment. "I'm sorry, it's just that you have such a unique look and I couldn't help myself."

"Do you think we could get together after class?"

"That wouldn't be appropriate. I'm still your teacher."

Terrick had smiled at her. "Not anymore. I'm actually dropping this class. It wasn't what I thought it was going to be and my company informed me that they're not going to pay my tuition anymore."

"Then do you think you could pose for me?" she asked with a huge smile on her face.

Terrick had posed for her several times before he and Celina acted on their desire for each other. To Celina, Terrick had been safe. All he'd ever talked about was having a family, his job, and marriage. Rena and John had approved of him the moment they met him. He had the proper manners and pedigree and, most of all, he seemed to love their daughter.

But something had been missing between the two of them and Celina never really put her heart into the relationship. She'd known that she didn't plan to marry Terrick the moment he gave her a three-carat diamond engagement ring. How could she marry him when she'd seen what happens to marriages? The pain, the disappointment, and the bitterness. She'd wanted no part of that and then the letter had come. Someone had submitted some of her drawings to the Harlem Renaissance Society and they'd fallen in love with her.

She'd been commissioned to design a mural for the revitalization project. It was to be a six-month undertaking. But Celina had turned this opportunity into an excuse to break things off with Terrick and get away from Chicago.

Her mother had called it running away. Celina had called it starting over. Now she'd found herself back where everything started. Her joy and her pain were wrapped up in one man—her daddy.

"Celina," Thomas said softly, tapping into her thoughts. "Yes?"

"You don't have to sit here and babysit me," he said as he set his empty bowl on the coffee table.

"I'm going to go next door and tell the guy "thank you" for keeping the yard up for you. Maybe he'll allow me to pay him for his service."

Thomas began to cough violently and Celina rushed to his side. "Daddy, are you okay?"

"Just a little fluid in my lungs," he said, his voice raspy from the fit of coughing.

"What's wrong? What did the doctors say?"

"Cancer."

Celina nervously chewed her bottom lip. "Are you getting treatment?"

Thomas shook his head "no." "What for, baby girl?"

Celina sighed and kneeled down beside her father. "Things are going to change. First thing in the morning, we're going to the hospital in Columbia."

Thomas was about to object when he broke into another fit of coughing. Celina gently rubbed his back. "Daddy," she murmured. "I'm not letting you go without a fight."

"I've lived my life," he whispered through his coughing. "I just want to make up for all the things that I've done to hurt you. That's why I asked you to come home."

"You can't give up," she said.

Thomas slowly stood up, then told Celina he was going to lie down in his room. She watched her father slowly amble down the hall, sadly thinking about how easily Thomas had decided to give up on living. Did he think he was that terrible a father? A better question was, did she agree? Celina shook the doubts from her head as she rose from the sofa. The past wasn't important because her main goal was making Thomas well.

While Thomas rested, Celina decided to go next door and thank the kid who'd been keeping the yard presentable. Celina knew the McRaes used to live next door.

She and Darius McRae had been born one month apart, he being older. They had been the best of childhood friends. When it came time to pick teams for neighborhood games of stickball, kick ball, and dodgeball, Darius had always chosen Celina first, despite the fact that she was a girl. After she and her mother had moved to Chicago, Darius and Celina lost contact with each other.

As she knocked on the door, Celina wondered what Darius was doing now.

The soft tapping on the door almost went unheard, but since Darius had been trying to sleep, he heard it and was ready to tell whoever it was to go away. All he needed was forty-five minutes of solitude. The hardware store had been buzzing like the chain saws he'd been selling all morning. Spring had finally sprung and Elmore was gearing up for its annual azalea festival. It seemed as if everyone in the city had come into the store that day. Darius was the third generation of McRaes to run the Downtown Hardware Store. His grandfather, Leon McRae, had moved to Elmore and opened the store in the late 1940s. When he died, Darius's father, David, had moved from North Carolina with his young pregnant wife, Marla, to take over the store.

When David and Marla had decided to retire and move to Palm Beach, Florida, Darius, who was facing a career crisis, moved back to South Carolina to continue the family legacy. He just didn't know it was going to be such a pain in the—the knocking grew louder. Darius pulled himself off the plush leather sofa. He'd hoped Richard, the assistant manager at the store, could go a few minutes without needing him. Darius walked to the door and snatched back the flimsy white curtain. The face that stared back at him looked familiar, but he had no idea who the curly-haired beauty was standing before him.

"Yes?" he said as he opened the door.

"I'm looking for the person who has been caring for my father's lawn," she said. Her voice had a midwestern accent with a northern influence.

"Your father?" he asked, trying to place the face. Their eyes met and it seemed as if they shared the same thought. "Celina Hart?"

"Darius McRae."

He opened the door wider and let her in. "Look at you," he said. "How long has it been?" The duo hugged each other tightly. Darius took note of Celina's luscious curves and the way she filled out the jean shorts and knit halter top. Spring in Elmore meant temperatures in the upper nineties and revealing outfits on the opposite sex.

Celina had the perfect body for those outfits, Darius surmised as he drank in her long, toned legs, small waist and ample behind. He sent his slow gaze upward and landed on her voluptuous cleavage. Part of him wanted to pull her shirt off and bury his face in between her breasts because there was no doubt in his mind that they were real and not silicone injected.

She definitely wasn't the skinny eight-year-old who used to play hide and seek with him twenty years ago.

Darius loved her natural look, the afro hairstyle suited her and highlighted her creamy skin and sparkling black eyes. The erotic thoughts that played in his head as he looked at her would've gotten him into so much trouble if someone could read his mind.

"It's been a long time," she replied. Celina licked her lips, then smiled. "So, is your son here?"

"Son? What are you talking about?" Darius furrowed his eyebrows, showing his confusion. "I don't have a son. Unless you know something that I don't know."

It was Celina's turn to be confused. She pushed her hair back from her forehead. "But my father said the young man who lives next door has been taking care of his lawn."

Darius smiled, revealing a set of perfect white teeth. "I see Mr. H. still sees me as that bowlegged kid next door."

Celina chuckled softly, sending an unexpected shiver down Darius's spine. He tried not to leer at her, but the woman standing before him didn't look a thing like the beanpole girl with whom he used to play tag. She was all woman and looked damned good.

"I must say I'm surprised to see you're still in Elmore," Celina said.

Darius led her to the sofa where he had napped earlier. "You must tell me what you've been doing with yourself," he said, still unable to take his eyes off her. Now he was leering and he didn't care.

Darius watched her mouth as she spoke, fixated on her thick lips, wondering if they were as sweet and soft as they looked.

"Hello," Celina prodded. "What have you been doing?"

"Oh, sorry," he said. "I was in Washington until last year. My parents packed it in and moved to Florida and I needed a change."

Celina nodded as she listened. "What were you doing in DC? Politics? Lobbying?"

"I worked in the attorney general's office. After nine-eleven, I decided it was time for me to rethink my life."

Celina reached out and placed her hand on his shoulder. "I know what you mean," she said. "That was a scary time in New York. You really had to take stock of what's important in life."

"Is that where you are? New York?"

Celina shook her head. "That's what my driver's license says, but I'm all over the place. Until I found out about my father I was working on a project in Paris." A painting on the wall above the fireplace caught her eye and she walked over to it. The print was one of hers. "Did you buy this?"

Darius tore his eyes away from Celina's round behind and looked at the painting. "Um, it was a gift. I'm not a big art person."

"Any idea who the artist is?" She smiled knowingly.

Darius shrugged his shoulders. "Like I said, I'm not into all of that. But I'm guessing you know."

Celina smiled and brought her teeth over her bottom lip. "It's me."

For the first time since he hung the picture, Darius looked at it. The painting was an impressionistic painting of a man and a woman embracing in front of a mirror. This was one of Celina's most famous paintings.

Darius followed her over to the painting. "Nice," he said, looking more at the artist than her work. She had the body of a model and curves he wanted to take a ride on.

"So, how much do I owe you for keeping up the yard next door?"

"Sign my painting," he said. "And join me for dinner."

Celina looked at Darius and smiled. "Is that it? I mean, you've done a lot of work on that lawn."

"For now, that's all I want. We've got a lot of catching up to do, Ms. Hart." Darius's voice was low and deep, catching Celina off guard.

She turned around and bumped into his hard chest. Instinctively, Darius put his arms around her.

"Well, I'm going to go. I'll stop by later with my paint-brush," she said, as she snaked out of his impromptu embrace.

Darius smiled and winked at her as she walked out of the house. "Looking forward to it," he said.

CHAPTER 3

As Celina walked into her father's house, she couldn't clear her mind of Darius. He oozed masculine sexuality. His skin was the color of Hershey's chocolate—the dark variety. And that body. He had rippling muscles that reminded her of the statue of David she had admired when she'd been in Italy. When he'd wrapped his arms around her, his strength surprised and excited her, and the thought of it made her body tingle.

Wait a minute, she thought. *You didn't come here to get busy with the neighbor. Get your hormones under control.* Celina walked into the living room and sat down on the sofa. The house was silent, indicating that Thomas was still sleeping. Celina's aim was to push Darius McRae out of her mind, but that became harder as she daydreamed about feeling his lips against hers.

A few moments later, Celina busied herself cleaning the living room, hoping it would erase her carnal thoughts of Darius, but she found herself gazing out the front window, looking over at his house, wondering what was going on inside.

The sound of Thomas's hacking cough returned her to reality as she rushed into his bedroom to see if he was all right. "Daddy," she said from the doorway. "Do you need some water or anything?"

Looking around the room, she saw that it needed a cleaning as well. With all the clothes on the floor, it was hard to tell what was clean or what was soiled. She wondered if his washing machine and dryer still worked.

"Baby girl, I'm fine," he replied through his coughs.

Celina crossed over to the bed and sat beside him. "If you were fine, you wouldn't have summoned me here," she said. "Daddy, I'm going to take care of you and you're not going to fight me on it."

Thomas smiled weakly as if he knew that he'd lose a fight with her if he tried.

"And," Celina continued, "if you need something, I'm here for you."

"Like I should have been when you were growing up. I've let you down and I know it's too late to make it up to you."

Celina looked longingly at her father. Part of her believed he was right, it was too late for her to be daddy's little girl. He had disappointed her in the worst way and taken away the security of a protective father that other little girls had. Sure, John had been there, but he wasn't her real father. That wound hadn't healed, but Celina told Thomas that it was okay. She was, after all, twenty-eight years old and didn't need Thomas to take her to the father-daughter spring dance. He needed her and she was going to be there for him, no matter what. Celina touched his forehead, checking for a fever. Thomas closed his eyes.

"I'm going to call your doctor and see what I should be cooking for you and when we can get an appointment in Columbia."

Thomas nodded. "I have medicine, but it makes me so tired. That's why the house is in the state it's in."

Celina stood up. "I'm going to fix all of that. I'll have this place looking good in no time. Do you want some more soup or anything to drink?"

"No," he said, and then drifted off to sleep.

Celina crept out of the room, heading for the kitchen to finish cleaning it. The knock at the door startled her as she began to mop the floor. "One minute," she said as she dropped the wooden mop on the floor. Opening the door, she was surprised to see Darius on the other side.

He was dressed in a blue and white vest and a pair of khaki pants that hugged his narrow hips and made Celina wonder if he preferred boxers or briefs. Her lusty thoughts shocked her because, after three years of celibacy, she didn't think that she had the desire to have sex. The last man to touch her was Terrick, the night before she ended their engagement, and it was less than a night of passion, making her vow even easier.

"Hi," she said breathlessly.

"I know you're probably busy with your father, but I'm grilling out tonight and I wondered if you wanted to join me."

"Why not?" she said. Celina, who usually turned down dates as if she'd been offered drugs, was genuinely looking forward to dining with Darius.

"Great. I have some steaks, chicken, and sweet corn on the cob."

Celina drew her bottom lip between her teeth. "I don't eat meat, not even chicken."

Darius's eyes widened in disbelief. "You went to New York and got all Yankeefied. You don't eat meat? If I remember, when we were growing up, you were the hamburger queen."

Celina rolled her slanted eyes and placed her hands on her hips. "For your information, I stopped eating meat before I moved to New York and I'm very proud of my southern roots, thank you very much. But that doesn't mean I have to eat artery-clogging meat."

"Calm down, CC, I was just joking with you," he said, waving his hands as if he were giving signals for a plane to land. A slow smile spread across his face, making Celina's heart race into overdrive.

"As was I," she found the voice to say. It was hard to concentrate on anything he was saying because all she could think about was tasting his kiss.

"I know how you transplants can be," he said. "So, tonight, around seven. I have to go back to work. With the big festival coming up, we've been busy."

Celina contained her giddy excitement, wondering how the moonlight would look bouncing off his cocoa brown eyes and creamy, dark skin. Then her mind wandered to tasting his honeysuckle lips in that same moonlight. Celina looked away from him quickly as the vision of his lips grazing hers blossomed in her mind. Darius bid her farewell and Celina returned to the task of cleaning the kitchen, all the while fantasizing about being alone with Darius in the moonlight.

On the drive to the hardware store, all Darius could think about was Celina. She must have been a milk drinker because it did her body well. If he had his way, they could skip dinner and feast on each other. He wasn't one to believe in love at first sight, but he damn sure believed in lust at first sight.

In short, he wanted her in his bed and sooner rather than later. Darius had given up on relationships that came with strings attached. The only strings he wanted to deal with were g-strings that were easily removed. Just thinking about Celina strutting around in a thong caused a tightening in his groin.

Celina aroused the most sexual part of him with her flirty smile and her intoxicating scent. She smelled like summertime, fresh flowers and sunshine with a smile as bright as the North Star. Darius wanted to bury his face in her cotton-soft hair and fill his nostrils with her fragrance until he was dizzy with desire.

He didn't have to worry about Celina putting pressure on him to make a commitment like so many other women he'd dealt with in Elmore because she had a life in New York.

Darius had a plan, and it involved Celina naked in his bed. She'd changed—grown up and grown sexy—and he knew he had to get next to her. Darius smiled as he walked to his car to head to work.

"Hey, boss," Richard called out when he spotted Darius entering the hardware store. "It has been jumping in here since you left. You'd think the governor was judging the competition this year."

Darius glanced at the crowd and nodded. "And this is calm?"

Richard shook his head and smiled. "At least we can pay the bills in full this month."

Darius nodded, then headed back to the office to check the day's receipts on his state-of-the-art computer system. The only thing Darius had changed about the way the store was run were the cash registers and the bookkeeping system. Everything was linked to the central computer in his office. With a few strokes of the keys, he was able to see how much his headache was worth. Darius smiled as he saw the bottom line.

Work quickly left Darius's mind and was replaced with visions of Celina kissing him while the embers from the charcoal grill burned out. His fantasy was so real that he could smell her, feel her touch on his cheek. He didn't notice the woman who walked into his office.

"I hope that smile is because you're thinking about me," came a woman's husky whisper.

Darius looked up and his smile was replaced with a scowl. "Tiffany, why are you here?"

"Because you don't return phone calls and you're always buried in this office," she said as she crossed over to the desk and hopped onto the edge of it. Tiffany crossed her long legs and faced Darius. Despite her beauty, this was one woman that he could do without. But it wasn't his fault that she'd been hanging around trying to make him her husband—a role that he didn't want. He'd told her that on several occasions, but Tiffany wasn't going to give up on having Darius or his bank account in her life, no matter how much he protested.

"As you can see," he said as he stood up and walked away from her, "I'm busy. The store is full and that is the only reason you were able to sneak back here."

She smiled brazenly and ran her hand down her ample chest. "You act as if this is the first time I've been back here." Tiffany hopped off the desk and closed the space between her and Darius. "Why are you fighting this? We fit. We belong together."

On paper, Tiffany Martin and Darius were a good match. She'd owned a fashion boutique three blocks up from the hardware store and seemed to have goals of her own. They'd met at a meeting of the Elmore business association shortly after Darius had taken over the store. Tiffany had asked Darius out for a drink after the meeting and he'd agreed—a decision he'd live to regret. Darius had hoped Tiffany was different from the other women he'd dated since he'd returned to South Carolina. He'd thought that, since she'd owned her own business, she was looking for more in a man than the size of his bank account, but he was wrong.

It hadn't taken long for Tiffany to show her true colors and Darius didn't like the picture. She'd started focusing more on his finances than anything else. That's when Darius vowed to make sure his relationships with women didn't extend past the bedroom. He didn't believe in dates. Just sex.

"Earth to Darius," she said, catching his thoughtful gaze.

"What?"

"Dinner, tonight? My place?"

He shook his head furiously. "No way. I have plans. And Tiffany, I'd appreciate it if you would leave and never come back."

Shock and disbelief distorted her comely face. "What?" She pushed her hair behind her ears.

"Did I stutter? You and I don't fit. You're not the kind of woman I want in my life and if you come in here again, I will have you arrested."

Tiffany searched Darius's face for signs of laughter, but his expression remained stoic. "You're serious? But I thought we were trying to build something."

Darius didn't respond, but instead reached for the door and held it open for Tiffany to leave.

She stomped hotly out of the office and glared at him. "You know what, Darius, you're going to rue the day you tried to play me."

Darius shrugged her comment off as an idle threat from a scorned woman. He ushered Tiffany out and let his thoughts return to his seduction of Celina.

CHAPTER 4

Celina looked around the kitchen as she washed her father's lunch dishes, satisfied that it no longer looked like the trash heap that she'd walked into hours ago. The floors sparkled, the counters shined, and the carpet looked decent. Everything reminded her of how things used to be when she was a child. Quietly, she walked down the hall to check on her father. He was resting peacefully. She'd awaken him a few hours early to make him eat a light dinner of chicken soup and half of a pimento cheese sandwich. Thomas smiled at his daughter as she filled his bowl and cut the bread for him.

"Thank God for you," he whispered when she set the food in front of him at the table. Celina didn't reply, just smiled at her father.

"Your mother raised you right. I know I should have done more. I'll always regret that."

"Daddy, please," Celina said in an exasperated voice. "Nothing can be done to erase or change the past." Secretly, she wished that he could.

Thomas nodded and ate in silence. Celina hoped she hadn't sounded too harsh, but she couldn't listen to him talk about a childhood that didn't include him. After he'd finished his dinner, Thomas went into his bedroom to watch an old western movie, leaving Celina alone with her thoughts of what could've been. What if her parents had stayed together? Maybe Thomas wouldn't be sick. "You're thinking like a child," she muttered as she washed the dinner dishes.

Celina looked out of the window over the kitchen sink while drying a bowl and spotted Darius in his backyard preparing the grill. He had changed out of his work clothes and wore a pair of well-worn jeans that hugged his slim hips. The pants dipped down and showed the top of his silk boxers, kind of like Usher Raymond. A white tank top covered his chest. Celina wondered if his body was as hard as it looked from afar. She sucked in her bottom lip as she watched him pour charcoal into the Weber grill, biceps bulging. When he wiped his brow with the back of his hand in a fluid motion, she nearly dropped the soup bowl. Despite her near accident, Celina couldn't take her eyes off Darius. She wanted to capture him on canvas so that she could have something to remember him by when she returned to New York, if she decided to leave.

The thought of staying in Elmore with Darius startled her because she'd never wanted to settle down before. Terrick hadn't induced these types of thoughts in her. She'd spent her adult life purposely sabotaging relationships and here she was ready to settle down in her hometown where the most she would paint would be landscapes of azalea bushes. No, Celina couldn't dare let a few moments of lust change everything she worked so hard for. Besides, Paris was waiting. If anything, she and Darius would have a brief fling, no strings, no emotional entanglements, and no one would get hurt.

Celina sighed and turned away from the window, trying to shake the thoughts of Darius out of her mind, but she couldn't. He invaded her mind like a thief in the night and it didn't take long for her to start staring out of the window again, watching his every move. *What am I doing? I'm not going to be here long enough to start anything with this man,* she thought, then headed down the hall to check on Thomas. He looked so small lying in his bed, nothing like the father she remembered.

"Daddy, are you okay?" she asked.

"Fine," he grumbled. "I told you, you don't have to babysit me."

Celina entered the room and walked over to his bed, then sat on the edge beside him.

"I'm not babysitting you. I just want to make sure you're all right." Celina gently patted her father's hand. "Daddy, I love you." *Despite everything,* she added silently.

Thomas smiled and squeezed Celina's hand. "I love you, too, but I want you to do something tonight other than fret over me. Have you eaten?"

"I'm going to get something later, but I just wanted to check on you," she said as she stood up.

Thomas nodded as if he were giving Celina his blessing to leave the house for a few hours. She walked into the living room, trying to kill the few minutes left before she planned to go over to Darius's house. And how in the world was she going to calm her raging hormones as she sat outside with him underneath the stars?

Darius watched the Hart house as if he were staking the place out. He'd already burned his NY strip steak, hoping to catch a glance of Celina as she headed next door. But the last thing he wanted to do was look anxious, no matter how much he was anticipating being with her. So, he was caught off guard when he felt her warm hands on his back. Her breath tickled his ear when she breathed "hello."

"Welcome to dinner, Ms. Hart," he said, stepping aside and leading her to the picnic table. He had covered the wooden picnic table with a red and white checkered cloth. In the center of the table, two candles flickered in the gentle breeze. "I wasn't sure what kind of wine went with grilled eggplant, so I have beer."

Celina laughed. "Beer and eggplant? Not bad," she said as she sat down, facing him. "Just for future reference, a nice Chardonnay works well with eggplant."

"So, are you saying there will be another dinner for us?" he asked calmly, though his heart was racing like a Nascar engine.

"Well, I might need something to do to pass the time," Celina quipped, then grabbed a beer.

Darius watched her take a dainty sip from the green bottle. How he wanted those lips wrapped around his. "How's your dad?" he asked, never taking his eyes off her lips as they caressed the bottle.

"As well as can be expected. He worries me, you know. One minute, he's like a little weak baby and the next minute it's like he doesn't need me. I know it's his pride, but I want to see him beat this thing."

Darius sat beside her and stroked her arm, not knowing what to say. If one of his parents had taken ill, he didn't know how he'd handle it. Despite the miles between them, he remained close to his mother and father. His loyalty to them was part of the reason he'd given up his career in DC to keep the family tradition alive.

She turned to him and smiled warmly. "I don't want to lay all of this on you," she said. "Let's eat."

Darius stood up and began placing the platters of roasted vegetables on the table. He handed her a white paper plate. "Dig in," he said. "I have to get my dinner off the grill."

As he piled the meat on a serving platter, Darius turned and looked at Celina as she gingerly cut into a slice of eggplant. He watched the blissful look on her face as she savored the taste. Darius smiled. His skills had paid off. He walked over to the table and set the meat on the far end of the table. "How is it?"

"Divine. Where did you learn how to cook like this?"

Darius grinned. "The best way to a woman's heart is through her stomach," he said.

Celina nodded as she took another bite of eggplant. "So, this is part of a plan? To get to my heart?"

"I didn't say that. Are you offering it?" Darius struggled to keep his voice cool like the wind.

Celina dropped her fork. "There is something I want from you," she said.

At that point, Darius would have said yes to anything she asked. He couldn't speak, though. Her voice had him hypnotized.

"Strip for me," she said.

"What?" *She didn't say what I think she did . . .*

"I want to paint you."

Darius shrugged his shoulders. "I don't know about that. I mean, I'm not a model or anything."

"That's why I want to paint you," she said. "And the background here is so natural, so beautiful."

Darius wanted to tell her that the only beautiful things he saw there were her face and her eyes, which twinkled like the stars dotting the sky. When she looked at him, it was as if she could see his soul. Darius shook his head and busied himself with fixing his plate. He was hungry, but not for the food he had cooked; he craved the unknown taste of Celina's lips. Were they as succulent as they appeared?

"Just think about it," Celina said, misreading Darius's silence. "It's not as hard as you think."

"I will consider it," he said.

"Thanks. And you have to give me this recipe," Celina said.

"Nope."

"Why not? Family secret?"

"You could say that. And the next time you want this grilled eggplant, this will be the only place you can get it," he joked.

Celina rolled her eyes. "Whatever."

Darius cut into his steak thoughtfully, trying to figure out how he'd ask her about her life back in New York and if there was someone special in her heart. He felt jealousy creeping up his back as he thought about the man sharing her life in Harlem. Was he an artist too? Probably a poet, but definitely not Mr. Wall Street. Then again, opposites do attract. Did they live together? Was he making love to her every night and modeling for her paintings as she'd asked him to do? Why wasn't he in Elmore to help with Thomas?

"Choking on all of that animal flesh over there?" Celina asked jokingly.

Darius chuckled. "Why didn't your man come with you?" he said, as he placed his knife on the table.

"Because I don't have one," she said before sticking a piece of eggplant in her mouth.

Darius smiled knowingly. "Now, I find that hard to believe. Celina, you're a beautiful woman. I know you have men beating down your door."

"That doesn't mean I answer," she mumbled. "Darius, why do you assume that I want a relationship? Maybe I like my freedom too much to be tied down to one thing, one place, or one person."

This was definitely a switch for him because most of

the women he knew wanted that exact thing—a house, a husband, and a settled life. Was Celina really that different? "Wow," was all he could say.

Celina looked at him and smiled. "Don't get the wrong idea. I don't hate men. But as an artist, I travel a lot and I don't want to argue and fuss with a boyfriend when I tell him that I'm going to Paris for a year. But what about you? You seem to have the more interesting story, anyway. You gave up the city to come back here. Why?"

Darius looked away from her. He had a story that he told about why he'd moved home for a simpler life. But it wasn't the truth. When anyone else asked, Darius would say that watching part of the Pentagon burn in 2001 made him rethink his life. Especially since he had been scheduled to have a meeting there that morning, but his car wouldn't start, and he'd waited for his emergency car service to come and give him a boost as the attacks happened.

He'd been on the phone with a paralegal when she released a bone-chilling scream as the plane hit the west side of the building. Hanging up the phone, he'd rushed into the house and turned on the TV to see if what his paralegal had said was true. Seeing the pictures sobered him. He wanted to do something to help, but he didn't know what. Like most everyone else who'd witnessed those attacks, he'd felt powerless, afraid, and angry all at the same time.

Then the phone calls had come pouring in, first from his mother, then several concerned friends. He'd heard from everyone close to him, except Renita—the woman he'd planned to marry. All sorts of crazy thoughts had run though his mind as he dialed her number, since she did work for the Department of Defense in the Pentagon. What if the plane had hit her office? What if she had been killed and he'd never gotten a chance to tell her just how much he loved her? He got the voice mail when he called her office, adding to his hysterics. Darius had pulled himself together enough to try her cell phone, but all of the networks were down and the call hadn't gone through. Finally, as he prayed for her to be all right, he called her at home.

"Hello?" she said breathlessly.

"Babe, I'm glad to hear your voice. Do you have any idea of what's going on right now?"

"Um, Darius, I'm late for w-work," she said.

That's when he'd heard the sound of another man asking her to come back to bed.

"Who's there?" he snapped, unable to believe what he was hearing.

She'd hung up the phone, leaving Darius seething with anger. He'd gone from thinking his girlfriend might be dead to wanting to wring her neck. After the passionate night of lovemaking that they'd shared, how could she be in bed with another man?

For the next few months, Darius had tried to go about his regular life, but he was heartbroken and angry. When he saw Renita, all kinds of evil thoughts danced in his mind and he'd been tempted to act on them. So, when his father had started talking about retiring and selling the hardware store, Darius had made the decision to return to Elmore and run the store. He bought the family's house and decided to settle in his childhood home.

Never did he imagine finding out that the girl next door had turned into a goddess.

"I ran away from a broken heart and decided to claim my legacy," he said, then told her the unedited version of why he left Washington. Celina reached out and stroked his hand.

"She was a fool," Celina said. "You're better off without her. Anyone who would cheat on their partner deserves to be alone."

I'd be a lot better with you in my bed, he thought, wanting to reach over and kiss her with everything inside of him. But Darius knew it wasn't the right time. Soon, though, he would taste her lips and feel her supple body pressed against his, tangled in his sheets.

For the rest of the evening, Darius and Celina kept their conversation light and jovial. She talked about her art, the time she spent in Paris, and how she was going to paint a mural on the side of her father's house. Darius told Celina how he planned to expand the hardware store and add a garden center. Celina glanced down at her watch.

"I didn't realize it was so late," she said. The evening air had turned cooler, but it was still comfortable.

Darius noticed that she was cool because her nipples peeked through her shirt and he couldn't help staring. Turning away, he said, "So, this is how the night ends?"

"And just what were you expecting, Darius McRae?" she asked, her voice like a midnight tease.

He stood up and walked over to her. He towered over her as she sat there looking up at him. He didn't care if it was too soon. He had to taste her lips. "This," he said as he captured her mouth with his.

Darius's swift move caught her off guard. But what surprised her more than anything was the way she responded to his kiss, melting against him as she rose to her feet to fully lose herself in it. She parted her lips and welcomed his tongue into her mouth. It was as if his kiss had awakened every repressed desire she'd ever had. No one had ever made her knees quake or her heart shiver the way Darius had with one kiss. It took every ounce of strength she had to push Darius away, despite the fact that her panties had grown damp with desire. Without saying a word, she ran from the yard.

When Celina got inside the house, she touched her lips with the tip of her tongue, still able to taste him. It was as if Darius had branded her lips and they would never be the same again. Celina liked his kiss a little more than she wanted to or should have. Shaking her head, she walked away from the door. She came to Elmore with a single focus and that was to care for her father. Nothing could change that and hopping into Darius's bed wasn't a part of the plan.

Celina tore down the hall to check on Thomas, hoping that seeing him would reorganize her priorities. She was happy to see that he was sleeping peacefully. That wasn't going to be the case for her tonight, she sighed, as she walked toward the kitchen. Not only could she taste Darius; his scent lingered on her skin, making it impossible to stop thinking about him. She inhaled deeply, letting the scent infect her nostrils and take her mind into his bedroom with her body pressed against his and those lips touching her in places that made her tingle all over.

The knock at the door startled her, but Celina didn't have to look out the window to know it was Darius. As she opened the door and Darius walked in, she tried to clear her mind of all of the erotic thoughts that he conjured. He stood inches away from her and she wanted to kiss him again and do more, feel more.

"Why did you leave?" he asked.

"Because you were out of line. I came to have dinner with someone I thought was a friend. Obviously you had other intentions." She figured if she turned her passion into anger that she could push Darius away.

"Celina, I didn't do anything you didn't want me to do. You kissed me back, as I recall. We're not children playing house. I know you wanted that kiss as much as I did."

"Animal instinct. Maybe I should have slapped you, then left."

Darius moved his head closer to her. "But you know you didn't want to do that," he said huskily. His lips were dangerously close to hers. Celina was afraid to move, because she knew their lips would touch and, despite her bravado, she would be powerless to resist him.

"Right now," Darius continued in a low, sexy voice. "You want to kiss me. But you're afraid you're going to like it too much. Just like the first time we kissed a few moments ago."

Celina stepped back and Darius stepped forward, closing the space between them and forcing her to face him. She sighed, resigning herself to the fact that he was going to kiss her again. He didn't, though. Instead, he took a step back.

"I enjoyed our dinner and I want to know if I can see you again," he said. "And if that means I have to stop kissing you, then that's what I'll do. So, will you see me again if I promise to be on my best behavior?"

The word "yes" floated from her lips before her head had a chance to remind her that Darius was a distraction, an extremely sexy distraction, that she didn't need or want.

"Tomorrow, I'm off all day. Let's go to the lake and maybe you can get some inspiration for another painting," he suggested, with a cunning smile on his lips.

Celina shook her head. "That isn't going to stop you from modeling for me. I don't care how beautiful the scenery might be."

"Why do I get the feeling that you are a hard woman to resist?" He tugged at her chin gently.

She turned her head away to hide the flush that colored her cheeks. "Well," she said, "I think I'm going to go to bed."

Darius took his cue to leave. Celina watched him walk away and released a sigh of relief. Or was it frustration? A few more seconds in his presence, and she might have invited him to join her in bed. Closing her eyes, she thought of Darius taking her into his strong arms and holding her against his hard body. The ripple of desire that tore through her body told her that she was going to have to fight those feelings. But did she really want to?

The telephone rang, interrupting her thoughts. "Hello?"

"Hey baby, it's Mom. How is everything?"

"Okay, I guess."

"And Thomas?" Rena asked. Concern poured from her voice.

"We're going to Columbia next week to have a battery of tests run on him."

Rena uttered a prayer. "I don't want anything to happen to that man."

Rena's concern surprised Celina. Had her mother forgotten the pain Thomas caused her? *Maybe this is what forgiveness is all about,* Celina thought.

"Tell Thomas he's in my prayers," Rena said. "And you are too, baby. I know you've had a hard time forgiving Thomas. Promise me you'll make peace with him before it's too late."

"I'll try."

"Do more than try. I'm going to go now. I love you."

"Love you, too." Celina hung up the phone with her mother's words echoing in her head.

CHAPTER 5

Darius climbed out of the ice-cold shower, but he didn't feel any better. Celina had lit a fire in his soul that water couldn't cool. Hell, ice wouldn't be able to put it out. Every time he closed his eyes, he saw Celina's face. When he licked his lips, he tasted her kiss. Darius had never longed for or ached for a woman the way he did for Celina. She was so damned sexy. Their kiss left him hungry to taste every inch of her body. Any woman who kissed with such fire had to be great in bed.

Darius knew he wasn't going to sleep a wink because his fantasies would keep him awake. Pulling a pair of cotton boxers onto his damp body, he headed out the front door to enjoy the clear night sky and pray for a cool wind that would rock him to sleep. As he stretched out on the hammock on the end of the porch, Darius noticed for the first time that his favorite relaxation spot looked directly onto the Hart porch.

He watched the door, hoping that Celina would walk outside because she couldn't sleep, either. Darius wondered if he had gotten under her skin the same way she had gotten under his. For all he knew, she was in the house having a conversation with her man in New York, because he didn't believe for one second that she was single. Jealousy surged through his nervous system, making him want to rush over there and snatch the phone from her hand. She didn't need him—a man who allowed her to face her dying father alone. Celina needed someone who would be a strong shoulder for her to lean on as she helped her father through his illness. If Mr. New York was too busy and too self-centered to provide that, then Darius would make sure he did.

Just as he closed his eyes, he heard the Hart's front door open. Celina stepped out into the silver moonlight. It bounced off her flawless skin, which was covered with a simple white cotton nightgown. It stopped midthigh. Darius's gaze traveled up her body, stopping at her ripe breasts, which protruded underneath the thin gown. Darius wanted to take them in his mouth and taste them and then travel down her taut body, sampling all of her treats and delights. Not wanting to frighten her, Darius continued to watch Celina in silence, letting his lusty thoughts heat him up all over again. He noticed that she had a sketch pad underneath her arm as she took a seat on the top step of the porch and turned her eyes upward. Darius wondered what inspired her art. Celina's paintings were very sensual and romantic.

Before dinner he'd done an Internet search of her work, finding countless sites dedicated to it. Her most popular paintings were of men and women touching, kissing, and being together. The sensuality of her work made him wonder if she was a passionate lover. Darius's mouth went dry as he watched Celina making long strokes on the paper, as the right strap of her gown slid down her shoulder.

"Weren't you taught that it is impolite to stare at people?" Celina asked.

He'd been spotted and all he could do was smile. "I

wasn't staring," he replied. "I was just trying to get some rest."

"Outside?" She turned to Darius with a sly smile on her face. "I know this is Elmore, but no one sleeps outside on purpose."

"I couldn't sleep and this is what I do when I can't sleep," he said, as he stood up and walked to the end of the porch. What he didn't say was that when he saw her in that skimpy gown, he knew that the only way he'd be able to sleep was if his bed were a block of ice. "What are you drawing?" he asked.

She shook her head, indicating nothing. Celina focused on Darius as he stood on the end of the porch. "I couldn't sleep, either, especially after the phone call I got when you left."

Darius hoped the call was from her inconsiderate boyfriend, ending their relationship when she needed him most. "Trouble in New York?"

She stood up, dropping her sketch pad on the porch. "What do you mean by that?"

"Nothing. I thought maybe your man called you with some bad news or something," he said, keeping his voice nonchalant. "Or an excuse as to why he isn't here."

"Darius, subtlety isn't your strong suit, is it?" Celina stood up and walked over to the fence that divided their yards. "I told you at dinner that I was single. Why don't you believe it?"

He shrugged his shoulders and placed his hands on the fence. Slow smiles spread across their faces.

"Remember when we used to climb this fence?" they said in unison, then broke out in laughter.

"Think you can still do it?" Darius asked.

Folding her arms across her chest, she gave him her hardest New York B-girl look. "Is that a challenge?"

"Do you accept?"

Celina answered him by grabbing the top of the chain-link fence. She stuck her foot through the metal links and climbed over the three-foot fence. As Celina leapt over the top, her gown caught on the fence, causing the back to rip. Darius struggled not to laugh as she tried to hold the gown together.

"Amused?" she asked, her face burning with embarrassment.

"Wouldn't you be? But I'll give you this, you've never backed down from a challenge, even when we were little."

Celina placed her hands on her rounded hips, forgetting for a moment that her gown was ripped to shreds. "And what does that mean?"

Darius smiled. "Do you want a T-shirt to cover your gown—or what's left of it, anyway?"

"Please," she said. "I'm so embarrassed."

Darius led Celina into the house, walking just one step behind her so that he could look at what the rip exposed.

"Red looks good on you," he said, catching a glimpse of her hi-cut bikini briefs.

"Darius McRae, you still don't play fair!"

"Still?"

Celina whirled around and held out her arm, pointing to a long faint scar. "Remember this? You just couldn't stand being beat in a race by *moi*, a girl. So, what did you do?"

Darius stifled a laugh. "I don't recall." He knew what he'd done, but he had to, since all of the boys in the neighborhood would've given him hell if he'd let Celina cross that finish line first.

Celina hit him in the chest. "You pushed me into old man Johnson's ditch and I cut my arm on a broken beer bottle. It took thirteen stitches to close this up, plus I had to wear a sling on my arm for two weeks in the heat of the summer," she said.

"And I got the spanking of my life," Darius said, incredulously. "I'll say we're even."

Celina hit him again, harder. "Am I supposed to feel sorry for you? I went to school that fall with two-toned arms."

Darius pulled her into his arms and held her close to him. "What can I do to make it up to you?" He gently stroked her forearm, feeling her body shiver underneath his touch. He knew he was casting a sensual spell on her and he had her at a disadvantage. She was standing before him barefoot in a ripped gown, stripped of her trendy clothes and city attitude. It took every ounce of self control in him not to tear the gown from her body and take her right there on the floor. How many women could look that sexy in a ripped frock? Her breasts pressed against his chest as he pulled her closer to his body. When he saw the flush on her face, Darius knew she felt his arousal through his shorts.

"Darius," she whispered. Her voice was a husky whisper. His reply was a tantric kiss on her lips that made her putty in his arms as he scooped her up.

Celina pushed against his chest, separating their lips. "This is so wrong. Please put me down."

Darius did as she asked, even though it was the last thing he wanted to do. "I'm sorry, I just couldn't help myself."

Celina straightened her torn gown as much as she could. "Look, we're both adults here, so I'm going to be blunt. I don't want a relationship. No promises of forever and happily ever after, just today and the here and now."

"Is that what you really want?"

"Yes," she said, "Just sex. And when, where, and how will be my choice. Good night, Darius."

Speechless, Darius watched Celina saunter out the door. No woman had ever been so blunt about sex. He was intrigued. *Just what are your terms, Ms. Hart?* Part of him wanted to follow her next door and find out what those terms were and when she planned to name the time and place. Instead, he decided to let things simmer, temporarily at least.

When Celina entered her bedroom, she pulled her ripped gown off and plopped down on the bed. What had gotten into her? She couldn't believe that she had said those things to Darius about having sex with him. Celina was so tempted to let him take her into his bedroom and have his way with her. The way he kissed, she knew that he would handle her body like no one else had. Closing her eyes, she imagined Darius ripping her already torn gown off and kissing her breasts until her nipples hardened against his lips. And with one hand between her thighs, he'd stroke her womanly center to near climax because it's been so long since she'd been touched and stroked there.

Lost in her fantasy, Celina didn't realized it was her own hand bringing her pleasure until she called out Darius's name and opened her eyes. Rising from the bed, Celina grabbed her robe, wrapped it around her body and headed into the bathroom to take a long cold shower. But she knew there was only one thing that was going to calm the fire raging inside her and that was Darius McRae.

But Celina wasn't really in the market for a fling. She had to make sure her father got the care that he needed to begin fighting his cancer. Still, Darius was a temptation that she wasn't sure she'd be able to resist. Closing her eyes, she imagined his hands roaming her body and making every nerve come alive with desire. *Stop it!* she thought. *This isn't why you're in South Carolina and since you've laid down the just sex edict, you're going to have to avoid that man at all costs.*

Groaning, she turned the shower on and regretted every word that she'd said to Darius. How was she going to handle it when he came to collect on what she'd offered?

You're an adult and you want him just as much as he wants you. It doesn't have to go any further than the bedroom. Sex, Celina could handle, but she wasn't trying to fall in love. Love, as her mother said twenty years ago, wasn't enough. Besides, she had no plans to stay in Elmore once her father was on the road to recovery.

Celina shut the water off and stepped out of the shower. As she dried her body, she decided that her best course of action would be to avoid Darius all together.

"This is lust. What we have here is sexual heat and when and if we give in to it, things will change," she said to her reflection.

CHAPTER 6

By Monday, Celina had traded her thoughts of Darius for concern about her father as they made the one-hour drive to Columbia for an appointment at the Palmetto Health Cancer Center, one of the premiere cancer treatment agencies in the southeast. The center, which pooled its resources with other major health centers in the state, had recently added former St. John's University cancer expert, Dr. Lewis Russell, to its staff.

Dr. Russell had a reputation for "curing cancer." He used the latest in cancer treatments to treat lung and throat cancer and he also adapted eastern medical tactics like using herbs and acupuncture. Celina was excited that her father was to see Dr. Russell and prayed that he would recover from his cancer or that the disease would go into remission.

Celina and Thomas walked into the doctor's office. She glanced over at her father, who didn't look as frail in his khaki pants and lime-green golf shirt, but he did seem nervous. "Are you all right?" she asked.

He nodded. "I don't like doctors, that's all. Every time I come to see one, I seem to get sicker."

The door to the office opened and Celina and

Thomas whirled around and looked at the man walking through the door. He didn't look like much of a doctor, with his Albert Einstein afro, colorful Hawaiian-style shirt, and a pair of lavender slacks. Celina thought his outfit was better suited for a Halloween costume or he at least deserved a citation from the fashion police.

"Good morning, folks," he said with a huge smile plastered on his face. "Mr. Hart, I just finished reading your file. I believe I can help you."

Thomas grunted. "I've heard that before."

Celina shot him a cautioning look. She wanted her father to keep an open mind about this treatment. Dr. Russell ran his hand through his wooly hair. His olive skin seemed to glow as he turned on his desk lamp. He continued laying out a course of treatment for Thomas.

"There's one thing," he said as he cleared his throat. "I want to admit you for at least a week. Your right lung has a number of cancer cells and before we suggest surgery, I want to try a different course of action."

"What do you mean?" Thomas asked. "Surgery?"

Dr. Russell opened a manila folder sitting on his desk and pulled out a sheet of white paper. "This is the course of treatment that I would like to start you on."

Thomas ignored it, but Celina took the paper from the doctor. "Acupuncture?" she asked. "What will this do to the cancer?"

Dr. Russell explained how acupuncture treats the entire patient, not just the illness. "The acupuncture relieves pain without the use of drugs, although, because Thomas's cancer is so advanced, we will probably have to use drugs and radiation as a part of his treatment."

"What are the risks with this type of treatment?" she asked.

Before the doctor could answer, Thomas banged his

hand against the desk. "Now wait a minute. I never agreed to any of this crap."

"Daddy, we're just talking," Celina said, placing her arm on his shoulder in an attempt to calm him down. Thomas picked up the paper.

"I'm not a human pin cushion and I ain't staying here. I have a good doctor in Elmore who can take care of me."

Celina pouted. "When's the last time you saw your doctor, Daddy? I thought you called me to come home because you wanted me take care of you?"

"Do you two need some time to talk?" Dr. Russell asked. "I understand if you do. This is a big decision."

"I'm not staying here more than a week," Thomas said. "I know I'm going to die. And sticking pins in me isn't going to change a damned thing."

Celina's eyes glistened with unshed tears. "Daddy, don't say that," she whispered.

"Mr. Hart, I want to make sure that doesn't happen, but you have to want it as well," Dr. Russell said.

Thomas looked at the tears in Celina's eyes. "I want that," he said.

Celina reached over and hugged her father.

Darius sat at his breakfast table picking at the banana nut muffin he should've been eating. He hadn't seen Celina since Saturday night, though he'd caught a glimpse of her walking to her rental car Sunday morning dressed as if she were going to church.

Maybe she was just all talk. I wouldn't be lucky enough to find a woman who can separate sex and emotions, he thought as he looked out of the window, hoping he would see her rental car in Mr. Hart's driveway. When he didn't see it, he remembered that she was going to take her father to the cancer center in Columbia.

The telephone rang, interrupting his thoughts of Celina. "Yeah?"

"Darius, I know you said you were coming in late, but we have a problem," Richard said.

"What kind of problem?" he asked.

"Vandalism. Someone broke the front window out last night," he said.

Darius swore under his breath. "Was anything taken? Who would do this? Damn it! I'll be there in a few minutes," he said as he pushed his chair back from the table, knocking over his coffee cup. No one had ever broken into the hardware store. Things like this just didn't happen in Elmore. After mopping up his mess, Darius threw on a pair of jeans and a T-shirt, then dashed out the door to go survey the damage.

When Darius got to the store, Richard was standing outside, sweeping up shards of glass. Darius looked at the front window. The glass had been completely broken out.

"Did you call the police?" he asked, rubbing his hand across his face.

The older man nodded. "It was probably some rowdy kids messing around and things went too far."

"I don't give a damn. This little joke is going to cost us hundreds of dollars that we can ill afford to pay out. Have you checked the inventory? If those little . . ."

"It doesn't look as if anything is missing. Darius, we have insurance for things like this. Calm down, boss." Richard paused, leaning on the broom.

"Things like this don't happen in downtown Elmore and I want to make sure a message is sent. If some bored kids want to throw bricks into businesses, they need to know there will be consequences." Anger flickered in his dark eyes. Richard backed off. Darius was nothing like his father. He had a quick temper and Darius blew up at things that David would have laughed off. Richard chalked it up to the time Darius spent in Washington. "Big-city residue," he'd named it, though he'd never say that to Darius.

"Rich," Darius said making an attempt to soften his tone. "I'm not upset with you. It's just the situation has me on edge."

"Are you sure that's all it is?" Richard started sweeping again.

Darius nodded, but he had more on his mind than a broken window and insurance claim forms. Celina. He'd much rather spend his time planning his seduction than dealing with this. "I'm going to go in and call the insurance company."

"All right," Richard said, not looking up from his sweeping.

Darius stalked into his office and picked up the phone to call his insurance agent. As he dialed the number, his cell phone began to ring. "What?"

"Grouchy this morning?" Tiffany said.

"I don't have time for you today."

"Trouble at the store? I saw the damage while I was on my way to work. Who knew a little brick could do that?"

"You're behind this, aren't you?" Darius snapped.

"What are you talking about? I wouldn't stoop to something that juvenile."

Rather than argue with her, Darius snapped his cell phone shut and continued his call to his insurance agent. He knew Tiffany had something to do with the vandalism and as soon as he could prove it, she was going to jail. He really wished she would grow up.

The hardware store didn't open until noon. Darius and Richard covered the front window with a piece of plywood. Customers chattered about what happened to the window and voiced their concerns about crime in

Elmore. Darius wanted to scream that this wasn't the start of a crime wave, but a scorned woman acting her shoe size and not her age.

"Darius," Richard called out from behind the register. "Mayor Hamilton's office is on the phone."

Darius looked away from his customer. "Take a message," he growled. "Better yet, tell them the donation for the festival is on the way." The last thing he felt like doing was being jovial. That woman was spiraling out of control and she needed to be stopped.

Richard shook his head, then relayed the message to the mayor's secretary. Darius handed his customer the drill bits he'd requested, then busied himself, straightening the items on the shelf in order to keep himself from being drawn into another conversation about the broken window.

By the end of the day, Darius was worn out. Between filing a police report, the business in the store, and the insurance paperwork, he felt as if he had been in a dogfight and had come out on the losing end. But his smile and energy returned when he pulled into his driveway and spotted Celina sitting on her father's porch. She seemed to be engrossed in her drawing. Darius wondered what she was furiously capturing on paper. Her head was bent over the pad, her curly locks spilling over its spiral edge. Darius wanted to bury his face in her hair and inhale its scent. He knew she smelled like roses and jasmine. Darius had her fragrance memorized. It haunted him at night when a cool breeze floated through his bedroom window. He wished she was standing outside his window when he smelled it so that he could invite her in.

He slowly eased out of the car, wondering if she saw him in her peripheral vision. He leaned over the fence, trying to find the right words to say. Celina looked up as if she felt Darius watching her.

"Hi," he said, once their eyes locked.

"Hello," she replied curtly. Celina hugged her sketch pad against her chest. Darius ignored the negative vibes he was getting from her and pressed forward with the conversation.

"How's Mr. Hart?"

Celina nodded. "He's going to be fine, I think. The doctor admitted him to the hospital for some intensive treatment. I wanted to stay, but the doctor said I would damage the 'chi' if I stayed there worrying about the treatments."

"The chi?"

Celina shrugged her shoulders. "It's some Asian medicine that works in conjunction with the clinical medicine."

Darius tugged at his bottom lip with his teeth as he and Celina locked eyes again. He didn't know what to say. Should he apologize for the other night?

"Celina, the other night . . ."

Celina stood up and turned toward the door. "You must stick to my ground rules. Rule number one: don't ever kiss me again."

Darius climbed over the fence, stalked to the porch, and stood one step beneath Celina, who was still clutching her notebook to her chest. "I can't promise you that. Remember, I don't play fair." Darius reached over and pulled Celina's chin up to his petal-soft lips. He gently brushed his lips across hers. Celina turned away, but Darius's lips followed her up the side of her cheek.

"Stop," she murmured, quickly turning her head toward his in order to look directly into his eyes.

Darius seized the opportunity to capture her lips and assault her with a mind-numbing kiss. She melted against him and Darius felt her body react to his kiss. He gently stroked her bare back, urging her to come closer to him. His desire pressed against the fly of his jeans and he wanted her to feel it so that she'd know what was in store for her, when she decided the time was right.

Celina pushed him away with a strange look flickering in her eyes. He didn't know if she wanted him or if she wanted to slug him.

"Darius," she said in a near whisper. "You *don't* play fair."

"But I do play to win," he said. He looked down at the sketch pad, which had fallen on the porch. The image on the paper shocked and intrigued him. Celina's face flushed with embarrassment. Darius leaned down and picked up the pad.

"What's this?"

Celina inhaled sharply. She'd been sitting on the porch thinking of Darius. The image of his sculpted body was emblazoned on her mind and when she started to draw freehand, it was easy to capture his face, body, and what she imagined he would do if he were lying on a sandy beach with a woman—a woman like her. The picture, while it wasn't erotic or pornographic, was sensuous and private. She'd never wanted Darius to see it. Showing him that picture would force her to admit that he had taken a piece of her mind and made it his home.

"It's nothing," she said, snatching the pad from his hand. She dashed for the door, hoping the added inches between them would allow her heart to return to its normal beating pace. She had no such luck because he quickly closed the space between them.

"This looks a lot like me," Darius said. His hand was dangerously close to touching her shoulder.

"I just started doodling and this is what I came up with. It doesn't mean anything," she said.

Darius nodded. "Celina, why don't you just admit it? You want to see what's between us just as much as I do." He traced the outline of her lips with his forefinger, sending Celina's system into overdrive. She backed against the glass door and Darius leaned into her. "Celina," he murmured against her ear. "Just admit it."

Darius smiled, then stroked her cheek. Celina grabbed his hand and looked into his eyes. "What do you want from me, Darius McRae?" she asked in a throaty whisper.

His eyebrow shot up. "I've already laid my cards out on the table. You know what I want and I don't care about miles or any of that. Celina, you're here now."

He pulled her closer to him. The heat from his breath sent shivers down her spine. Celina turned her lips toward Darius, allowing him to capture them and lock her up in a lustful kiss that shook her to the core. She wrapped her arms around him, pressing her body against him, feeling his every throbbing muscle. As he ran his hands up and down her back, a hailstorm of emotions rushed through Celina as he touched her.

Darius effortlessly scooped Celina up into his arms. He pushed the door open and rushed to the sofa. He gently laid Celina on the cushions.

For a split second, she wondered if she was making a mistake. But when he kissed her on her neck, turning her insides to jelly, she couldn't think anymore. Slowly, Darius peeled Celina's clothes from her body, lavishing her satin skin with kisses each time he exposed a piece of her copper-colored flesh.

Celina's body responded instantly to Darius's touch and he handled her body like an expert, touching her in places that aroused her and elicited hot lust from every pore of her body. As Darius ran his hands between her thighs, Celina released a primitive growl. She hadn't been touched like that in years, hadn't felt butterflies fluttering in her stomach since she lost her virginity on prom night years ago.

Darius kissed her inner thigh gently, his tongue like a paintbrush drawing on her tender skin. She clutched his back, clawing at his T-shirt until she pulled it over his head. Darius continued painting lust across her thighs, slowly venturing up to the warm folds of skin that housed her passion. With wide strokes, he touched her most sensitive spot, sparking a sensation that she'd never felt before. Soft moans escaped her throat as she felt a warm trickle stream down her thighs. Tightening her legs around his neck, she pushed his face closer to her pulsing mound of female sexual energy. Celina's legs quivered as Darius picked up on her desire and increased the speed of his tongue flickering inside of her, touching her G-spot, and making her explode. Darius traveled up her body, leaving a sweet, sticky trail across her muscular thighs, her taut stomach, and perky breasts, before planting a soul-searing kiss on her lips. Celina devoured his tongue as if she were a starving woman. And she was. Starving for love, attention, and tenderness. As she kissed him, she allowed herself to wonder what it would be like to fall in love with Darius McRae. To move back to Elmore and paint pictures of Darius all day. She wondered what it would be like to sit on the hammock on his porch and paint the bushes as they began to bloom. The thoughts of his tenderness and the love he wanted to offer calmed her fearful heart and part of her wanted to lose herself in his love.

But she didn't want to get hurt and that stopped her from giving him everything that he wanted from her. As

Darius throbbed against her, she knew everything was going to change.

"I need protection," she said huskily. She knew Darius thought she was talking about birth control, but that wasn't all the protection that she needed. She needed protecting from being hurt. *This is just sex,* she thought. *Don't overthink it.*

Darius reached into his discarded jeans and pulled out his wallet. He pulled a condom from behind his bills.

Celina propped herself up on her elbows. "You carry condoms in your wallet?"

Darius chuckled. "It's something my father taught me a long time ago: always be prepared—"

She silenced him with a kiss, coaxing his tongue into her mouth. She sucked it furiously, as if she were receiving sustenance from him. Darius moaned excitedly as she deepened her kiss, their tongues dueling for position, and his hands roamed her body. She responded to his touch, lighting up like a Roman candle. Neither of them could wait any longer. As Darius dove into her body, Celina shuddered, feeling his pulsating shaft pressing deeper and deeper into her. She clutched Darius's back as his lips brushed against her neck. She tightened her muscles against his burgeoning manhood. Darius howled in ecstasy as he and Celina continued their sensual grind until they tumbled off the sofa, still wrapped around each other like mating snakes. Celina's nails bit into Darius's shoulder as the waves of an orgasm began to attack her system. Darius held her close as he recognized what was happening to her. "You feel so good," he whispered in her ear as he slowed his sexual pace. Celina uttered an incoherent sentence. Darius gently stroked her cheek as they pulled apart from each other.

Celina stood up and quickly gathered her clothes.

Darius stared at her. "What's wrong?" he asked.

"This, this was wrong." Celina dressed and dropped her head in her hands. *What have I done?* she thought.

Darius rushed to her side and wrapped his arms around her waist. She threw his hands from around her, then pulled her shirt over her head.

"We both wanted this," he said as he reached out to stroke her back.

Celina jerked away. "This doesn't change anything. What I said still stands. We're friends, nothing more." She walked over to the door and opened it. "Consider this a one-night stand because this will never happen again."

"I don't believe that," he said confidently. "What we just shared was only the beginning.

"As long as you know the rules," she said.

"Rules?"

"No attachments, just sex."

"I don't have a problem with that, but are you going to be able to follow your own rules?" Darius asked. "You're not Carrie Bradshaw and this isn't Manhattan."

Celina rolled her eyes. "And just what is that supposed to mean? Do you think men are the only ones who can have sex and walk away? Besides, my priority isn't keeping your bed warm. I came here for my father. This is a by-product. You know what, forget the rules, this is the one and only time we'll do this. If you don't mind, I need to shower." She nodded toward the door.

"I'll leave for now," he said. "But this isn't over, not by a long shot and you know that." Darius winked at her as he walked out the door.

As much as Celina wanted to tell him that he was wrong, she knew things between them had just gotten started.

CHAPTER 7

For the next two weeks, Celina spent her days in Columbia and her nights avoiding Darius. The only reason she didn't stay at the hospital with Thomas was because his doctor asked her not to. She wanted to hide from Darius because every time she saw him, she thought about the night that they'd spent together. She had to remain steadfast and stay away from him. Darius wasn't what she needed in her life right now.

Thomas had been responding well to his treatments, gaining weight and not coughing as much. Celina had to focus on her father, not her growing desire for Darius.

"What's wrong, Celina?" Thomas asked as she stared out of the window.

"Nothing," she replied. "I was just thinking about how you fought to stay out of the hospital and look at you now."

Thomas smiled and sat up in the bed. "Just like your mother, you make me a better person," he said.

Celina bristled underneath the compliment. She wondered why, if Rena was so good for Thomas, he broke her heart the way he did. She wanted to ask him that, but decided that it was a conversation they could have at a later date.

"When are the doctors letting you come home?"

"Maybe in a day or so. I might be back in time for the festival."

Celina stood up and walked over to her father's bedside. "The azaleas are looking pretty this spring," she said.

"Celina, I'm glad you came home. I never thought I needed anyone. Maybe I just never wanted to need somebody, but having you here is making this easier for me."

"I want to see you get well," she said. "You have a lot more living to do."

Thomas nodded in agreement. "I see that now. I owe you a lot."

She took her father's thin hand in hers. "No, you don't. I'm going to head back before it gets too late," she said. "Call me if you need anything."

"I will. How is that boy next door? Has he cut the grass this week?"

"Um, I hadn't noticed. But I'll take care of it," she said as she dashed out the door to avoid any other inquiries about Darius. On the drive home, all Celina could think about was Darius. She didn't want to admit it, but she missed him. He seemed to be respecting her wishes by leaving her alone. Then again, she didn't leave him much choice. Celina left early in the morning and returned late at night. Before leaving Columbia, she would stop at a mall and read a copy of the *New York Times* while sipping overpriced coffee at a coffee shop or she would wander around window-shopping for hours.

Celina pulled her cell phone out of her purse and dialed her mother's number. She slowed down as she slid her hands-free ear bud inside her ear.

"Hello?" John Malcolm said.

"Hey, John, is my mom there?"

"Yeah. Is everything all right?" His voice was peppered with concern.

"More or less, everything is fine."

"And your father?"

"He's good. The treatments are working pretty well. He may be coming home tomorrow."

"Excellent. I'll get your mother." Celina listened as John called out for Rena.

"Celina, are you OK?" Rena asked when she came to the line.

She sighed before saying, "Mom, how did you find it in yourself to love again after Daddy?" Celina pulled over into the right lane on the interstate. Traffic was light and she was thankful.

"What kind of question is that?" Rena said. "You've never been in love because you've never allowed anyone to get close enough to you. Terrick was a good man and you could be married and working on a grandbaby or two."

"Ma, I'm just so . . . I met someone and I don't want to be hurt. Right now, he seems like a great guy, but I know it isn't going to last. And Terrick and I had absolutely no chemistry, so there would've been no grandbabies."

Rena sighed heavily. "Celina, every man is not your father. What happened between Thomas and me was just that, between him and me. It doesn't mean you're going to meet the same fate. If this man makes you feel special, give him a chance. Get to know him. That's what happened with me and John. When it's right, you know that it's right. If you're having these thoughts about him, then he must be something special."

"I'm scared, Mom," Celina said. "Just like every man isn't Daddy, every man isn't John, either."

"Well, baby, life isn't easy and you're going to have

some pain. But you can't keep running and hiding behind a canvas," she said.

"I don't do that," Celina protested, then slammed on her brakes as a car darted in front of her.

"Oh no? What about your fiancé? Why did you give Terrick the ring back?"

"Because I wanted to move to New York," she said. "And he wasn't the man that I wanted to spend the rest of my life with. I wasn't hiding from anything."

"That's bull and you know it. Terrick would have moved there too and he still asks about you. The man is heartbroken to this day. He could've been the one and you tossed him aside like leftover trash. Don't do the same thing with this new guy."

Celina muttered an expletive at the car in front of her, which seemed to brake for no reason. She darted into the other lane. "Ma, traffic is crazy, I have to go."

"All right, Ms. Road Rage. And remember what I said. Pain is a part of life and running away all the time is no way to live."

Celina clicked the phone off and focused on the road. She knew Darius would be at home when she got there and it was time for her to stop running.

As the sun set on Elmore, Darius smiled. This was why he'd moved back to South Carolina. The beauty of nature was all around him, from the birds chirping above his head, to the butterflies dancing around the flowers in the yard. He sipped his beer slowly, bathing in the warmth of the fading sun rays. The only thing that would've made this scene better would have been having Celina in his arms. Darius noticed her evasive tactics and he had had just about enough of her game. That's why he'd left work early, because he was going to make her face him whether she liked it or not.

He scratched his head and rubbed his face. Somehow he had to win her over.

The sound of an approaching car made him stand up. He hoped it was Celina returning from Columbia, but as the tan Lexus came into view, he realized who it was. Tiffany pulled her car into the driveway and slammed the door as she got out. Her purple sundress blew in the gentle summer breeze, exposing her golden thighs. Months ago he might have been aroused; now he was repulsed.

"What do you want?" Darius asked.

"I don't appreciate you starting rumors about me," she snapped.

He rolled his eyes and sat on the hammock, nearly knocking over his half-empty beer bottle. "If this is why you came here, then just leave."

"For the record, I didn't break your window," she said as she walked up the red brick steps. Tiffany ran her finger down the center of Darius's chest. "But you did break my heart."

Slapping her hand away, he glared at her. "How did I break your heart? Tiffany, you have issues and maybe you should go see a counselor or something."

She leaned forward, pressing her ample breasts against his chest. "Darius," she whispered, "you know you want me."

Before he could reply, another car approached. As he feared, it was Celina. She had to have seen him. The way Tiffany was draped over him, there was no way he could explain what was going on without looking like a liar. He could feel Celina's eyes boring into him like a boll weevil making a nest. Darius pushed Tiffany away, and she turned and looked at Celina as she got out of her car.

"Who is she?" Tiffany asked, when she noticed Darius's eyes following Celina as she walked up the steps. "She can't be someone you're remotely interested in."

"Why don't you just leave and find someone else to pester?" Darius said.

Tiffany smiled as she watched Celina slam the door behind her as she walked into her house.

"Looks like you're going to be a free man if you were depending on her for some loving," she said before flouncing off the porch and getting into her car.

Darius watched helplessly as Tiffany drove away. How was he going to explain this? He knew what things looked like and this was the reason Celina didn't want to enter into a relationship. Darius toyed with waiting for Celina to come over to his place. *I might as well wait for a cold day in Hell,* he thought as he leapt over the fence separating their yards. Darius knocked on the door, holding his breath as he waited for Celina to open it.

"What do you want?" she asked.

"I want to talk to you," he said.

Celina folded her arms across her chest and raised her right eyebrow. "Looks like you had your hands full on your front porch," she said angrily.

"I know what that looked like," he said. "But it wasn't what it seemed . . ."

Celina threw her hand up, stopping Darius in mid-sentence. "I don't need an explanation. You don't owe me anything, Darius. You're free to do whatever you want to do."

He ran his hand across his face, searching for the right words to say. Nothing he thought of saying sounded right and the look on Celina's face told him that whatever he said was going to be met with some resistance. Still, Darius had to try to make her see the truth.

"Celina," he said, wrapping his arm around her waist

and pulling her against him. His words floated out of his head as she focused her angry glare on him. She looked as if she was poised to spit fire.

Pushing out of his arms and backing against the door, she said, "Darius, what do you want from me? I mean, there you were with a half-naked woman standing on your porch. But it wasn't what it looked like, right? Let's just be adults and let this thing go."

"No, I'm not going to do that. Tiffany means nothing to me and I'm not a perfect man. I've made some mistakes."

"And so have I. My latest one was getting tangled up with you."

Darius grabbed her arm, pulling her against his hard chest. His lips were centimeters away from hers. "I'm not going let you walk away. You can say we're just friends but there is something else going on here."

"Maybe in your mind," Celina said. She pressed her hand against his chest in an attempt to push him away, but Darius grabbed her hand and kissed it gently. Celina stepped back from him and opened the front door. "Why don't you just leave? We have nothing else to say to each other."

Shaking his head, he didn't move. "Your little attitude isn't going to push me away, even if that is what you want."

"I'm not my mother and if I can't be number one, I won't be number two," Celina snapped.

"What?"

Celina fell silent as if she regretted her admission. Darius cupped her chin in her hands.

"Talk to me. You laid out all of these rules, you claim you just wanted sex, but that's not true, is it?" Darius asked gently.

"I don't want to be hurt," Celina blurted out. "I don't want to get my hopes up about you to have them crushed."

Darius stroked the side of her face with his thumb. "I would never do anything to hurt you," he said. "You have to trust me, believe in me."

She shook her head as fat tears rolled down her cheeks. "I-I can't," Celina whispered. "I wish I could, but I can't." She stepped back from Darius and pushed against his chest. "Please go."

Darius stood firm. He wasn't going anywhere.

CHAPTER 8

Celina walked away from Darius, wishing she could take back everything she had said to him. She'd given him too much information and now she knew he wasn't going to walk away, but Tiffany was a reality. She knew there was something going on with the two of them and she wasn't going to let him make a fool of her. Darius would deny that he and Tiffany were still intimate; that's what men did when they were caught.

How many times had her father denied there was something going on with the other women he had been with?

"Talk to me." Darius said.

"Why are you still here?" she asked, her eyes flashing anger.

He sighed as he reached out and grabbed her shoulder.

Celina placed her hand on top of his and moved it from her shoulder. "Please, just go."

"No, not until we work this out. Celina, I want and need you in my life," he said, nearly pleading with her.

"And her, too?" she spat out. "What does Tiffany mean to you?"

Darius threw his hands up. "I told you—nothing. She was a mistake. I was messed up when I got involved with her, but I'm not that person anymore."

"How do I know that?" Celina asked. "Am I just supposed to take your word for it? Darius, you're full of it and I'm not going to let you hurt me. I came home early tonight because I wanted to . . ." Her voice trailed off and she turned her back to him.

"You wanted to what?" he asked.

"Nothing," she said, knowing that she couldn't open up to him now. Her mother might call it running, but Celina was being smart and getting away from Darius would be the wisest thing for her to do. She didn't want to admit it, but she was falling for him. Celina stood in front of the leather recliner, holding on to the arm of the chair, hoping it would prop her up and give her the strength to push Darius out of her life.

"This is just wrong," Celina said.

Darius walked over to her and pulled her into his arms. She pressed her hand against his chest, but he wouldn't let go.

"No it isn't, Celina. If this is about Tiffany—"

She shook her head furiously. "I watched my father hurt my mother with a parade of women and I would never stand for that. You're not going to do that to me."

"I wouldn't want to," he said. "You're the woman I want. Nothing is going to change that. I don't need a harem."

She inhaled sharply as he leaned in closer to her, his lips nearly touching hers as he said, "Why can't you let me inside that wall?"

"I'm afraid," she said as Darius twirled a strand of her hair around his finger.

"Don't be," he said, then brought his lips down on top of hers.

Celina surrendered to his kiss, but was she going to be able to surrender to his love? She abruptly broke off the kiss, fresh tears shining in her eyes. "Darius," she said. "I-I can't do this."

"Can't or won't?" he asked. "You can't let fear keep you from experiencing life."

Celina turned around and looked at him, wanting so badly to be able to trust him. But how could she ignore what she'd seen? How could she ignore her heart? *I'm here for my father, not for him and not to fall in love with him.*

"Darius, right now is not a good time for this. We can't . . ."

"Can't what? You won't let anything happen, Celina. We're here, right now. You want me just as much as I want you. After what we've shared, I can't get enough of you. Fighting it isn't going to change how you feel." He walked over to her and stroked her back.

"Promise me that you won't hurt me," she said, finally giving into what she felt.

"That's one promise I will keep," he said as his lips brushed against hers.

Celina took a step back. "But we have to take things slowly," she said. "I don't want us to make mistakes by rushing into this. If we're going to build something real together, it can't just be based on physical attraction."

Darius nodded in agreement but he didn't say a word. The last thing he wanted to do was give her an opportunity to change her mind.

Celina closed her eyes and inhaled sharply. Darius's scent was intoxicating and she felt dizzy. But it was time, she told herself. It was time to allow herself to love.

"Why don't we have a quiet dinner tonight?" Darius asked. "We could drive up to Myrtle Beach and have some seafood and talk."

"I need to stay close to home in case the center calls

me about my father," she replied. "But I would love to have dinner with you tonight."

Darius smiled. "All right, I'll break out the grill and some wine."

"That sounds good," she said.

Darius stepped back and headed for the door. Celina followed him, trying to quiet her doubts about him and the journey they were about to embark on. He turned around and kissed her gently on the forehead.

"You won't regret this," he said.

I hope not, she thought as she smiled at him.

Darius walked home with extra pep in his step. He had made inroads with Celina. Now he had to prove to her that all men weren't out to hurt her, though he knew it was going to be a hard sell. However, he was up for the challenge because he wasn't going to be satisfied until her heart was his completely.

The last woman who'd moved him this way was Renita, even though she proved not to be worthy of his love. Besides, Celina and Renita were like night and day. Celina had a vulnerability that made him want to protect her. She was strong and at the same time fragile, like the petals of a rose.

The night had to be special. As Darius prepared for dinner, he ignored the blinking light on his answering machine. The outside world would have to take a backseat as he readied himself to prepare his famous grilled eggplant, stuffed mushrooms, and a green salad for Celina. The phone rang as he chopped bell peppers and leaf spinach and he ignored that as well. He had too much to do to be distracted by whomever was on the other line.

After washing and drying the vegetables, Darius

walked up to his bathroom and took a long shower. As the water beat down on him, he thought about the rain and making love to Celina while the water cascaded around them. He closed his eyes, imagining her curly hair pressed against her face as the rain fell. He could feel her soft lips tickling his neck and her tongue dancing on his earlobe. Darius was so engrossed in his fantasy, that the water got cold as his body heated up, anticipating making love to Celina. He shut the spray off, dashed out of the shower, and wrapped a towel around his waist. He headed for the bedroom and took a pair of black slacks and a white golf shirt from his closet, but he wasn't satisfied with the outfit. *We're not going to a business meeting,* he thought as he reached for a pair of linen shorts and a goldenrod oxford shirt. He dressed quickly, because he still needed to get the candles ready for the dinner table, since he and Celina would eat inside tonight and, if he were lucky, she'd be his tasty dessert.

After putting the candles and the place settings on the table, Darius headed for the kitchen to finish cooking the meal. He pulled a salmon steak from the freezer for himself, squeezing lemon juice on the frozen fish, then dropped it in a glass pan with some parsley and chives. Darius slid the pan in the oven. While the food cooked, he dimmed the lights in the dining room and throughout the house. Next, he opened the curtains so that when the sun set and the moon and stars began to dot the sky, they would provide the perfect backdrop for their dinner.

He walked into the kitchen and grabbed the salad to set in the center of the table. He looked at his watch. It was almost time for Celina to come over.

* * *

Celina stood at the front door with her sweaty hand on the doorknob, her heart beating like an African drum. With her other hand, which was just as sweaty, she smoothed her knee-length black halter dress with red Chinese embroidery around the neckline. Luckily, she didn't stain it. Convinced that her dress was fine, she started tinkering with her hair, which she'd pulled up into a bushy ponytail, and not a hair was out of place. *All right, you can do this. Besides, the man has seen you naked,* she thought.

Swallowing her fears, she opened the door and stepped onto the porch. Casting her eyes upward, she took in the natural beauty of the setting sun, which gave her the urge to grab her sketch pad and colored pencils. Celina made the short trek across to Darius's house. She took a deep breath before she knocked on the door.

When Darius opened the door, he took Celina's breath away. He radiated. The golden shirt he had on made his dark skin glow.

"Hello," he said. "You look beautiful."

Celina blushed. "Thank you."

"Come in, dinner is almost ready," he said, stepping aside to allow Celina to walk in. She couldn't deny how beautiful everything looked and how great it smelled. The candles flickered on the table and filled the room with a golden glow and the scent of jasmine and honeysuckle.

"You went all out, didn't you?" Celina said as Darius led her into the dining room. One thing that impressed her about Darius was his style and the fact that his house didn't look like a typical bachelor pad. Everything was in its place. And he had a love of music, and fine food—those were major pluses in her book. She never expected to find someone like Darius in Elmore and she never expected to find herself falling in love, either.

"Please, sit down," he said, pulling out a chair for her.

"Thank you," she said. "You're such a gentleman."

Darius sat down beside her. "I'm glad you're here," he said as he reached over and grasped her hand gently. "Celina, you're the most intriguing woman I've ever had the pleasure of meeting."

He smiled and leaned in to kiss her on the cheek. As his lips touched her skin, shivers of delight ran down her spine. The feeling excited her and surprised her all at the same time. *Change the subject, quick, or we won't be eating dinner at all,* she thought. "Darius, what's for dinner?"

He stood up. "I think you will approve. I have grilled eggplant and sun-dried tomatoes, stuffed mushrooms, and a salad."

"Sounds divine," she replied. Darius walked into the kitchen and Celina took a full breath for the first time since she walked into the house. Being close to Darius frazzled her senses. She had to stay in control of herself, but he made her feel things and want to do things that she'd only fantasized about.

Celina surmised that it was time to give in to what she was feeling as she watched Darius walk into the dining room with the trays of food. Rising to her feet, she took one of the trays from his hands. "Looks like you were struggling there," she said, placing the tray on the table.

Darius set the other tray on the table and stroked Celina's cheek. "I know we said we were going to wait, but I want you so much, I'm about to explode," he said.

Before Celina could say a word, Darius had pulled her into his arms and captured her lips hungrily. She moaned softly as he slipped his sweet tongue into her mouth and probed the crevices as if he were on an expedition. Her body responded naturally to his touch, his kiss, and she didn't fight it when he untied her dress and barely noticed when it pooled around her feet. But when she felt his hands against her breasts, Celina pulled back.

"We-we can't do this," she whispered. "Not now."

Darius leaned in closer to her. "Celina, you want me just as much as I want you. Don't fight what's in your heart."

"How do you know what's in my heart? You're more interested in what's between my legs," she snapped.

Darius placed his hand over Celina's heart, which was beating rapidly like an engine in overdrive. "This is how I know," he said. "Your heart is talking to me and it is saying the same thing mine is saying. When are you going to start listening to it?"

She couldn't breathe when he pressed his lips against her neck. Every word he'd said to her had been true and she was trying to find some thought to push him away, to give her an excuse to run again. She couldn't find one.

"Do you still want me to stop?" he asked.

Celina shook her head. "Don't stop. Please, don't stop."

Darius scooped Celina into his arms and carried her into the bedroom. In the darkness, Celina's doubts whispered in her ear, telling her that she was setting herself up to be hurt, just like her mother.

Darius laid her on the bed, looking down into her dark eyes. She looked up at him, not knowing what to say or if she should say anything, but words failed her. If she had said something, it might have been the wrong thing. She desperately wanted to believe that she and Darius were building something real and that he wasn't like her father had been when he was married to her mother.

As he unbuttoned his shirt, revealing his sculpted chest, a surge of lust ripped through Celina's body. She wanted to feel his skin against hers, his manhood deep inside her. But what more could he offer her?

Darius kissed her lips gently. "I want you to love me," he said. "Don't hold back. I'll protect you."

"Are you sure you can do that?" she asked breathlessly.

"Yes," he replied confidently, then gently kissed her neck. Celina exhaled and her stomach trembled as Darius's hand brushed across her smooth belly. Then he gently removed her satin and lace bikini panties, stroking her inner thighs with his thumbs as he slid the delicate material down her legs.

She moaned as Darius played her body like a classically trained pianist, slipping his finger into her valley of sexuality, making her thighs quiver. She responded to his every touch like a musical note. Darius slid in between her legs, positioning himself on top of her, pressing her breasts against his chest. Their hearts seemed to have one beat, their bodies one yearning.

Celina took his earlobe into her mouth, gently biting it as he wrapped her legs around his waist. She was so hot she felt as if flames had engulfed her body and it was going to take Darius to put them out.

As Darius entered her awaiting body, neither of them realized that they hadn't protected themselves. Celina pulled Darius closer to her, urging him to dive deeper into her body. She wanted him to lose himself inside her and she wanted to lose herself in his love. He answered her silent request and thrust his hips into hers, digging so deeply that she felt as if he'd touched her soul. She closed her eyes as she exploded from the inside out. Never had she experienced such passion and such intense pleasure. Darius wrapped his arms around her, not ready to pull back. Her warmth and wetness made it hard for him to control himself, but he held out until he knew that Celina had been satisfied. Then he allowed himself to climax.

"This feels so good," Darius said as they lay in one another's arms. He kissed her on the forehead.

"I wish it could be like this forever," she said. Her words surprised her.

"It can be." Darius propped himself up on his elbows, peering at Celina. He knew that no other woman would ever again share his bed or his heart. "All you have to do is believe that we are meant to be. When you start overthinking things, that's when you run into trouble."

"I want to believe that. I need to believe that," she said, tightening her grip around Darius's waist. Celina glanced down at his naked body. "Oh my God."

"What's wrong?" he asked.

"I can't believe this. Darius, you didn't have on a condom. How could you do this?" Celina bolted up in the bed, shattering the afterglow of their lovemaking.

"I'm sorry," he said. "I wasn't thinking."

"Do you know what this could mean?"

"Celina, I swear this isn't something I did on purpose. If you're worried about a disease or anything like that, I've had a physical and everything was negative."

She wrapped the sheet around her naked frame and sat up in the bed. "That's good to know," she said. "And the same is true for me. I had a battery of tests before I went to Paris. But that's not the only thing that we have to worry about."

"Celina, you don't have to create trouble or something to worry about. Everything is going to be fine. Do you trust me?"

Celina nodded. She did trust Darius. She just hoped this trust wouldn't come back to bite her in the heart.

* * *

Darius looked into Celina's coal-black eyes and the look of fear that shone in them filled him with guilt. He should've protected them and used a condom. The last thing that he wanted was a child out of wedlock. Even though times had changed, in Elmore people still believed that it was marriage first, then children.

Celina swung her legs over the side of the bed. "I have to go," she said.

Darius grabbed her shoulder. "Don't go. Stay with me tonight."

Celina shook her head furiously. "I-I can't stay," she said. "I have to go."

Darius turned her around so that they were facing one another. "Have to or want to? I thought you were going to stop running or did you just say that to get me into bed?"

She looked at him and forced a smile. "You're not funny," she said.

"I'm not trying to be. How are you going to leave when we haven't even had dinner yet?" Darius stroked her forearm. "You can sit here and I'll bring our plates in. We can have dinner in bed."

Celina swatted his hand away. "Umm, I think we should get out of this bed," she said as she reached down and picked up her discarded panties. Darius pounced on her playfully, gently kissing her on the lips. Celina responded to his kiss, just as he knew she would, then she placed her hand against his chest and pushed him away.

"You still aren't playing fair, Darius McRae," she said breathlessly.

"And you love it," he joked.

Celina playfully slapped him across the chest. "I thought you were going to feed me?"

Darius stood up and smiled. "I will, but you have to put your dress on before I feast on you again," he said.

Celina slowly and seductively stood up. "Maybe that can be arranged," she said as she slid her dress over her hips.

Darius walked up behind her and tied her dress. Then he kissed her on the neck. Celina shivered underneath his touch.

"We'd better get to that dinner," she said as she turned to walk away.

Darius watched her as she sauntered down the hall, his eyes focused on her hips as they swayed from left to right. *It should be a crime to look that damned good,* he thought. Darius knew he had to keep his hormones in check, at least until they got through dinner.

Darius and Celina sat across from each other, eating in silence, stealing glances at each other as if they were in high school, sitting across from each other in the cafeteria. Celina caught his stare and she seemed to blush. "Why are you looking at me like that?" she asked, placing her fork on the side of her plate. "Do I have food all over my face or something?"

He shook his head. "It's like asking why do people stare at the *Mona Lisa.* Celina, do you realize how beautiful you are?"

"You don't have to blow smoke," she said. "You've already gotten me into bed tonight."

Darius walked over to her and stood over her chair. "Why do you say that? I don't say things that I don't mean and you are the most beautiful and intriguing woman I've met in a long time."

"This is so new to me," she said.

He raised his eyebrow. "This?"

"The heat between us." Her voice was barely a whisper. "For so many years, I never let anyone get too close, even when I was engaged to be married. I'm sure Terrick would've been a good husband, but the passion was never there."

"It's called falling in love."

Celina nodded, "That's what I was going to tell you earlier today when you were with Tiffany. When I saw that, I just wanted to retreat into the house and never speak to you again. My first thought was, *he's just like every other man who claims to love someone, but can't keep it in his pants.*"

"I would never do anything to hurt you," he said, cupping her chin in his hands. "Your love means more than anything to me."

Tears threatened to fall from her almond shaped eyes as Darius brought his lips to hers and softly kissed her. When Celina wrapped her arms around him, he felt her opening up to him and he couldn't be happier. Dinner was completely forgotten as Darius lifted Celina from her chair and carried her back to the bedroom where they made slow, gentle love all night.

CHAPTER 9

She arched her back like a lazy cat, stretching her hand out and touching Darius's face. Everything seemed a little unreal to her. Here she was, lying in bed with this man, opening her heart to him and feeling more satisfied that she'd ever felt. All she could do was pray that this feeling would last.

Being with Darius calmed her, made her happier than she had been in years, and she couldn't help wondering if she'd cheated herself all this time in an effort not to be hurt.

Mother was right, she thought, looking at Darius's sleeping frame. *I have to take a risk and live my life.*

Now Celina was going to have to face another demon— forgiving her father. She sat up in bed, realizing that she hadn't checked on Thomas. What if someone had called the house looking for her? The red numbers on the digital alarm clock read 7:30. Normally, she would be on her way to Columbia. She rose quietly, trying not to wake Darius, but she did anyway. He sat up and looked over at Celina, who was dressing at the foot of the bed.

"Good morning, sunshine," he said, then climbed out of bed, walking up behind her, circling her waist with his strong arms. "I know you weren't going to leave without saying good morning or good-bye?"

"I didn't want to wake you, but I have to get moving. My father may be released from the hospital today."

Darius dropped his arms from around her waist. "You're driving up there this morning?" Celina nodded as she slipped into her dress.

Darius clasped his hands together and looked at her. "You know," he said. "I don't like you driving all that way alone. And you come back so late sometimes. Why don't I go with you?"

She shook her head. "That's not necessary. I'm a big girl, Darius. And you have your own responsibilities here."

He cocked his head to the side and looked at her. "I know that. But these trips have to be hard for you. Celina, you don't have to go through this alone because I'm here for you."

She didn't want to grow dependant on Darius and though she would have loved to have someone to talk to about what was going on with her father, she didn't think he would be able to tear himself away from his business long enough. "Darius, I really don't need you to go with me," she said.

"I don't care, I'm going with you. So you might as well get yourself together and meet me at the car," he said. "I'm not taking 'no' for an answer."

"Whatever," she said, flinging her hair back.

"I'll be ready in fifteen minutes," he said as he walked Celina to the door.

She turned around and looked at Darius. This man was determined and all she could do was roll with it. The look in his eyes told her that he wouldn't easily be deterred.

"Fine, I'll see you in a little bit," she said as she walked out the door. As Celina strode across to her father's house, she couldn't help but smile. Darius had entered her life and made one of the hardest times in her life much easier to handle and, he'd opened her heart to something she never thought she would feel—love. Celina had thought she loved Terrick. That's why she'd accepted his engagement ring, but he didn't fill her with the excitement that Darius did. He didn't make her feel secure, safe, and alive. Terrick couldn't make her body come alive with sensual sensations the way Darius did. He was a great friend and nice guy, but he didn't set her soul on fire. Darius McRae did that with just the sound of his voice. Celina wondered if this feeling would last and she silently prayed that it would as she ran into the bathroom and took a quick shower. As she stepped out of the shower and wrapped herself in a towel, there was a knock at the door.

"Darius, is that you?" she called out as she dashed to the front door and pulled the curtain back. Celina turned and looked at the clock on the wall. It had been fifteen minutes since she left him. Celina opened the front door. "Sorry, I'm running a little behind."

Darius smiled approvingly at the towel she covered herself with. "That's okay, I'll wait. Want some coffee or something to eat before we go?"

Celina shook her head. "I can pick up something at the hospital, but if you want some coffee, help yourself," she said as she led him into the kitchen. Celina pointed to the antiquated coffeemaker on the edge of the breakfast bar. "Dad has some Sanka in the cabinet. I have to get dressed," she said, then disappeared down the hall. Celina listened as the cabinets slammed, indicating that Darius was about to brew some coffee. She quickly dressed in a pair of black and white yoga pants and a matching tank top. She tied the black jacket around her waist, then slipped on a pair of black thong sandals. When she walked into the kitchen, Darius was fumbling with the coffeemaker.

"How long has your father had this thing?" Darius asked.

"It's been here since I was a child," she said with a laugh. Celina walked over to him. "Let me help you with that." She removed the ceramic coffee carafe from the bottom of the coffeemaker and filled it with water from the faucet, opened the back of the machine, and poured the water in. Then she removed the filter basket and poured coffee grinds in the filter.

"We have a sale on coffeemakers at the store," Darius said. "I'll even give you one. It shouldn't take all of this to make a cup of coffee."

"It's not so bad," she said as the coffee began to percolate. Celina reached into the cabinet above her head and pulled out two ivory mugs. "Sometimes old things are just fine. This coffeemaker reminds me of Sunday mornings, rushing off to church, and my parents being together."

Darius walked up behind her and wrapped his arms around her waist. "But it never hurts to try something new," he whispered against her ear. "Look at us. You were so adamant about not even giving me the time of day unless it was on your terms. Now we're making new memories with your old coffeemaker."

Celina sighed. "Darius," she said as his lips brushed against her neck, "don't start something that we can't finish. We have to go."

"I know," he said. "But I want to hear you say it again."

Celina whirled around and locked eyes with him. "Hear what?" she asked. Darius stroked her hair and smiled. She grabbed his hand. "What is it that you want to hear?"

"You saying that you're falling in love with me," he said.

She exhaled loudly. Did he not understand that she needed to get to the hospital? Why was it so important for him to hear her say again that she was falling for him?

"Come on, Darius, we have to go," she said.

"All right," he said, "but don't go changing your mind on me between here and Columbia."

"I'm falling for you, Darius McRae, faster and harder than I've ever fell for anyone," she said unabashedly. Celina stood on her tiptoes and kissed Darius firmly on the lips. "Can we go now?"

Satisfied, Darius nodded and the couple headed out the door. Darius walked over to the driver's side and stopped Celina from opening the door. "Why don't you let me drive?" he suggested as he slid the keys from her hand.

"And I thought chivalry was dead," she said as she gave up the keys and walked over to the passenger side of the car. Darius smiled as he released the electric locks and watched Celina get into the car and cross her legs at the ankles.

When he eased into the car, it was her turn to stare, taking note of how Darius moved like fluid, smooth and cool. Even the way he switched the car on was slick, like a TV detective—or maybe it was the rose-colored tint through which she saw him. Darius had come into her life and carved a space in her heart—something that she'd never expected to happen.

Celina didn't know that love could feel good like this; she didn't realize the splendor of it all. All she'd seen and imagined was the pain that her father had caused her mother all those years ago.

Darius and Celina rode to the hospital in silence because she fell asleep. He glanced at her as she dozed off while he headed down the interstate, knowing that he was right and she needed him to travel with her. He reached out and gently stroked her thigh, careful not to wake her up because she needed her rest. Darius wanted to protect Celina at all costs, not wanting her ever to be hurt by anything. If he could have found a cure for her father's cancer, he would have. He wondered if Thomas was getting any better and how Celina was really dealing with all of this. From the short time that he'd known her, he knew that she was good at bottling things inside. Darius admired Celina's strength and the fact that she could do for herself, but allowed him to reach out to help her as well. She was the perfect blend of independence and sass tempered with a little bit of southern belle innocence.

In short, she was perfect. Everything that Darius had ever wanted or hoped to find in a woman. He smiled as thoughts of the wedding march and Celina dressed in a white gown danced in his mind. The last woman who made him think about marriage was Renita. But it was her thirst for other men that killed his dream of making her his wife. Celina wasn't like that. Darius knew she just needed one man to love her and he was going to be the one to do it.

He thought about Celina's life in New York. As beautiful as she was, was she really single in the Big Apple? Women like her didn't come around often and some man was a fool to let her roam the city alone.

But what if she wasn't alone? What if she had a boyfriend in New York waiting for her to return from Paris?

Celina sat up and looked over at Darius. "Are we there yet?"

Darius smiled as he turned off at the exit marked for the medical center. "I can imagine how you were as a kid in the car," he said.

Celina rolled her eyes. "You drive like an old man," she said, running her tongue over her lips. "I would have been there by now."

"Woman, you wound me. Just because I don't drive like a bat out of hell doesn't mean I drive like an old man," Darius replied as he turned onto the street from the exit ramp.

Celina chuckled. "Yes, it does," she said as she slid her petite feet into her thong sandals. She wiggled her golden toes, causing Darius to nearly run a stop sign as he fantasized about taking each toe into his mouth, sucking them as if they were imported chocolate. The car jerked forward as Darius slammed on the brakes. Celina placed her hand on the dashboard, bracing herself.

"All right, I apologize," Celina said. "You don't drive like an old man."

"Sorry," Darius said. "I got a little distracted."

Celina raised her eyebrow at him. Darius shrugged his shoulders, not wanting to let her know what distracted him. Celina gave Darius directions to the medical center. He muttered under his breath as cars haphazardly entered traffic, cutting him off.

"Road rage?" Celina ribbed.

"Everybody in Columbia can't be in this much of a hurry," he said, as he moved into the left lane so that he could turn into the medical center's entrance.

Celina shrugged her shoulders. "Everyone doesn't drive like they're in Elmore," she said with a smile.

Darius looked at her as he pulled the car into a parking spot. "I bet you drive like a maniac in New York."

"Actually, I prefer the subway," she said as she opened

the door and stepped out of the car. "It's safer and cheaper."

Darius watched Celina as she got out of the car. She stretched her arms above her head, exposing a small sliver of flesh, sending sparks of arousal though Darius's body. He looked away quickly. He hadn't come to the hospital to lust after Celina; he was there to support her as she checked in on her father. After all, the man was sick, near death. But he couldn't help thinking about the time they had spent in his bed and watching her wrap a sheet around her lean body, hiding the breasts that he loved and the thighs that he wanted to be between.

Darius walked over to Celina and linked his arm with hers, wanting everyone to know that she was his woman and his heart was hers.

Celina felt so comfortable with Darius that it frightened her, because she could see herself growing to depend on him more and more. But love wasn't about dependence and she knew that he was merely offering his support to her because he cared. Still, the prickly voices in the back of her head questioned whether this feeling would last. *Don't get too comfortable, because your home is in New York.*

She leaned against him as they rode the elevator up to the fifth floor where her father's room was, doing her best to ignore the negative thoughts as the doors to the elevator opened and they stepped off, heading down the hall for room 537.

Boisterous laughter poured from the room—a sound that Celina had never heard before. Her father, she surmised, had probably charmed a few nurses. She slowly pushed the door open. "Mom?" she exclaimed when she saw Rena sitting at the foot of Thomas's bed.

Rena stood up, hugged her daughter, and then smiled approvingly at Darius. Celina knew her mother had recalled their conversation from a few days ago and put two and two together.

"Is this little Darius McRae?" Rena asked. "You certainly aren't little anymore."

"No ma'am," he said as they hugged.

Celina looked from her father to her mother. She hadn't seen the two of them looking that happy at the same time since she was a child. Celina walked over to her father, who looked a lot healthier than he had when she brought him to the center.

"How are you feeling?" she asked as she kissed him on the forehead.

Thomas nodded. "Better, much better." His gaze fell on Rena, who was catching up with Darius. Celina followed Thomas's gaze. Part of her—the child that never grew up—was happy to see her parents together again. But why couldn't things have been like this before? Maybe they never would've divorced. Then again, it took cancer for Thomas to curb his cheating ways.

"Mom, what are you doing here?" Celina asked, wondering how John felt about her rushing to her ex-husband's side.

"I came to check on you and your father. Is that a problem?" Rena raised her eyebrow.

"Not at all," she said, knowing that it wasn't the time to question her mother.

"John is at the hotel. I thought you could use a break and John and I decided to come and help you with Thomas," she said. "But, Mr. Hart looks as if he is going to be just fine." Rena walked over to Thomas and ran her hand over his forehead. Thomas looked as happy as a little boy in a candy store.

"Mom, can we talk outside?" Celina said, wanting to understand how her mother could be so civil to the man who crushed her heart.

Celina shook her head slightly as she and her mother walked outside and a few feet away from Thomas's door.

"What's wrong?" Rena asked.

"I don't get this, Mom. You and Daddy divorced, but here you are. You don't owe him anything and I'm sure that John can't be too happy about you dropping everything to come down here."

Rena reached out and stroked Celina's hair. "Child, your father and I will always have one connection and that's you. I never wanted Thomas to suffer. John and I prayed about our decision to come here and we felt as if this was the right thing to do. It doesn't change how I feel about John. And speaking of feelings, you and little Darius look pretty cozy together. Was he the man you were talking about on the phone a few days ago?"

"What?" Celina said, though she couldn't deny it—she was glowing and it was all because of Darius.

"He's handsome, well-mannered. I remember how you two used to run around the neighborhood together. This is cute," she said.

Celina smiled as her mother took her down memory lane.

Celina and Darius had been about seven years old and they ran into the house because Rena had been baking cookies and they smelled it from the backyard.

"Ma! Are those chocolate chip cookies?" Celina said, as she burst through the door.

"Is that how you ask for cookies?" Rena had said. "If you and Darius want to have some cookies, go wash your hands and have a seat at the table. You know, one day, you two are going to be baking cookies for your children."

Celina and Darius looked at each other and stuck their tongues out. "No way," they said in unison.

Rena knew what the smile on her daughter's face meant and she couldn't have been happier about it. "I'm glad Darius has opened your eyes to the wonders of love."

Celina relaxed her shoulders and leaned against the wall. "Is that why you're here? Because you still love Daddy?"

"Yes, and because I love you. Celina, you shouldn't have been going through this alone. I should've been here sooner. It's a good thing that you have Darius."

Celina nodded. Darius was a special blessing that she hadn't expected. He'd opened his arms to her and provided her with a shoulder to lean on. "Let's go back inside before they realize that we're talking about them," Celina said.

When Celina and Rena walked into the hospital room, Thomas was sitting up in bed and Darius was pouring him a cup of water. Darius smiled at Celina as she walked in. "Is everything all right?" Celina asked.

Thomas nodded. "What about with you two?" he asked as he focused his gaze on his former wife. Rena walked over to Thomas and placed her hand on his shoulder.

"We're fine. And I'm going to leave you in the capable hands of our daughter." Rena bent over Thomas and kissed his cheek tenderly.

Thomas clutched Rena's hand. "Thank you," he said, his eyes glossing over with unshed tears of gratitude. "I'm really glad you came here."

Rena patted the back of Thomas's bony hand and Celina's heart swelled because in that moment, she had her family back together. Then she began to wonder why they lost it all to begin with. If her parents still loved each other, why couldn't they make it work? Was that just the way love went?

Darius walked over to her and wrapped his arms around her, bringing his lips close to her ear. "Are you OK?"

Celina turned around, thinking that she didn't want love to turn into pain and she didn't want to be hurt the way her mother had been by her father. How could she be sure that Darius wouldn't break her heart?

"Can you give me and my dad a minute?" she asked. "I need to talk to him in private."

Darius nodded and turned toward the door. "Can I get either of you something from the vending machines?"

"Nah, son, we're fine," Thomas said.

"When are you coming home, Daddy?" Celina asked when they were alone.

"Tomorrow, I hope," he said as he made himself comfortable in the bed. "I have a few more tests to go through."

Celina sat on the edge beside him, noticing that her father wasn't coughing nearly as much as he had been. She wrapped her arms around herself and focused her stare on her father. "That sounds good," she said. "You still love her, don't you?"

Thomas smiled despite himself. "I never stopped loving your mother," he said. "She is and will always be my first love."

"Then what happened?" she asked. "If you still love her, why didn't things work out for you two?"

Thomas shrugged his shoulders. This conversation was long overdue. He had always known that he'd have to answer for what happened between him and

Rena. "Celina, I made mistakes. I won't deny that," Thomas said.

"But why? Why couldn't you love us enough to keep our family together? I've struggled with this for years. I wanted to believe you loved me, but it's been hard," she said, her eyes sparkling with years of tears.

Thomas's heart hurt as he looked at the pained look in his daughter's eyes. "Maybe it was my ego, but I never thought your mother would leave. Celina, your mother and I were very young when we got married. I still had a lot of growing up to do. By the time I became a man, your mother was long gone. In Chicago, the first time I came to visit, I knew I was going to bring my family home."

Celina nodded as she recalled the visit. She and Rena had been living in a modest two-bedroom apartment on the south side of Chicago. Until she and her mother had moved into that apartment, Celina had never seen a roach unless it was on the Discovery Channel. Celina had hated that apartment and she thought her father had come to take them back to Elmore when he showed up on their doorstep. Immediately, she went into her room and started packing. Then Thomas had walked in and beckoned her to sit on the bed. When he told her that she wouldn't be returning with him, her heart had broken into a thousand pieces.

"Rena was making a good life for you and for herself. She had that job at the art gallery," Thomas paused and looked at Celina. He searched her face for understanding, but her expression was blank. He cleared his throat and continued talking. "That day, when I saw you and your mother, I knew you didn't need me. So, I checked out of your lives. Rena asked me to stay in Chicago, thinking that a fresh start away from Elmore would fix everything that had gone wrong between us, but I was too afraid to start over. I had a good thing at home and I wasn't about to give that up. Everybody knew my name, I had steady work and Chicago was just too big. I knew I couldn't be what you and your mother needed. I couldn't step up and be that husband and father that you and Rena needed. I thought I was doing the right thing."

"The right thing?" she said. "Daddy, I needed you." Celina blinked rapidly to hold back the tears that threatened to fall.

"And I'm sorry I wasn't there, but when I saw how well you and Rena were doing without me—" He stopped talking and looked out the window, then said. "Celina, I made your mother cry so many nights. But that day, she looked so beautiful and so happy. I knew I wasn't going to make her that happy because I was jealous of her. Your mother had the strength to get out of Elmore and I never could. I loved you and your mother so much, I just had to let you go."

Celina knew what her father said should have made sense, but it didn't. When he let Rena go it was as if he let her go, too. And if he loved her mother so much, wasn't he supposed to fight for her and make things work?

"How can you say you loved us? Daddy, you abandoned us. You let your ego keep you from your family. That's inexcusable and I don't know if I'll ever forgive you."

Thomas turned away from Celina. "I don't expect you to understand or even forgive me," he said. "But I want you to know, that boy loves you."

"What?" Celina said, wiping her eyes with the back of her hand.

Thomas smiled and stroked his daughter's hand. "Darius McRae loves you. I can see it in his eyes and I know he isn't going to run like I did. He's a better man than I was."

Celina looked away from her father and stared out the window, wondering if Darius's love was fleeting or if he was there to stay. Was she ready to risk her heart and find out?

CHAPTER 10

Darius stood outside Thomas's room, not knowing how Celina would be after speaking with her father. He knew that her father's abandonment had a lot to do with how she felt about love and why she'd been holding back from him.

Come on, D, you have to let her work through this if you're going to have a shot with her, he thought as he walked over to the window at the end of the corridor. As he looked over the Columbia skyline, his cell phone rang. Darius flipped the silver phone open. "Yeah?" he said.

"Where are you?" a female voice demanded.

"Who is this?"

The woman on the other end of the phone sighed heavily. "Now you don't know me? Darius, I'm not going to be ignored."

"Tiffany? Why are you calling me? I made it pretty clear that I don't want anything to do with you."

"Because you didn't return my calls last night. I guess she let you in huh? She can't compare to me. You'll see."

Darius snapped the phone shut. Seconds later it rang again. "Stop calling me. I don't have time for your games."

"Darius," Richard said. "What's going on?"

"Sorry, Rich. What's up?"

"Well, we have another problem at the store," he said. "I'm beginning to think that someone is targeting us."

Darius clenched his jaw tightly, causing the muscle on the side of his face to twitch. He knew who was targeting his store and why, but she was going to stop.

"What happened now?"

Richard sighed, then began telling Darius about the fire that broke out in back of the store. Someone had broken into the storage shed and burned the azalea bushes. The fire destroyed the shed, but only caused minor cosmetic damage to the store's siding. Darius muttered a string of curses.

"Calm down," Richard said. "Boy, sometimes I swear you're going to have a heart attack before you're forty."

"Rich, I'm sorry, but these childish games have to stop."

Richard grunted. "You think you know who's doing this?"

Darius nodded his head furiously before telling Richard he knew who was doing all of this. He might not have been able to link Tiffany to the fire and the vandalism at the store, but he knew it was only a matter of time before he could, and when he did, there would be hell to pay.

"I hope the police plan to look into this. Things are getting serious. Fire is nothing to play with. Someone could have been killed."

"We're lucky that someone didn't get hurt. Who do you think is doing this?" Richard asked. "People are starting to talk and we're losing business."

Darius sighed heavily into the phone. "Tiffany is behind all of this and when I prove it, she's going to jail. You'd think that a grown woman would know how to deal with rejection. I'll see you this afternoon." Darius closed his phone just as Celina walked out of her father's room.

Her eyes were blurry and rimmed with faint red lines. She walked over to Darius and embraced him tightly.

"What's wrong, sweetheart?" he asked, noticing her emotional state.

Celina buried her head in his chest and sobbed silently before saying, "My father and I had a long talk that stirred up some emotions." She clung to Darius as he gently stroked her hair.

"Did it help?" he asked. Celina nodded. Darius kissed her forehead. "Then, that is all that matters. Isn't that part of the reason you came home?"

Smiling though her tears, she knew that he was right. "I got some of the questions I had for the last twenty years answered. Maybe this will be the turning point in my relationship with him."

Darius nodded and smiled at her, all the while wondering how he was going to keep Celina from getting involved in his mess with Tiffany. "The doctors are getting ready to take Daddy up for some tests. Why don't we go get some lunch?"

Darius nodded and wrapped his arms around Celina's waist and led her out the door. "You know," he said. "I know a quaint little bistro near the mall where we can eat."

"That's fine," she said as they walked out to the car.

Darius watched Celina as she slid into the car, reaching into her purse and retrieving her round sunglasses to hide her puffy eyes. Darius admired her strength and the class she displayed in dealing with her father's illness. Watching her move through it without falling apart just solidified the fact that she was nothing like the clingy, self-centered women who had tried to wedge their way into his life.

Celina caught his intense stare as she snapped her purse shut. "What?" she asked.

Darius just continued to smile at her, finding himself at a loss for words. "Nothing," he said. "I just admire you."

"Admire me?" she asked.

"Yes, look at how you're dealing with this situation. You're a strong woman and that's commendable. You didn't have to come back and help your father, but you did. Put your career on hold and came back to a place that you don't know to help a man who left you. How many other women do know who are that selfless?"

She wiped a tear from her cheek. "I don't know. It just seemed like the right thing to do and I needed answers from him before it was too late."

Darius started the car and reached for her hand. They rode in silence to the restaurant. He knew that Celina was consumed with thoughts of her father and he wished there was something that he could do to ease her mind and her pain.

Just love her, he thought as they pulled into the parking lot of the restaurant. He got out of the car and opened the door for Celina, who was still silent and deep in thought.

"When is your father coming home?" Darius asked as he opened the door to the bistro.

"Tomorrow, I think."

They walked into the restaurant and sat in a corner booth. Darius took Celina's hand in his. She sighed and cocked her head to the side. "You know," she said, "this might not be the right time for this, but once my father comes home, I'm going to have to go back to New York."

Darius's heart dropped to his stomach. "Oh," he said,

not wanting to think about her leaving at all. He thought about the time that he and Celina had spent together, wrapped in each other's arms, her lips against his. Her heart beating against his. His desire for her began to grow. Celina looked at Darius, seemingly reading his sexual thoughts.

"Are you OK?" she asked.

"Not at all," he said. "Celina, you just do something to me. And thinking about you leaving or not seeing you again aren't the thoughts that I want to have right now."

She blushed underneath his comment and his hot stares.

"So, is that all I am to you? A really hot fantasy?" Celina probed.

Darius walked over to her side of the booth and pulled her into his arms. "You're more than that," he whispered, his warm breath tickling her ear. "I've never met anyone like you before in my life. What man can resist you? You're charming, classy, strong, and brilliant."

Celina pressed her hand against his chest. "Why don't we go outside and eat, since it's such a nice day," she said.

"All right," he said as he waved for the waitress and pointed to the patio.

Once they were moved outside to a table underneath a yellow umbrella, Celina turned to Darius and smiled at him. "I have a request."

"What's that?"

"Strip for me. I still want to paint you."

Darius smirked. "All right," he said. "Why don't we do it tonight, before I lose my nerve."

Celina smiled at Darius. "I'll be gentle," she said, as she leaned over the table and kissed him on the cheek. "Thank you."

After Darius and Celina finished their lunch, they

headed back to the hospital. This time, Celina's mother and stepfather were in Thomas's room.

"You guys are still here?" Rena said when they walked in the room.

"Yes, we are," Celina said as she hugged her mother. "We're leaving soon, though."

John walked over to his stepdaughter and hugged her. "Hey, sweetie," he said. "You look great. And happy." John glanced sidelong at Darius, slipping into protective father mode. "And who are you?"

Darius cleared his throat and introduced himself to John.

Thomas sat up in the bed. "John, I've already checked him out. He lives next door. He might be good enough for our little girl," Thomas said.

Darius laughed because he hadn't met a woman's family in years, but here he was being scrutinized by Celina's parents. He felt as if he were back in high school, about to head to the prom.

After a few hours of the five of them laughing and talking, Celina and Darius headed back to Elmore. Celina slept all the way home and Darius replayed their lunch conversation over and over again. He knew she felt the connection that they had and he wasn't going to let her run away from it. Now, how was he going to convince her to stay?

As they pulled into the Elmore town limits, Celina sat up in the passenger seat. She hadn't realized she was so tired. She looked over at Darius as he passed the road that led to their houses.

"Where are we going?" she asked, raising her eyebrow with curiosity.

"I have to make a quick run to the hardware store," Darius said. "Then, I was hoping you'd watch the sun set with me."

Celina smiled. "Only if you take me to get my sketch pad first. Remember, you made a promise."

Darius chuckled and nodded. "Yes, I did. I'll take you after we leave the store," he said. He pulled around to the back of the hardware store and parked the car.

Celina looked at the burned-out storage shed. "What happened here?" she asked.

"Electrical problem, probably. I'll be right back," Darius said.

She was skeptical about his explanation because she was sure if an electrical short had caused the damage that she saw, Darius would have let one of his staff members handle it. Celina watched Darius walk into the hardware store. Once he disappeared inside, she got out of the car to get the scoop on what was really going on. Though their voices were muffled, she could tell Darius was having a heated discussion with someone.

"I don't give a damn," Darius bellowed. "Call the police now."

"D, how do you know it was her?" the man asked, his voice terse. "Everyone knows her and it will be a town scandal."

Celina wondered who they were talking about and what "she" did. The voices came to an abrupt halt. Celina stepped closer to the door to see what was going on. She saw the same woman who was on Darius's porch walking toward them. "You keep running into trouble, don't you?" she said.

"Tiffany, don't play coy like you didn't set this fire," Darius barked. "I told you to stay away from this store."

She placed her hand on her hip and rolled her eyes. "And I won't be ignored," Tiffany said. "You can't toss me aside like I'm a piece of trash. Darius, we had a good thing."

"Had? Tiffany, we never had anything. When are you

going to get it through your head that you and I never had a relationship and we are not going to?" Darius asked. Then he grabbed her by the arm and led her toward the front of the store.

Celina was confused by Darius's reaction to the woman and a little put off at the way she said Darius tossed her aside. Was that really his style—use a woman until he grew tired of her? Curiosity got the best of her and she walked into the store to find out what was going on. She crossed over to the man who Darius had been talking to and asked, "What's going on?"

"Little Celina Hart, is that you?" Richard asked.

She smiled tensely. "Yes, it's me. But I haven't been called 'little' in a long time," she said as she looked at him, trying to place who he was.

Richard smiled at her again. "You don't remember me, do you?"

Celina shook her head. "I'm sorry, I don't."

Richard took her hand in his. "Your father and I used to smoke cigars together in the back of your mother's house."

Celina remembered him. "Mr. Ingram," she said, then gave the man a hug.

"When did you get into town?" he asked as they separated.

Celina told him that she had been back in Elmore for about a month and that she had come there to take care of her father.

"I had no idea he was so sick," Richard said solemnly.

"No one did. He did a good job of hiding his illness from everyone," she said. Richard patted her on the shoulder. "But he is doing better now. Darius and I went to the hospital to see him today."

Richard smiled at Celina. "So, that's what's different about my boss."

She furrowed her brows. "What do you mean?"

Richard released a low chuckle. "You can tell when a man is in love and boss man is definitely smitten. I knew it wasn't that one," he said, nodding his head toward Tiffany. "Although she *is* having a problem taking 'no' for an answer."

Celina folded her arms underneath her breasts. "Is she doing something to hurt Darius's business?"

Richard shrugged his shoulders. "I don't know if she's the one who broke the window and burned that shed back there, but Darius isn't going to let her or anyone else get away with that. He has some temper."

She fell silent, not knowing what to make of what Richard told her. She had never seen Darius out of control or angry, until she saw him with Tiffany. Darius looked as if he could snap that woman's neck as they argued in the distance. "A temper?"

Richard nodded. "City residue. Where are you living now?"

"New York."

Richard grunted at her reply. "You kids love leaving here for a big, dirty city. But somehow you come back. You come back for the homegrown food and the love," he said.

"What do you mean by that?" Celina asked.

Richard smiled, then walked away without answering Celina's question. Maybe he was right, but she certainly didn't come home to fall in love. Darius's temper didn't quite sit well with her. Then again, maybe this woman had done something to him that elicited this kind of response from him. Could Darius become violent? *Wait a minute,* she thought, *Darius isn't like that. This woman is probably responsible for burning his shed and breaking that front window. Anyone would be angry about that.*

Celina walked to the front of the store where Darius and

Tiffany were arguing. "Darius," she said. "Is everything all right?"

Tiffany looked at Celina, giving her the once-over as if she was sizing her up.

Celina returned Tiffany's glare with one of her own. "Problem?" Celina asked.

Tiffany turned on her heels and headed out the door. Darius turned to Celina and pulled her into his arms.

"I'm sorry you had to witness that," he said. "There's been a lot of stuff going on here and I'm 100 percent sure that Tiffany is behind this. She's acting worse than a child but she's taking things too far now."

"What have the police said?" she asked. Darius shrugged his shoulders. Celina hugged him tightly. "Let's get out of here so we can still catch that sunset," she whispered in his ear. "And don't forget, you still have to strip for me." Celina flashed Darius a devilish grin.

"You don't have to ask me twice," he said. Darius waved to Richard. "See you in the morning."

Richard smiled. "Have fun, you two," he said.

Darius drove Celina to her house so that she could retrieve her sketch pad. He sat in the car while Celina ran into the house. She grabbed her pad from the edge of the sofa, then walked into the kitchen and picked up her charcoal pencils. Celina was ready to go. Darius smiled at her as she walked to the car. He pushed the passenger side door open so that she could slide in. "All right," she said. "Let's go."

CHAPTER 11

The sky began to change colors, fading from powder blue to burnt orange, then a faint purple. A lone star dotted the sky as the sun began to descend. A soft breeze blew across the lake, causing the tranquil water to ripple slightly. Celina pushed her hair back off her forehead and looked up at Darius as he leaned on the trunk of a nine-foot oak tree on the bank of Lake Elmore.

"Move your arm a little to the left," she ordered as she continued to sketch Darius's image. Celina tried not to focus on his crotch, but his semi erect penis seemed to point directly at her. Celina swallowed hard as she forced herself to focus on his face.

"How much longer?" he asked. "It's starting to get cool over here."

"Not from where I'm sitting," she mumbled. "Just a few more minutes."

Darius tried to hold his pose and a straight face, but he broke out into a smile.

"Please, please don't smile," Celina said.

Darius tried not to smile, but he broke out laughing.

Celina dropped her sketch pad and glared at him. "You're not a good model."

Darius walked over to Celina, standing in front of her. "Really?"

She slowly stood up, pressing her hand against his chest. "That's right, because good models do as they're told," she said. "I guess I'll have to finish this from memory."

Darius reached around Celina's neck and unclasped her halter top. "Well, let me give you something else to memorize," he whispered against her ear, then pressed her body against his as her breasts spilled from the flimsy shirt.

She started to protest, because they were out in public and anyone could walk by and see them, not to mention the animals that she was sure they'd scared away. But when Darius assaulted her neck with the sweetest kisses, all her reservations flew away with a group of ducks that had floated into the air. She melted against him as his tongue brushed across her neck. Then Darius scooped Celina into his arms, gently laying her back on the plaid blanket that they had spread on the ground earlier. He straddled her body, his fingers dancing around the waistband of her denim cutoffs before he peeled her clothes from her body, kissing each piece of skin he revealed.

Celina's body writhed under the touch of his hands, the lick of his tongue, and his gentle biting. Though Darius's hot erection pressed against her thighs, he didn't glide into her body right away, which she desperately wanted him to do. Instead, he continued teasing her body with his hot kisses. As a cool breeze blew over their bodies, Celina shuddered, every nerve in her body standing on end. With her senses stimulated, all Darius needed to do was kiss her on her neck to bring her to a near climax. She gripped the back of his head as he suckled her breasts, tickling her nipple with his tongue.

Arching her back, she pressed herself into his mouth, wanting and needing more of his lips, tongue, and teeth.

Darius wrapped his hands around her back, giving her more of what she'd been silently begging for. Celina sat up, breaking off her kiss with Darius, and looked into his eyes, which were clouded with love, lust, and desire. For a second she wanted to stop and run away because the feelings were too intense. Darius wasn't having that, though. It was as if he sensed her apprehension when he leaned in and said, "I need you."

Her chest heaved up and down as Darius molded her against him. She wrapped her legs around his waist, inching closer to his erection. He reached into the discarded canvas bag behind them and pulled out a condom package. Darius slid the protection across his erect penis in one quick motion. Celina's breath caught in her chest as she felt Darius throbbing against her thighs and her body quivered with anticipation and fear. Being next to Darius ignited so many emotions in her. Her body ached for his kisses, his touch, and the feeling of him inside her. Her heart yearned for his love, his warmth, and his tenderness. Celina still wasn't certain that she could give Darius everything he wanted or the love he deserved. She was still afraid of the hurt that she knew love caused. Seeing the change in her, he slowed his sensual assault on her body.

"What's wrong?" Darius asked, cupping her face, forcing her to look into his eyes. Celina tried to silence Darius by kissing him, but Darius turned away. "Talk to me," he said. "If you don't want to do this or . . ."

"Nothing's wrong," she said, attempting to look away. But he held her face between his hands, not giving her a chance to turn away.

"I know you're holding back," he said. "I just don't

understand why." He ran his index finger down the side of her arm. "You don't have to hold back from me."

"I'm not doing that," she replied unconvincingly.

Darius clutched her round bottom and pulled her closer to him. "Celina, I want more than your body. Why don't you let me in here," he said, pointing his finger to her chest. "This is what I want more than anything else."

Celina felt even more exposed and naked than ever with Darius lying on top of her. He'd seen her body before, but in this moment, it felt as if he saw right though her soul. He seemed to see every part that she'd tried so desperately to hide from him.

She uttered the words, "I'm afraid," as if she were a child stuck in a thunderstorm. "I don't want to be hurt."

Darius pressed his lips against hers, pecking her gently. "You don't have to worry, Celina. I'll never hurt you." He moved his mouth across hers, tracing her lips with his tongue. Celina closed her eyes, shutting out the voices of doubt in her head. Darius felt her body relax.

"Make love to me," she moaned. Darius was more than happy to oblige her request, reaching down and spreading her legs apart. Following a bead of sweat down her flat stomach, Darius's tongue traveled down her body, causing her heightened senses to stand even further on end. When he slipped his hand between her thighs, her legs shook almost violently as he peeled apart the folds of wet skin hiding her tender bud. Then he pulled his finger out of her and sampled her womanly juice.

"You taste so good," he whispered as he pulled her against his erection.

Celina was rendered speechless as Darius took control of her body. She clutched his shoulders and moaned his name as he took her to the heights of passion. The way he moved against her, stroking her body in all of the right places, she was sure he was a student of the Kama

Sutra. As he dove deeper into her core, Celina pressed her hips into his, offering him more of her body, despite the fact that she was near climax.

He went in for the kill as he leaned in and planted a sensual kiss on her neck. She melted against him, climaxing powerfully. Darius had branded her his and, as much as it excited her, Celina was still frightened by the prospect of falling deeper in love with him. Every day wouldn't be like this, every day wouldn't be just pleasure and bliss. When would he tire of her and walk away?

Ignoring her negative thoughts, she rolled her hips into his. "Darius," she moaned before burying her mouth in his neck.

Now it was Darius's turn to explode as her tongue danced across his neck. Just as he knew her body, Celina also knew his. Her tongue found every crease and crevice to drive him wild. Their bodies were in sync, but would their hearts ever be? Celina tried to push those thoughts out of her mind as they began to climax. Darius pulled the blanket around their naked bodies, using the edge of it to wipe the sweat from their faces. He drew the shape of a heart in the moisture that had collected above her breast.

Celina laughed at the gesture. "What is that? You giving me your heart?"

"Yes," he replied seriously. "Can you return the favor?"

Celina rolled out of his embrace and picked up her discarded clothes. That was a question she wasn't ready to answer. "It's time for us to go," she said, kicking out of the blanket.

Darius stood up and pulled on his shorts, then turned his stare toward Celina. "It's time for us to stop playing this game. This stopped being about sex a long time ago."

"Darius . . ."

He threw his hand up stopping her from finishing. "Let me be totally honest with you. I never wanted this to happen. I didn't mean to fall in love with you, but how could I not? You're everything I've ever wanted and all the things I didn't know I needed."

"How can you be sure?" she asked. "People fall in and out of love like the weather changes. I may be what you want now, but what happens tomorrow or when I return to New York?"

"I love you, distance isn't going to matter. I know you have your issues with relationships because of what you saw your father put your mother through, but I'm not him."

She turned her back to him and Darius grabbed her by the shoulder forcing her to face him. "I don't play fair and I don't give up on something that I want," he said. "Your attitude about love may have pushed a lesser man away, but Celina Hart, mark my words, you will be mine."

I already am, she thought as she looked at him without saying a word.

As Celina dressed, Darius struggled with his desire for her. Just the way she pulled her shorts up over her hips and reached around to tie her halter top turned him on like a light switch.

Darius stood in front of her and pulled her into his arms. His heart was beating in overdrive. When Celina was that close to him, his body lit up like a firecracker. Every nerve stood on end. He somehow found the voice to say, "Celina, you and I will be together, all the way. I just have to make you believe that you can love me without being hurt or afraid." Darius stroked her bare back. She fell silent. "Baby," he whispered. "Talk to me. What's on your mind?"

"We need to get cleaned up," she said, pulling away from him.

Darius shook his head, he could feel his temper beginning to flare. She was hot and cold, holding back her true emotions from him and it was grating on his nerves. What more could he do to show Celina that he loved her and wanted to protect her from all harm? Hadn't he shown her that he was someone she could depend on? Someone who loved her? Celina stared at him, seemingly reading his mind.

"Darius, I need some time," she said. "This is really new to me and I don't know how I'm supposed to respond and react."

Darius sighed. He wanted to know how much time she was going to need and what was going to happen when she returned to New York. The lyrics of Bonnie Rait's "I Can't Make You Love Me," began playing in his mind. Had he turned into Tiffany and many of the other women who had come into his life? They all pressed him to give them something he didn't want to give. Was he doing the same thing with Celina? Maybe their connection was purely physical and she was only going to give him her body and nothing more.

"Fine," Darius said, ignoring the questions running through his mind. He gathered their things and stalked to the car with Celina nearly running to keep up with him. Darius stopped short of the car then turned around and glared at her.

"Celina, I can't do this. I love you so much it hurts, but you keep holding me at arm's length as if I'm going to do something to break your heart. When you look at me it's as if you don't believe that I love you, and it's breaking *my* heart."

She walked over to him and stroked his face gently. "Darius, I don't want to do that to you. But I'm . . ."

"Afraid, I know. You've said it over and over again. But have I given you a reason to feel that way? What more can I do?" he asked as he grabbed her hand and held it over his heart. "You feel that? This is yours, all you have to do is reach out and grab it."

"But Darius, my life is in New York. My art and my . . ."

He silenced her by placing his finger to her lips. Darius stared into her eyes. "Your life can be anywhere you want it to be. You've said it yourself, you can find art anywhere. What's wrong with here?"

"So, because you say you love me, I'm supposed to pack up and move here? What happens when you decide you don't love me anymore?"

"Would you rather I packed up and moved to New York? Either way, here or there, I will never stop loving you," he said.

Tears pooled in her eyes as he stared at her. Darius wanted to kiss her and never let her go. "Celina," he said. "I need to hear you say it. I don't want to waste your time or mine if you don't feel for me what I feel for you."

"Darius, don't do this to me," she said as she clutched her sketch pad to her chest.

"Do what? Love you? Ask you for answers that I deserve?" Darius pulled her into his arms and kissed her forehead. "Celina, if you need time, I'll give you time. Just don't expect me to wait forever and allow you to play with my heart because you think that's what *I'm* going to do to *you*. In this time that you need, are you going to consider having a life with me? Or is this a smoke screen for you to push me away?"

Celina shook her head and laughed sarcastically. "You know, I didn't come down here for you. My father is my priority and he needs me. This relationship is secondary and I can't look beyond today until I know what's going to happen with my dad."

"And I would never take you away from that," Darius said. "You're here for your father and I'm here for you."

"As long as I give you what you want, right?" Celina snapped. "Damn it, this was a mistake, you and I should've never hooked up and confused everything."

"What's confusing?" he asked, closing the short distance between them.

"The way I feel," she said. "Yes, I've been holding back and trying hard not to love you, but every day you show me something new and I want to . . . We'd better go."

Darius nodded and they got into the car. They rode in silence back to their houses. He didn't know what to say or how he could say anything without sounding as if he was being overbearing. *I've said enough,* he thought as he pulled into her driveway. *Celina has to decide what the next move will be.*

She climbed out of the car without saying a word and Darius followed her lead. He started for his driveway, but stole one last glance at Celina as she walked up the front steps. She didn't look back. Darius held his breath as he walked back to his house. What was he going to do, he wondered. What else could he do to show Celina that he loved her? Darius walked into his house and plopped down on the sofa. Thoughts of Celina clouded his mind until the telephone rang. *What is it now,* he wondered as he reached over and picked up the cordless phone from the charger on the oak end table. "What is it?" he asked when he picked up the phone.

"Darius," Tiffany said. "This is getting ridiculous."

"What's ridiculous is you breaking windows at my store and burning my shed with thousands of dollars worth of azalea bushes in it. What's ridiculous is you acting like a child and trying to prove a point."

"I'm tired of the police questioning me every time something happens to you," Tiffany snapped. "Why are you doing this to me?"

Darius slammed the phone down, unable to listen to

another word from her. He knew she was going to try something else and the only way to stop her would be to catch her in the act. Walking over to the window, Darius stared helplessly into the night sky, watching the twinkling stars. Tiffany was a problem he didn't want to deal with, but she needed to be handled. Why couldn't the police find some sort of evidence that linked her to the vandalism and arson at his store? Nothing like this had ever happened in Elmore before. Darius was so deep in thought that he didn't see Celina walk up his front steps. Her rapping at the door startled him. Darius opened the door, thinking it was Tiffany. When he saw Celina, he smiled.

"I want to talk to you," she said. "Actually, I want you to just listen."

Darius stepped aside and watched Celina walk in. She stood next to the sofa until Darius nodded for her to sit down.

"I do care about you," she said without looking at him. "You have opened my eyes to what love can truly be, but I still can't be sure that I'm ready for this. What I feel when I'm with you can't last forever."

Darius sat beside her, held her face in his hands, and brought her eyes to his. He could tell it was hard for Celina to open up to him. He stroked her hand as if he was telling her it was all right to tell him what was wrong.

She squeezed his hand and continued. "I have sabotaged every relationship that I have ever had."

"Why?" Darius asked.

Celina twirled a strand of hair around her finger and looked at Darius. "Love hurts. I want to skip the pain," she said in a voice barely above a whisper. "I know you say you would never hurt me and you love me, but what happens when that changes?"

Darius shook his head furiously. "Love doesn't have to

hurt. I'm not saying that we won't have difficulties, but together we'll get through them. I've watched my parents work through a lot during their marriage."

Celina slipped her hand from underneath his. Then she stood up. "But what if we can't do that?" she asked. "I didn't have such great role models."

He shook his head. How could a woman that beautiful, a woman whose paintings screamed love and showed that she obviously wanted love, say that she didn't believe love would last? Darius knew Celina yearned to be loved, wanted to be touched tenderly, and it was up to him to show her that love was going to last. As passionate as she'd been every time they made love, he knew she wanted it and craved it just as much as he did. *You need to let go of the fear of what your father did,* he thought as he lost himself in her teary eyes.

"You'll never know until you give yourself a chance to be loved," he said, leaning into her. "And I'm talking about more than something physical." Darius let her go.

"What do you mean?" she asked.

"Celina, when we make love, it's more than sex. Then when we're done, you seem to retreat into this 'I don't want to be hurt' mode. We couldn't make love the way we do if we didn't have more than lust holding us together. I know that you love me. You just don't want to admit it."

Celina walked toward the door. "What do you want from me?" she asked as she reached out for the doorknob. Darius stopped her from leaving, placing his hand on top of hers.

"The question is, what do you want to give me? You know where I stand and how I feel."

She looked up at him, her black eyes reminding him of a young doe caught in the headlights. "I-I don't know," she said.

Darius leaned into her, his lips dangerously close to her ear. "I'll tell you what I want from you," he said. "I want you to open your heart and whatever is holding you back from loving me, let it go." He took a step back from her. Darius reached around her and opened the door. "You can go if you want to."

Celina raised her right eyebrow, then reached for the door. Instead of walking out, she closed the door and turned to Darius. "I don't want to go," she said. "I want to stay here with you." Celina fell into Darius's arms and he squeezed her tightly. She'd finally said what he'd needed to hear.

CHAPTER 12

Celina woke with a start. Her neck was aching, her back throbbing, and when she rolled over her lips collided with Darius's nose. They had fallen asleep sitting on his sofa. A half-empty bowl of popcorn sat at their feet. Blinking her eyes, she focused on the TV, its screen filled with snow, and humming faintly.

Darius stroked Celina's arm. "Um," he said. "What time is it?"

She shrugged her shoulders. "We missed the movie," she said as she stood up and stretched.

"Are you going to spend the night?" he asked.

"I don't know, you know I have such a long way to go to get home," she joked.

Darius stood up and pulled Celina back on the sofa, then pounced on top of her. "You're not going anywhere," he said as he brushed his lips against hers. "I make a really mean cheese omelet."

Celina seductively licked her lips. "So, you want me to stay so I can sample your omelet?"

Darius reached out and stroked her hair. "Yeah," he said. "That's one thing you can sample."

Celina reached up and grabbed his hand. She looked

into his eyes and wondered if this was love. The look that she saw on his face was like nothing she had ever seen, not even when she was with Terrick, who'd made declarations of love all the time. When Celina had announced to him that she planned to move to New York, he hadn't done a thing to stop her. She never really believed that what she and Terrick had shared was real love, anyway. Slowly but surely, she was starting to believe that Darius did love her. Now she needed to learn to love him back. It wasn't going to be easy, because that nagging voice kept telling her it wasn't going to last.

"So," he probed, "are you staying?"

"Yes," she said breathlessly. "Isn't it time for you to go clean up your room, hide the dirty socks and everything like that?"

Darius gently bit Celina on the cheek. "I'm not a college frat boy. My room is presentable, for the most part. Besides, who said you were sleeping in my bed?"

Celina pushed him off her and stood up. "As if there was any doubt of where I would sleep," she said haughtily, then headed down the hall. Darius dashed after her and grabbed her around the waist. They laughed and played like two middle-school students, running through the house playing tag in the middle of the night. They finally collapsed on the bed, covered in sweat. Celina turned to Darius, wanting to tell him that she loved him. It was on the tip of her tongue. She wanted the word to pass through her lips, but she couldn't say it. Darius looked at Celina.

"We're not as young as we used to be, are we?" he asked, breathing heavily.

"Not at all," she replied. Both of them sighed, then broke out laughing. She smacked his arm. "No one told you to chase me through the house. We're just lucky you got rid of Mrs. McRae's china cabinet."

Darius chuckled low and long. "Do you remember my seventh birthday when little Marvin nearly broke the glass?"

Celina nodded, reflecting on the memory. "Your mother swooped down on him like Batman or something. She said, 'Didn't I tell you children not to run in my house? Out! All of you, go outside and don't come back.'"

Darius rolled off the bed because he was laughing so hard. Celina leaned over the edge and looked down at Darius. How could anyone not love him? He was absolutely gorgeous, had a wonderful sense of humor, and he was the most gentle lover Celina had ever known. He awakened more than lust in her. He'd opened her frightened heart to the possibility of love.

"You OK?" Darius asked when he caught Celina's stare.

She forced a smile and said she was tired. Darius seemed to buy her excuse because he was tired, too, and crawled into bed with Celina. She rested her head against his chest and drifted off to sleep.

Darius held Celina as if she were a fragile china doll. He didn't know if she was really sleeping or if she was faking it. In the silence of the room, he took the opportunity to explore the nuances of her, starting with her hair. He loved the wooly texture of it. Inhaling, he took in the jasmine scent. She reminded him of the most exotic flower, one that didn't have a name. Slowly, he slid his finger down her arm. Italian silk had nothing on her skin, which was smooth and unblemished. Darius wondered if she fought acne as a teenager the way he had. Whatever awkward stage she'd gone though, she was a beautiful butterfly now.

Focusing his gaze on her lips, Darius wanted to kiss her, but he was afraid that he would wake her.

How did this happen? How did I fall for you so fast and so hard? No other woman has ever moved me the way you do. It's only going to get better. I wished you could see that.

As he was about to drift off to sleep, the telephone rang. Darius eased his arms from around Celina and reached over to pick up the phone.

"Yeah," he whispered into the receiver.

"You hung up on me earlier. I don't appreciate that," Tiffany said.

"When are you going to stop calling me?" Darius slid off the bed and walked into the bathroom. "It's one o'clock in the morning."

"And there was a time when I called you at one in the morning and you wanted me to rush right over," she said. "I guess that would be a problem now that I've been replaced, huh?"

"Times have changed and you have proven yourself to be a crazy . . ." Darius stopped in midsentence as Celina walked into the bathroom.

"Darius," Celina said. "What's going on?"

He dropped the phone and looked at Celina with a guilty expression on his face. "Nothing," he said.

"Who was that?"

"Wrong number," he said.

Celina folded her arms across her chest. "Please don't do that," she said as she pushed her hair back off her forehead.

"Do what?"

"Lie to me. Who was the woman on the phone?" Celina put her hand on her hips and looked into Darius's eyes. "I mean, no one gets out of bed to tell someone they have a wrong number."

"Tiffany," he said, looking away from her.

Celina huffed and pushed her way into the bathroom. She closed the door in Darius's face.

"Celina, there is nothing going on with me and Tiffany, even though that's what she wants."

The bathroom door opened. Celina looked at Darius with anger flickering in her black eyes. "I've heard this song and seen this dance before," Celina said. "If there's nothing going on, then why did you sneak out of bed to talk to her?"

"Not from me you haven't," Darius said. "It isn't a song and dance. It's the truth. I didn't want to wake you and . . ."

Celina rolled her eyes and turned her back to him. "Save it. It's funny how this Tiffany woman keeps popping up."

"Celina, it's not like that. I think she's the one who has been causing all of the trouble at the store."

She narrowed her eyes into little slits. "Darius, spare me, okay? You're just like him."

He was confused. Who was Celina talking about? Then he realized that it was her father. "Celina, I know what you're thinking and it isn't true."

Celina jerked away from him. "What I'm thinking is, I've made a huge mistake being here. Darius, I refuse to let you play me for a fool."

He grabbed her arm, forcing her to look him in the eye again. "Do you think that's what I'm doing?"

Celina snatched away from him. "You tell me," she snapped. Celina bolted over to the side of the bed, grabbing her clothes.

"I'm not going to let you run out of here. You're not going to sabotage this relationship, not when I know that we love each other."

"I'd like to see you try and stop me," she said as she pulled her shorts up over her legs. Darius pushed her back on the bed, pinning her shoulders down.

"I know you love me as much as I love you," he said.

Celina pushed against his chest, but Darius wouldn't release his grip on her. "I'm not going to let you go," Darius whispered. "Tiffany isn't a threat to us. The only thing that can hurt us is you walking out that door."

"I'm not staying here," she snapped. "What are you going to do when I return to New York? Tell Tiffany that I didn't matter? I know this game. I watched my father run it on my mother for years. I'm not going to be your flavor of the month and fall for your lies of love."

Darius stood up, ran his hand over his face and forced himself to calm down. "When are you going to realize that I'm not your father and you're not your mother?" And you can't believe what we have is a lie."

"You're right," Celina said as she pulled her shirt over her head. "Because I'm not going to wait ten years to leave."

Deciding to give Celina her space, he watched her storm out the front door because he knew it wasn't over. What he didn't know was that a shadowy figure sat across the street watching his house.

The next morning, Darius woke up praying the night before was a dream. Yet the cold sheets on the left side of the bed let him know that he was alone. Even if he could smell the faint scent of Celina in his bed, she wasn't there. He refused to let her fade away like her jasmine scent. Leaping out of the bed, he took a quick shower, dressed, and dashed out of the house hoping to catch Celina before she headed to Columbia. When he stepped onto the front porch, he spotted her getting into her rental car.

"Celina!"

She turned her head and looked at him with disgust clouding her eyes. "Leave me alone, Darius," she said.

He didn't heed her warning, as he leapt over the fence dividing their yards and stood in between her and the driver's door. "Baby, I don't like the way things ended between us last night. You made everything seem so final."

"That's because it is," she said, making an attempt to close the door. He wouldn't let the door go.

"Look me in the eye and say that," he said. "Celina, tell me that you want me to leave you alone and that you don't care about me, then I will walk away."

Celina turned her head away from him. "Say it," he whispered, bringing his face closer to hers. "Tell me to leave and I'll do it, but as long as there is a chance for us, I'm going to be right here in your face."

"Leave me alone, Darius," Celina said. Her voice was shaky and thin and she wasn't fooling Darius or herself.

"You don't mean it," he replied. "You don't mean it at all."

"How are you going to tell me what I mean?" she snapped. "Darius, I'm not going sit here and listen to you lie about what's going on with you and Tiffany and how much you love and care about me. Darius, we had great sex. That's it. Don't try to make it more than what it is."

"You know it's more than that," Darius exclaimed. "You know we have more than a physical connection. You couldn't give yourself to me the way that you do if you didn't love me."

Celina threw her head back, as if she knew Darius wasn't going to leave until they worked something out. "Look," Celina said. "I have to go see my father. I don't have time for this. I have to get to my father."

"When will you have time for this? For us? Celina, I'm not giving up on you and I won't let you give up, either," he said, pounding his hand on the side of the door. "Don't shut me out when I love you more than I've ever loved anyone."

"Love me? How can you love me when you still have another woman calling you and showing up at your house and I'm just supposed to believe that you're so in love with me? That you can't live without me and you would never do anything to hurt me?"

Darius squared his shoulders. "That's exactly what I'm saying. Celina, open your heart to me and let me show you what I'm saying is true. Am I a perfect man? No, I'll make mistakes, but I will never hurt you or cheat on you. You mean too much to me."

Celina started the ignition. "I have to go," she said. Darius closed her door and started to walk away. Celina rolled the window down, "Maybe we can talk when I return from the hospital."

Darius, who was walking away feeling dejected, perked up when he heard what Celina said. He turned around and looked at her. "I would like that," he said. She backed the car out of the driveway and headed down the street.

As Celina drove to Columbia, she tried not to think about him and the scene in the driveway, but she couldn't help herself. She wanted to believe that he loved her and that he was going to be true to her. What was going to happen when she left? Because she would be going back to New York and eventually she wanted to return to Paris to finish what she'd started there.

Yet, she was conflicted over her feelings for him. When they were together, he made her feel so special, like nothing mattered but them being together. However, that woman kept showing up and Celina wasn't naive enough to believe that Tiffany was coming around without provocation. No woman could be that desperate, could she? Celina shook her head as she drove onto the interstate, trying to quiet the contradictory voices in her head. On the one hand, she wanted to see where this thing would go with Darius, but there was no way she'd let him hurt her. Could he stay true to her and resist Tiffany's temptation? *If I don't trust him, then I obviously don't love him.* The lie burned in her brain because she knew that she loved him more than she wanted to admit.

By the time she arrived at the hospital, her mind was muddled with thoughts of Darius and the love he had professed to her. How could she be sure that he really meant it? Celina walked into Thomas's room. She was surprised to see her mother sitting at his bedside.

"Mom, what are you doing here?" Celina asked as she walked over to Rena and kissed her on the cheek.

"Well, John and I are leaving today and I wanted to visit with Thomas before we left," she said.

Thomas smiled at his former wife and his daughter. "Your mother is a good woman," he said as Celina leaned over and kissed him. "She's been here for a while, giving us a chance to catch up." He reached out and stroked Rena's shoulder.

"It was good for me, too," Rena said.

Celina watched her parents in awe, not knowing if she'd stepped into the twilight zone or not. There had been a time when the mention of Thomas's name sent her mother into a bitter tirade. Looking at them smiling at one another now didn't seem real.

"So," Celina said. "Are you getting out of here today?"

Thomas nodded. "Yes, I am, thank goodness."

"That's great," Celina said. "I have everything at the house ready for you. Have you all had breakfast?"

Thomas shook his head. "Not unless you count this cardboard hospital food," he said, pointing to the tray.

Rena rose to her feet with a smile still planted on her lips. "Why don't I go get us something to eat?" she said. "There is a nice restaurant near the hotel that has the best grits, pancakes, and eggs."

Celina nodded, happy to have a reprieve from eating tasteless and overpriced food in the hospital cafeteria.

"Well," Rena said. "I will be right back."

Celina sat down beside her father and took his hand in hers, gently stroking it. "What's going on with you and Mom?" she asked.

Thomas shrugged his shoulders. "We had a long talk about our lives together," he said. "We got through a lot of our past problems."

"She forgave you?" Celina asked.

Thomas nodded, gave her hand a squeeze, and smiled. "Are you going to forgive me?"

Celina turned her head away from her father. What could she say? She needed to forgive him and she needed to let go of the pain that she felt her father had caused her. She found that was much harder than she thought it would be. Celina feared that her father would disappoint her again and she'd go back to the place where she was at twelve years old. Even though she was a grown woman who didn't need her father to escort her to the father-daughter picnic, those years without him had scarred her deeply. And she'd been taking it all out on Darius.

"I have forgiven you," she said.

"Have you? I mean, Celina, we've never really talked about what the divorce did to you. Your mother told me a little bit today."

She held her breath as Thomas talked. "I never realized that you knew about my affairs," he said. "As hard as I tried to hide them from your mother, I never thought about how you'd feel if you found out."

"The whole town knew. You can't keep secrets in a place like Elmore," she mumbled.

Thomas nodded. "I know and I'm sorry that I ever hurt you or Rena. And just because I was a cheat, that doesn't mean that the man who loves you will do the same thing to you. I cheated on your mother because I was a young fool and didn't know that I was going to ruin two of the best things that ever happened to me. If I could turn back the hands of time, there are two things I'd change. I would've never started smoking and I never would've hurt your mother."

"She seems to be over it," Celina said, slipping her hand from underneath Thomas's.

"But you're not, are you?" His eyes shone with tears as a few drops of water slid down Celina's cheek.

She shook her head, then took a deep breath. "I'm not," she said. "Watching you hurt Mom has made it hard for me to trust a man when he says he loves me. I remember when you used to tell Mom how much you loved her and how she was your everything. Then you'd go and stay out all night. Did you tell those other women the same thing?"

"Sweetie, I know what I did was wrong and I hurt your mother, but just because I messed up, it doesn't mean every man is going to do that. I did and still do love your mother. It's hard to explain why men do some of the things that we do. I was running from responsibility, from my own failures. Your mother made me focus on being a family man, paying bills, and I didn't want to do that. We were so young when we got married and I thought there was something in the streets for me and I went looking for it. Darius isn't like that."

"How can I be sure?" she asked. Closing her eyes, she tried not to cry. Hot, fat tears spilled from her eyes anyway.

Thomas stroked his daughter's hair. "How many men do you know who would give up the bright lights and big city for Elmore to take over his parents' business? Is everything always going to be happy between the two of you? Not always, but I know that you need to give that man a fair chance."

"What?"

"Don't judge Darius because of what I did. He is a good man and a hard worker. He's always shown me nothing but respect and I know he will do the same thing with you."

Celina raised her eyebrow at her father. "Darius and I aren't going to work. I mean, I'm going back to New York soon and then there's the project in Paris. There are going to be too many miles between us for this to work."

"It looked like you two were working the last time you were here. Celina, that man loves you. You have his nose open so wide I can see his brain when he talks. Don't lose him. Don't be like me and run from what could be the best thing to ever happen to you."

Celina silently mulled over what her father said. Maybe he was right, but she wasn't willing to risk it. She had a plan. As soon as they returned home, she was going to hire a nurse and get as far away from Darius as she could. Once she returned to her art and New York, Darius would become a wonderful memory that she could push out of her mind. *So, I'm running, it's not like I haven't done it before,* she thought as she faced her father.

"I can't stay in Elmore forever," Celina whispered, more to herself. "What happens when I return to New York?"

"No one can see into the future, but what happens if you never allow yourself to see what Darius's love feels like? Let your heart guide you," Thomas said. "And, who said that I'm ready for you to go back to New York?"

Celina smiled at her father. "Maybe I can stay for a few more weeks," she said as she leaned over and hugged him.

Rena walked in with three steaming boxes of food. "Well, this looks promising," she said. "I wish I had my camera."

Celina and Thomas laughed at Rena as she set the Styrofoam boxes on the foot of Thomas's bed. The three of them dug into the hot grits, fluffy eggs dripping with cheese, and buttery toast. While Thomas and Rena enjoyed crispy strips of bacon, Celina enjoyed her eggs.

"I still can't believe our child is a vegetarian," Thomas said in between bites of bacon. "She grew up on this stuff and hamburgers, too."

Rena smiled. "That's what happens when people move up north," she said. "And you know Celina has always followed her own beat."

"Stop it," Celina said. "It's a much healthier lifestyle and I like it."

Rena raised her eyebrow. "That's the problem with you young kids these days. You let TV and books tell you how to live. My mother lived to be one hundred, and she ate pork, beef, and chicken—cooked with lard."

Celina rolled her eyes. She'd heard this speech the day she had given up meat and men. "And," Rena continued. "Prince Charming doesn't exist, and Oprah can't solve all of your problems. You keep running away from love and I'm never going to have a grandchild or two to spoil."

"All right, mother, I get it," Celina said exasperatedly. She dropped her plastic fork in the box, suddenly having lost her appetite.

"Do you? Where is Darius?" Rena asked, folding her arms across her chest and dropping her own fork.

"At home, the last time I checked," she said, avoiding eye contact with her mother.

Rena shook her head. "Here we go again. So, what phantom issue is ending this relationship?"

"Our relationship is not over because it never started," Celina said. "And I don't want to talk about it."

Rena picked up her cup of coffee and shook her head. "I know you don't, you never do. I'm not arguing with you today. I'm way too tired."

Celina stood up and walked over to the window, avoiding looking at either her mother or her father. How could she tell her mother that she couldn't give herself to Darius because she had watched love destroy her and she wasn't the forgiving type?

"What do you want me to say?" Celina asked, as Rena walked over to her and placed her hand on her back.

"Celina, I want you to be happy. I was blessed to fall in love twice. I just want you to open yourself up to love once. I know you love Darius and he loves you. Don't let your hang-ups keep you from being happy."

Celina nodded as her mother stroked her back. "Am I supposed to give up New York to be here with Darius?"

"No, you two can work out a compromise or something. That is, if you love him enough. And what's so special about New York, anyway? You didn't have a problem jetting off to Paris to paint. Why is it so hard for you to admit that you have feelings for that man?"

Celina nodded again. She'd been trying to fight it and deny it, but she did love Darius and she didn't want a life if he wasn't in it. He still had to prove to her that he had no hidden skeletons that would leap out of his closet and break her heart. Then again, there was Tiffany. What was it about that woman that gave her the creeps?

CHAPTER 13

Darius tried to focus on his work at the store, but all he could think about was Celina. Was she really going to bolt out of his life because of a misunderstanding? This didn't really have anything to do with him; it was more about her fear. If he could only get inside that dark space and shine his love so that she could see that he wasn't Thomas Hart.

"Darius," Richard called out from the doorway of Darius's office.

"Yeah?" he said, thinking, *what now?*

"Chief Wayman is out here for you."

Darius nodded, thinking the mess with Tiffany was going be over soon. Maybe she had been arrested, which would've brightened his otherwise dark day.

"Send him back," he said as he pulled out a bottle of Jack Daniels and two shot glasses. The burly lawman walked into Darius's office with a scowl on his pie-shaped face.

"Chief," Darius said offering the man a drink.

Wayman shook his massive head and didn't take the seat that Darius had offered him, either.

"What's going on, Darius?"

Confused, Darius shrugged his shoulders. "You tell me. This is about the fire and my window, right?"

"I'm here about two adults trading accusations and using my police department as some sort of go-between. Tiffany said someone threw a brick through the window of her house last night and she said you did it."

Darius poured himself a shot of the brown liquor and downed it in one gulp. "That's a damned lie. Last night I was at home with Cel . . . a guest."

Wayman sat down and took the bottle from the middle of the desk. "Darius, I like you, always had nothing but respect for you and your family." He paused to pour himself a drink. "But you and Tiffany need to handle this immature beef between the two of y'all without involving me. I don't have time to answer calls from you two because she's jealous of your new girlfriend or vice versa." Wayman gulped his drink, then headed for the door. "If this is a lover's quarrel, just send some flowers and get it over with."

"Wait," Darius said. "That woman has cost me $10,000 in the last month. She has to pay for that. If she isn't responsible for the fire and the brick through my window, then who is?"

"I need proof that she did anything. I'm talking to you just like I talked to her when you said she was the one who did all this stuff here. This is getting really old. I have less trouble out of the so-called gangsters in town."

Darius rolled his eyes. "Chief, that woman is crazy and someone is going to get hurt."

"That's not going to happen. You watch too much television. This is Elmore, not Los Angeles or Washington, DC." Wayman turned and walked out of Darius's office.

Darius poured himself another drink. There had to be some way to prove that Tiffany was behind all of this. Darius downed his drink and poured himself another one.

Richard walked into the office and closed the door. "What's going on?" he asked.

"I feel like I'm in high school again," Darius said as he reached for his bottle of Jack Daniels, but Richard moved the bottle out of his reach.

"Youngblood, Jack can't get you out of this." Darius dropped his head on the desk. Richard looked at his boss and shook his head. "I got a feeling this is about more than Wayman's visit."

Darius nodded slowly. "I messed up, bad," Darius revealed.

Richard rocked back on his heels, thinking that his young boss's temper had gotten him into trouble. "What happened?" he asked.

Darius relayed the events of the night before and Richard shook his head, fighting back the laugh that danced in the back of his throat.

"When are you young cats going to learn not to lie about simple things? You know that woman is out to get you and Celina could help you if she knew the truth about what's going on."

"But I don't want her involved. Celina has . . . Never mind."

Richard shook his head. "You and Celina need to talk and then you need to find out if Tiffany is playing the role of psycho girl and press charges against her. If my woman gets out of bed to take a late-night phone call, I'm going to think the worst too. And you know women overthink everything."

Darius stood up and ran his hand over his face. What Richard said sounded easy enough, but he knew Celina's trust issues were going to make it hard for him to convince her that he was telling the truth about Tiffany.

Darius looked at the bottle of Jack Daniels sitting on his desk, knowing that there were no answers in the bottom of it. He needed his head to be clear. "All right," Darius said, "I'm going to take off for a little bit."

Richard saluted his boss. "I'll hold things down here," he said. "Go get that woman."

Darius headed home so that he could wait for Celina to return. No matter what it took, he was going to have to convince her that he was telling her the truth about Tiffany's antics. The last thing he expected to find when he arrived home was the Elmore fire department pulling up to his house. Darius stopped his car, ran up to his front lawn and looked for the fire.

"What's going on?" he demanded. Darius didn't see any smoke or flames. One of the firefighters looked at him and shrugged his shoulders. "Where's the fire?"

"We got a call that there was a fire here," the firefighter said as he put his gear on. "We're going to check out the structure and see what's going on."

Darius uttered an expletive and headed to his car to grab his cell phone. He'd dialed Tiffany's telephone number.

"Hello?" she said sweetly.

"I'm tired of your games," he snapped. "Stop it right now."

She laughed. "Well, Darius, how are you this afternoon? I take it that the police have been to see you about my window."

"Look, stop this madness," he demanded. Darius clutched the phone so hard that his knuckles turned white. "You know I didn't do anything to your window. Now you have the police breathing down my neck. And you have the fire department at my house."

"I have nothing to do with the fire department being at your house," she said unconvincingly. "But if you're going to continue to blame me for something I didn't do, then you're going to get the same treatment. How is your new girlfriend?"

"That's none of your damned business. Is this about my relationship? Tiffany, I don't want you and that isn't going to change. You can set fires and throw all the bricks you want and I still wouldn't want anything to do with you. You need help."

"Darius, who said I still wanted you? Maybe I just want to watch you squirm. You aren't going to get away with treating me like I'm a piece of trash you can toss away because you're done with me. I won't be ignored."

"This isn't a damned movie. When are you going to realize that we never had anything to begin with, Tiffany? You're a leech and I don't need you in my life." The dial tone sounded in his ear. Darius tossed his cell phone into the ditch.

The fire chief walked over to Darius. "We didn't find a fire or anything."

"Who called you all?" Darius asked through clenched teeth.

"We got a call from 9-1-1," he said. "Must have been some child playing a prank."

Darius wanted to tell the fire chief the child was a grown woman with a grudge, but he shook the man's hand and thanked him for checking. Darius walked into his house as the massive fire engines drove away. He flung himself on the sofa and stared up at the ceiling. Things were going to get worse before they got better. He could feel it.

Celina smiled at Thomas, who was napping while she drove. She was glad her father was coming home and that they were working toward repairing their tattered relationship. Celina knew it was only going to be a matter of time before she and Thomas had significant roles in each other's lives and that he'd beat this cancer. He didn't seem like the same shell of a man that she'd found when she'd first arrived in town.

Celina's smile started to fade when she thought about what else was waiting for her in Elmore. Darius. She knew that when she got home Darius was going to be there waiting and she was going to have to make a decision. Was she going to allow him in her life or was she going to just pack up and head back to New York before her heart got broken?

Running from love wasn't going to be an option and leaving now would probably undo all the progress that she and her father had made. Besides, Rena was right; she needed to open her heart and let Darius in. She couldn't run forever. She knew she cared about Darius and leaving him would be one of the hardest things that she would have to do. But the situation with Tiffany worried her. The temptation for Darius to cheat on her was very strong and she didn't want to be hurt. What man could and would turn down a woman desperate to give him her body? She knew Tiffany was that kind of woman. Lust was all over her face that day Celina saw her leaning over Darius on his front porch.

Thomas snorted as he sat up in the passenger seat and looked at his daughter. "You all right?" he asked.

"I'm fine, Daddy. Maybe I should be asking you that, being that you're the one who just got out of the hospital."

Thomas smiled. "I haven't felt this good in years. Seeing your mother was good, but having you here is the best medicine that I could ever have. I love you, Celina. Now you just have to make yourself as happy as you made me."

"How do you suppose I do that?" she asked, even though she knew the answer to that question.

"With Darius McRae," he said. "That man loves you and I know you could kiss the ground he walks on, too. Y'all probably been in love with each other since you were born. I remember watching you two play when you were children. I'd always had a sneaking suspicion that you two would end up together."

Celina shook her head. "Don't worry about me. I'll be fine. We just have to make sure that you get well, all right? We're going to get you a nurse and we're going to have to make sure you have food in the house and . . ."

"Don't start dodging the subject," he said. "What about you and Darius? You are going to talk to him before you go back to New York, aren't you?"

"Yes, Daddy, I'm going to talk to Darius." *Even if it's just to say good-bye.*

Thomas smiled and nodded. "That's good."

When Celina pulled into the town limits of Elmore, she felt her chest tighten. She was only a few minutes from seeing Darius. What was she going to say to him? *Just speak from your heart,* she told herself as she turned into the driveway of her home. Celina glanced over at Darius's house, wondering if he was still at the hardware store. Thomas slowly got out of the car and bent over to retrieve his bags. Celina, however, was quicker, and grabbed them.

"Daddy, why don't you go inside and let me get your bags for you? Then I'll come and fix you something to eat," she said. Celina heard Darius's front door close and, from the corner of her eye, she saw him standing on the porch.

"Hey there, young man," Thomas called out.

"Mr. Hart, how are you?" Darius replied.

"Good, good. Why don't you come over here and help Celina with my bags and join us for dinner?"

Celina shook her head at Thomas's less than subtle matchmaking attempt. Darius walked over to the Hart house and stood next to Celina.

"How are you today?" he asked.

"All right," she said softly.

Darius took the black bag from her hand. "That's good to know," he said.

Thomas ambled up the front steps and unlocked the front door. He was going to go inside and get into his bed. His plan was to tell Celina that he was too tired to get up for dinner and to eat in his room, forcing her and Darius to eat alone. Maybe then they would fix whatever was wrong between them. He remembered being young and in love; the ups and downs of it all. Thomas stole one last glance at the couple before walking into the house.

Celina waved at her father, then turned to Darius. "He's not slick," she said as she pushed her hair back.

"But I like his technique," Darius said as he gave Celina the once-over.

"What? Did you lose something?"

"I don't know, you tell me." Darius smiled and walked toward the front door.

"Darius," Celina said as she followed him. He kept walking, about two steps in front of her. Celina caught up with him and grabbed his shoulder.

Darius opened the front door and set Thomas's bag in the chair next to the door. Then he pulled Celina into his arms. "Celina, I love you so much, I ache for you. The last thing I want to do is cause you a moment of pain. I'm not going to let you walk out of my life. If I have to follow you to New York, I will. If I have to buy every piece of your art to start an art gallery, I will, just to have a part of you next to me."

Celina held his face in her hands, stroking his cheeks with her thumbs. "Darius," she whispered. "I don't know what to say."

"Say what's in there," he said placing his hand over her heart. "Say what's resting right here in your heart."

"I love you," she blurted out. "I didn't mean to fall in love with you and I didn't even want to. But I did. Darius . . ." He silenced her with a kiss, leaning into her, pressing his body against hers and she melted against him. Darius buried his hand in Celina's hair, pulling her mouth closer to his. Celina savored the taste of his tongue, nearly devouring it as he probed the sweet crevices of her mouth. His kiss seemed to fill her with the essence of his love and she was lost in it, forgetting that her father was just down the hall, that she needed to be preparing dinner, and that she'd spent the better part of her day trying to convince herself that she didn't love him. Darius broke the kiss off. "Your father is going to come after me with a shotgun if he sees us."

Celina raised her right eyebrow at him. "I wouldn't worry about that if I were you. He thinks you're good for me."

Darius smiled. "I've always liked your dad. He's a smart man, you should listen to him."

"Listen, I've got to cook my dad something to eat, but we need to talk."

"You seem to forget I was invited for dinner."

Celina opened the door and held it open. "Then I'm going to put you to work, grill master."

As they walked into the house, neither of them noticed the angry glare that followed them.

* * *

Darius sat at the bar with Celina, watching her as she chopped celery and carrots. "Are you going to help me or just watch me do all the work?" she asked as she dropped the knife.

"I like the view," he said, then rose to his feet. "What do you need me to do?"

"If you don't put that chicken breast on the grill, my poor father is going to starve," she said.

Darius took the meat from the counter and placed it on the small indoor grill after seasoning it with a little salt, red pepper, and onion powder.

"That smells good," Celina said. "It almost makes me want to eat chicken again."

Darius playfully smacked Celina on the bottom with the dish towel he had draped over his shoulder. "Come on back to your roots. You were raised on this. How does one survive without eating meat?"

"And I was raised on breast milk, but you don't see me putting it in my coffee," she ribbed. "Besides, does this body look or feel as if it's been deprived of any nourishment?"

Darius dropped his head and chuckled low. "You're wild, baby," he said.

After dinner was done, Celina fixed a plate of chicken breast, wild rice, and steamed broccoli for her father. Darius set the table for him and Celina. He looked up as he set a pair of plates on the table and watched Celina walk down the hall. The sway of her hips put him in a trance. He had a vision of her naked body lying beside him, her fuzzy hair fanned out over the pillow. Darius licked his lips as he thought about kissing her regal neck, moving down her svelte body using his tongue as a guide, tasting the tangy essence of her womanhood. Darius felt his sex growing against the zipper of jeans. No woman had ever aroused him the way Celina did. Just the thought of her filled him with lust, love, and desire. Darius walked over to the refrigerator and fixed himself a glass of water, hoping that it would cool him. Somehow, he had to get her to stay in Elmore, in his life and in his heart, no matter what it took.

"Is everything all right?" Celina asked when she returned to the kitchen.

Darius set his glass on the edge of the bar. "Yeah. Let's eat." Darius walked over to the table and, in a chivalrous move, pulled out Celina's chair. Then he brought over a bowl of rice and the roasted vegetables she had prepared. Celina looked up at him and smiled.

"Darius," she said. "I was going to run away. I was going to go back to New York and not look back."

He nodded. "I felt as if that was your plan, but I wasn't going to let you get away with that."

Celina smirked. "And just how were you going to stop me?"

Darius turned her chair around, then knelt down in front of her. "By any means necessary," he said.

Celina wrapped her arms around his neck and brushed her lips against his. "I need details."

Darius ran his hand between her thighs. Her skin felt like silk against his fingers. "Meet me outside when the sun goes down and I'll show you," he said, in a low, sexy growl.

Celina cleared her throat. "Let's eat," she said.

"I'd love to," he said as he ran his finger down her thigh.

Celina smiled and shook her head. "You're so bad, but I was talking about food."

Darius stood up and smiled. He walked over to his chair and started eating, never taking his eyes off Celina. He couldn't wait for the sunset.

CHAPTER 14

After dinner, Darius headed back to his place, allowing Celina to spend some time with her father. She told him that she was worried about Thomas because he hadn't come to dinner. She walked into his bedroom and found him sitting up in bed watching an old western. His empty plate sat on the foot of bed. Celina picked up the plate and took its place. "Daddy, are you all right?" she asked.

Thomas nodded, turning his head to look at his daughter. "I just needed a little rest. I wanted to feel my own mattress under my butt."

"Do I need to call your doctor?" she asked, placing her hand on her father's forehead, checking for a temperature.

Thomas patted Celina's knee and shook his head. "Why don't you quit worrying about me and enjoy your life."

"Meaning go find Darius?" she said with a smile on her face.

Thomas nodded. "But I don't think he's lost. Did you two enjoy dinner? Have you offered him some dessert?"

"Daddy!" Her face flushed with embarrassment. "I didn't make any dessert."

Thomas smiled knowingly. "I'm sure the Dairy Queen is open and you two could share an ice cream cone or a milk shake."

Her blush faded. If she and Darius were going to share dessert tonight, it wasn't going to come from the Dairy Queen. "I'm going to wash the dishes and then visit Darius," she said as she headed for the kitchen with the plate. While washing the dishes, she glanced out the window at Darius, watching him as he set a citronella candle in the middle of the picnic table. *What is he planning?* she thought as she dried the dishes. Celina couldn't wait to find out, so she dried her hands on the dish towel and headed out the door. Creeping up behind Darius, moving like a sleek cat, Celina covered his eyes with her hands. "Boo."

Darius whirled around, taking Celina into his arms. "I knew it was you," he said, dipping her as if they were ballroom dancing. "I could smell you."

"Should I be offended by that?" Celina pushed Darius away.

He grabbed her delicate hand. "No," he said, kissing her on the cheek. "You just smell like the biggest and sweetest honeysuckle bush in Elmore. That's one of the many things I love about you."

Celina relaxed in his arms. "And," Darius continued. "I was watching you in the window. I saw you when you left."

"I forgot, you don't play fair."

Darius groaned and released Celina, nearly causing her to fall. "When are you going to let that go? You're going to keep punishing me for what happened twenty years ago?""

She pointed to the faint scar on her arm. "When this disappears, I'll forgive you," she joked.

Darius walked over to her and drew her face into his hands. He gently kissed the smooth skin on the bottom of her chin. "What if I kiss you every time you remind me that I made you fall? Will that make you feel better?"

Celina nodded and motioned for Darius to move down lower. His lips danced against her neck, slowly moving down to her collarbone. Darius wrapped his arms around Celina's waist, lifting her up onto the picnic table. A soft moan escaped her throat as Darius's fingers grazed the top of her waist. He unzipped her shorts with one motion. Celina closed her eyes as Darius began to pour hot kisses over her body. Celina's body came alive underneath the heat from his mouth and tongue as he suckled her breasts through her halter top. Celina wrapped her legs around his waist, pulling him closer to her body. She wanted him inside of her. Darius had awakened her sleeping desire, making her come alive. She tugged at his white tank top and pulled it off his sexy body. Celina stared at his chest. It was better than any work of art she had seen in Paris or New York. He was quickly becoming the inspiration for her art and her life. She never knew love felt like this because she'd always thought love equaled pain and sadness. Darius showed her instead that love was tender, sweet, and kind.

"Wait, wait," he said as she pulled at the waistband of his shorts. "I have to protect us and I want to take you inside. I have something special for you."

Celina stroked his hard penis. "I know."

Darius smiled and caressed Celina's arm. "It's not just that, although that is a *big* part of it." He took her hand in his and led her inside through the back door. Celina was greeted by flickering candlelight and a pathway of pink, white, and red rose petals. A dozen yellow, pink, and white roses sat in the middle of the oak coffee table in the living room. Beside the roses were a bowl of ice and a tray of fresh summer fruits, blocks of sweet melon, strawberries dripping with chocolate, whipped cream, and cherries.

"What's all of this?" Celina asked. "And when did you have time to do all of this?"

Darius placed his finger to Celina's lips to quiet her. "Remember I said I wasn't going to let you go?" he said.

Celina stared at the bounty of fruit in wide-eyed wonderment. "You really don't play fair. I love chocolate-covered strawberries."

"Well, this is just part of our dessert tonight."

"Part? What more do you need?"

"Your naked body. You taste better than anything on this table and I'm going to feast on you all night." Darius motioned for Celina to sit down on the sofa. She did as Darius gently commanded, then he took over, lifting her leg and slowly moving down her lengthy leg to her foot. He removed her sandal, then picked up the can of whipped cream, spraying it on her toes. She shivered with delight as his warm tongue licked the cold cream from her digits. Bracing herself for what was next, Darius spread her legs apart and moved in between them. He made her feel like a belt the way he molded her around his body. Darius plucked an ice cube from the bowl and slid it across her lips, then covered her mouth with his. The kiss was hot, deep, and wanton. Celina responded just as passionately, wanting to rip his clothes off and have him right there on the sofa. But Darius was just getting started.

He pulled back from her, then picked up a strawberry and drizzled the chocolate sauce across her chin, down her neck, and across the top of her chest. Smiling, he untied her halter top, pulled it off, and ran the juicy berry across her breasts, paying close attention to her diamond-hard nipples. Darius feasted on Celina as if she were the strawberry, licking the chocolate from her chin, traveling down her neck. He took her rock-hard nipple into his mouth, drawing moans of pleasure from her. The sensations that shot though her body made her back arch as his tongue darted across one nipple and then the other, while his hand eased down her taut stomach to remove her shorts. With speed and skill, he peeled them from her body and exposed the red satin thong she was wearing. The sight of the flimsy undergarment made Darius smile.

Celina took note of the look on his face. "You're not the only one with surprises."

"I see and I like."

Celina stroked the side of his face. "I love you," she said. The words felt so natural when she said them. Just as being with Darius felt natural. It was like breathing. Being this close to him made her think about the future, weddings, babies, and painting in the backyard while he looked on. These were feelings that she'd never felt before, even when she and Terrick had been engaged. Pausing, she froze in place and opened her eyes.

"What's wrong?" Darius asked, noticing how quiet she had gotten.

Smiling, she replied, "Nothing."

Darius began massaging her thighs. He reached for a piece of honeydew melon, placed it in his mouth, and offered it to her. Celina bit into the melon, then fell into Darius's kiss.

"Tastes good," she said as she chewed on the fruit.

Darius kissed her again. "I like that much better," he said when he broke off the kiss.

She wrapped her arms around his neck and pulled him closer to her, covering his lips with hers. Then she deepened her kiss, savoring the sweetness of his mouth. Darius pulled Celina onto his lap, pushed her thong aside, and entered her with his finger. Celina cried out in delight as Darius moved his fingers up and down inside of her. It felt as if he was spelling out his name inside of her, branding her forever, and at that moment, she wanted that to be the case. She wanted to belong to Darius and wanted him to belong to her. She tightened herself around his finger, moving up and down. "Make love to me," Celina moaned. "I need you."

Darius removed his finger, stood up, and then scooped Celina into his arms. He carried her into the bedroom and gently laid her on the bed. She watched Darius as he stripped out of his clothes. Every time she saw his body, she couldn't help but marvel at how magnificent it was. Celina was in awe of his chest, his strong arms, and his legs. She smiled as he climbed into the bed, moving slowly and deliberately. He wrapped his arms around her, pulling her against his hard body. She moaned in anticipation of feeling his hardness inside her. She waited as Darius reached over on the nightstand and picked up a condom, but decided she couldn't wait any longer for what she wanted and took the condom from his hand. Celina opened the package, then took Darius's throbbing penis in her hand and rolled the layer of protection onto him. Pouncing on top of him, she rubbed her wetness against his hardness, urging him to take her to that place of passion she longed for. He eased inside her, gripping her hips as she moved back and forth. Her breasts jutted out as she rode him like a motorcycle, grinding her hips against his, relishing the hot friction between the two of them. Sweat beaded on her body and Darius clutched her back, pulling her even closer to him, seemingly meshing her body with his, making them one. Their hearts were beating in perfect sync. Arching her body, she released herself and moved up and down with the rhythm of a classic jazz song. The heat they'd generated could've kept Elmore warm and cozy all winter.

He groaned Celina's name over and over again as she brought him to the brink of an orgasm. Celina seemed possessed, unyielding in her desire to be filled with his love. She continued riding him, making his toes curl. Unable to take anymore, he pulled her against his chest, but Celina wasn't finished with him yet. She teased his neck with her tongue, causing him to mutter unintelligibly. As she traveled down his body, lashing his nipples with her tongue, Darius shivered.

"Oh, Celina," he cried as she pressed her head against his chest. Wrapping her arms around his back, she snuggled against him tightly, never wanting to let him go. "Wow," Darius said after a few minutes of cuddling. "What has gotten into you?"

"You."

"Come again?"

Celina propped herself up on her elbow. "I feel like I can let go with you," she said. "You freed me and I like being free. It's like I can't get enough of you."

Darius kissed her on the forehead. "If this is you being free, then I like it too," he said.

Celina sighed and looked into Darius's eyes.

Darius stroked her hair. "What is it?"

"I know this isn't the right time, but what are we going to do when I go back to New York?" Celina stretched her arms above her head and closed her eyes. *Way to kill the mood, genius.*

"Why do you have to go back to New York?" he asked.

Celina furrowed her brows. "Why wouldn't I go back to New York? My life is there, my work, and the city has become a huge part of me."

"What about me? I thought I was becoming a part of you?"

Celina sat up and turned her back to Darius. "You are," she said. "But I can't just stop being who I am because I'm in love with you. Darius, you have your career and I have mine."

"Yeah, I know that. But, it's not like you're punching a time clock or working in an office building. You can paint here and . . ."

"Darius, this isn't open for discussion. I'm going back to New York. There are no galleries in Elmore. How am I going to get my work seen if I'm here?"

Darius sat up and placed his hand on Celina's shoulder. "Then why don't we build a gallery? With your reputation, the art world will travel here."

"What?" she asked. "Are you serious?"

Darius nodded. "Elmore needs some culture and who better than Elmore's own to bring it here? And, if you have to go back to New York, at least you will have a reason to return."

Celina smiled as she mulled over the idea. "All right," Celina said. "But for the record, as long as you're here, I'll have a reason to come back."

Darius pulled Celina into his arms and kissed her gently. "I love you," he said.

Celina reached down and stroked his manhood. Darius responded by pouncing on his lover, showering her face with kisses.

As the sun crept over the horizon, Darius looked down at the woman in his arms. He had to convince her to stay in Elmore because he didn't want a long-distance relationship; he wanted something permanent. *I want her to be my wife.*

Celina began to stir in his arms and her eyes fluttered open like the gentle wings of a monarch butterfly.

"Good morning, sunshine," he said.

Celina smiled. "It is, isn't it?"

Darius stroked her hair, then kissed her on the forehead. "Want some breakfast?"

Celina yawned and stretched, then shook her head no. "I have to go check on my father and call the agency about a private duty nurse. I'll come by the store today for lunch. My treat."

"I like the way that sounds. I need to cut your father's grass anyway. I'll get on that before it gets too hot," he said.

Neither of them made an effort to move. Celina even squeezed Darius's waist a little tighter. A few moments later, Celina was on her way home and Darius was out in his storage shed getting his lawn mower and weed eater together. All he could think about, though, was being with Celina and building a life with her. He closed his eyes and relived the night before. He could feel her touch, taste her kiss, and smell her feminine scent. When Darius felt a hand on his back, he thought it was Celina. Then he turned around and saw Tiffany. "What in the hell are you doing here?" he demanded as he jerked away from her.

"She's cute," Tiffany said. "Convenient and easy, from the looks of it. How long have you known her, Darius? Five minutes. You never let me spend the night."

"Because I never wanted to see you in the morning. Tiffany, when are you going to stop this? You're stalking me."

She frowned and folded her arms under her breasts. "How long are you going to keep this one? A week? A month?"

"If you don't get off my property, I'm going to call the police," Darius snapped.

"Whatever, Darius," she said as she turned to walk out of the yard.

Darius banged his hand against the side of the storage shed. How was he going to get this woman out of his life and out of his relationship with Celina? He had to stop Tiffany from showing up at his house. He didn't want Celina to get the wrong idea, but the reluctance of the police to believe that she was the one wreaking havoc on his life let him know that he was on his own. Tiffany was acting unstable and he feared that it wasn't going to be long before she went too far. He couldn't allow that to happen. Stopping her wasn't going to be easy because she hid her tracks very well.

Darius pulled the lawn mower out of the garage and headed next door. He attacked the grass with fury, using every bit of his muscle strength, but it did little to dissipate his anger. He muttered profanities as he walked up and down the yard, cutting the grass down to half an inch. Tiffany was trying to turn his life into a living hell and he wasn't going to have it.

Darius had finished mowing the backyard in record time because his anger pushed him. Pulling his wet, white T-shirt from his body, he tossed it across the yard. Darius looked toward the house and saw Celina standing on the back porch with a glass of water in her hand. Masking his fury, he smiled and walked over to her. Even in a pair of gray sweat shorts and blue tank top, with her wooly hair braided back in three thick cornrows, she looked sexier than any Victoria's Secret model.

"You're working extremely hard out here," she said.

Darius took the water she offered. "Well, I needed to get this done," Darius said.

Celina folded her arms across her chest. "Do you always curse like a sailor when you mow the lawn?"

Darius sighed as he downed the glass of water, then decided that he needed to be honest with her. "No," he said. "You know everything that's been going on at the store, right?"

Celina nodded. Darius continued, even though he didn't want to. "I know who's behind it." He walked over to her and tugged at the bottom of her shirt. "Come here." He pulled her into his arms.

Celina focused her gaze on him. "Have you told the police?" she asked.

"Yes. They're not taking this too seriously. Tiffany hasn't admitted to doing anything, but now she's resorted to stalking me. Everything crazy around me started happening right after I told her that I didn't want anything to do with her. This morning, before I came over here, she was outside my home."

"She was what?" Celina exclaimed.

Darius nodded. "She must have been outside the house since last night because she saw you leave. She made a veiled threat."

"What are we going to do about her?"

Darius looked at Celina and wanted to smile. In a way, he was glad to hear her say *we*. But on the other hand, he didn't want her to get involved with this madness. What if Tiffany tried to do something to hurt Celina? Darius couldn't have her in the middle of this. "Celina, I want you to let me handle this."

"You know what, if this woman is going to be a problem for you, there's no way I'm going to stay out of this."

Darius knew it was pointless to argue with her. He could see the New York coming out of her. But more than anything else, he could see the love in her eyes.

Darius smiled at her. "All right," he said. "But I don't want to think about that right now."

"We have to," she said. "If that woman is stalking us, she's breaking the law." Celina moved away from Darius. "The police need to do something and I'm going to call . . ."

"Celina, let's just sit on this for a minute. The police aren't going to do anything until something else happens."

Celina untwisted the end of one of her braids. "If you think that's best," she said. "But, this woman has to be stopped." Darius agreed with Celina 100 percent, but he remembered what the chief said when he was last in his office. Tiffany had him just where she wanted him. He was vulnerable.

"Darius," Celina said, "don't worry about her. We'll get through this. Besides, I was thinking about your gallery idea."

Darius's eyes brightened. "Really?"

"Now, keep in mind, I'm just thinking about it. A lot of artists have galleries in their hometowns, why can't Celina Hart? Then I could split my time between here and New York," she said. "More importantly, we'll be spending more time together."

Darius hid his disappointment. He didn't want her part-time, he needed her all the time. "That sounds like a plan," he said finally, not wanting to give his disappointment away. Darius handed her the empty glass. "Let me finish up the yard."

Celina smiled and turned toward the back door. "Darius, I love you," she said.

"I love you, too," he said then started the lawn mower again. *Do you love me enough to leave New York?* Darius wondered as Celina disappeared inside the house.

CHAPTER 15

As the weeks passed, Celina felt less and less like returning to New York. It wasn't like she was missing anything there and she obviously wasn't missed because she hadn't received any calls about work. Then again, most people in the art community thought she was still in Paris. "Why not stay?" she thought aloud as she washed the pots she'd used to cook breakfast. Thomas walked down the hall and smiled at his daughter at the sink.

"Celina," he said. "When is the nurse coming?"

"She should be here in about an hour," Celina said as she placed the last dish in the cupboard. "Is everything all right?"

Thomas nodded. "I was just wondering when Velma was going to get here."

Celina looked at her father, who was starting to look like himself again. He was gaining some weight and his face was no longer gaunt. His daily breathing treatments made him talk without wheezing. Celina prayed that the cancer was in remission.

"Are you sweet on Ms. Velma?" Celina asked as she dried her hands on the dish towel.

Thomas smiled. "Maybe Nurse Velma is sweet on me.

Look at me. Who wouldn't be?" He spun around as if he were a model on the runway.

Celina broke out into laughter. This was the Thomas she remembered. Cocky, sure of himself, and in control. Celina walked over to Thomas and hugged him tightly. "I love you, Daddy," she said. Thomas hugged her back and Celina felt hot tears on her shoulder.

"Daddy, what's wrong?" she asked.

"Baby, it's what's right. You came here and saved my life. I know I can't make up for the twenty years I wasn't there for you, but I'm going to try."

Celina shook her head, "Daddy, you don't have to do that. The past is the past and there's nothing we can do to change that. Maybe we should just concentrate on our future."

Thomas tweaked her chin the way he did when she was a child. "Your mother did a fine job with you."

Celina smiled. "I'm going to go to the lake and paint for a while. Are you sure that I don't need to stay here and chaperone you and Ms. Velma?"

"Are you going back to Paris?" Thomas asked as she walked down the hall. Celina shrugged her shoulders. She knew what a great opportunity it was to have a chance to be a part of the Guimard project in Paris, but she didn't want to leave Darius. Would Darius go to Paris with her? Did he even like Paris? *Maybe on our honeymoon,* she thought. The words in her head shocked her. Celina wasn't the kind of woman who dreamed of marriage and babies, but Darius made her want all of those things. Walking into her bedroom, she grabbed her sketch pad and pencil set. She knew Darius was working this morning and she would have a few hours to work. Celina dressed in a pair of lavender flood pants and a pink tank top, then stuck her sunglasses on her head. Celina was walking out the door when Velma walked in.

"Good morning, Miss Velma," Celina said.

"Morning, Celina. Just look at that hair," she said as she stroked Celina's hair. "Where are you headed this morning?"

"Down to the lake. I'm going to draw for a while. We don't have this kind of nature in the city," she said.

Velma smiled. "Well, have fun," she said as Celina headed out the door. "I'll take good care of your daddy while you're gone."

Celina got in her car and headed for the lake, not paying any attention to the car following her down the road.

Darius tried to focus on the inventory count, but his mind kept wandering to Celina and the day that he'd have to watch her walk out of his life. She made it clear that she was going back to New York. Maybe he could let Richard run the store and he could go with her and return to practicing law. Certainly some of the firms that had wooed him when he was in Washington would love to have him on their staffs. Then again, with as much time as had passed, he probably wasn't even a blip on their radars anymore. Darius dropped a box of nails, causing the sharp tacks to fall all over the floor. Swearing under his breath, he kneeled down to clean up the mess. He needed to get his head back into business, but with all that had been going on lately, he couldn't focus on one thing for too long.

Richard rushed over to help pick up the nails. "Darius, what's going on with you?" he asked.

A grunt was the only reply Darius gave the older man.

"Is Tiffany still giving you problems?"

Darius nodded and closed his eyes. "That's the least of

my worries right now. I think Celina's going to be leaving soon and I'm wondering if I should go with her."

Richard ran his hand over his face. "What about this place? You came here to keep your family's legacy alive. Love is grand and all of that, but shutting this place down would be like a slap in the face to your parents. They trusted you with this place."

"I know, but I love that woman," he said. "I can't see my life without Celina in it."

Richard nodded and looked at his young boss. "How does Celina feel about this? Has she asked you to give up everything for her?"

"We haven't really talked about it. I do know I'm not going to let her walk out of my life."

"You really love her, don't you?"

Darius nodded. "More than I've ever loved any other woman."

Richard smiled. "Then, youngblood, you need to tell Celina how you feel and let her know that you want to move to New York with her. If she loves you as much as I think she does, she's not going to want to give this up." Richard stood up and looked at Darius. "So, I guess this place is going to close down after all?"

Darius shook his head. "No, not if you agree to run it for me. I mean, you're just like family."

Richard smiled. "I would be honored. Are you sure this is what you want? You said you wanted to get away from the big city and New York is as big as it gets."

Darius sighed. Richard was right, he'd had his fill of the fast lane; but if he couldn't get Celina to stay, then he was going to have to go with her. Darius's cell phone rang before he could reply to Richard. He looked down to see who was calling, but the number was blocked.

"Hello?" he said.

"She's not cute," Tiffany said. "She's not attractive at

all. All of that nappy hair. Is that what you want, Darius? I mean she can't hold a candle to me."

"What are you talking about and why are you still calling me?"

"I'm talking about your new woman," she replied. "Wouldn't it be a shame if she fell in the lake and drowned?" Tiffany laughed and Darius's blood ran cold.

"Tiffany, don't do anything foolish. Leave Celina alone."

"Celina. That's her name?" Tiffany said. "Wonder how it will look on a slate stone?"

"Tiffany," he said. There was no response. Darius looked at his phone and it said call ended. Rushing to his car, he had to get to Celina before Tiffany did something to hurt her. Richard called his name, but Darius didn't hear him because his single focus was getting to the lake and stopping Tiffany's bullshit. If anything happened to Celina, he'd never be able to live with himself and would more than likely spend the rest of his life in jail because he'd kill Tiffany if she hurt the woman he loved.

Darius drove like a maniac to the lake, running through stop signs, turning down alleys, and driving across empty fields. Once he arrived, he saw Celina's rental car parked on the side of the road. He pulled his car behind hers and dashed out of the car and scanned the area for her along the banks. When he didn't see her, his heart plummeted to the bottom of his stomach. Was he too late? Had Tiffany done something? Darius ran through the gate leading to the lake.

"Celina!! Celina, where are you?"

He heard a rustling in the bushes. Darius whirled around and looked to see what was making the noise. A small rabbit came hopping out of the bushes. Darius swore and continued walking along the bank of the lake.

"Celina!" Darius looked down on the ground and saw her sketch pad. Darius picked it up and looked at the drawing. It was of the lake and it looked as if she was drawing a man and woman coming out of the center of the lake. Darius was really worried now. He looked down in the water and saw a pencil floating in the water. Darius started taking his shoes and shirt off so that he could dive into the water and search for Celina. Then he heard a splash. He looked up and saw Celina swimming to the shore. She stood up when she reached the shallow water, revealing her black lace bra and matching panties.

"Darius, what are you doing here?" she asked.

"Looking for you," he said, unable to take his eyes off her wet body. "Have you seen anyone around here?"

"How did you even know I was here? I thought you were working at the store today?" she asked.

Darius looked at Celina, trying to make sure she wasn't hurt.

"Darius," she said, touching him on the shoulder. "What's going on, baby?"

"Tiffany called. She was out here watching you." Darius saw Celina shiver. "I don't want you traveling alone," he continued. "I don't know what kind of games Tiffany's playing or what she might do. I don't want to take that risk."

"Darius, wait, I understand what you're trying to do, but I'm not going to become a prisoner in my own hometown because of this woman. I live in New York. I can take care of myself."

"Celina, you didn't even know she was here. How can you take care of yourself when you don't know what the threat is? You shouldn't swim alone, anyway."

"You know what the threat is? This woman is crazy and nothing is going to stop her unless she gets what she wants or one of us stands up to her. I'm not going to let that woman rule my life," Celina said.

"I don't want to see you hurt. If anything ever happened to you I would never . . ."

She flung her hair back and faced Darius. "Nothing's going to happen to me and I won't hide from that woman." Celina pulled her shirt over her head. "You will not run my life!" she yelled out across the lake. "You may play crazy, Tiffany, but you don't scare me."

Darius pulled Celina into his arms. "I'm not going to let her and I'm not going to lose you, either," he said. A rustling in the bushes made Darius and Celina turn around. The same white rabbit came hopping into the clearning. Neither of them noticed the crouching figure in the bushes. Celina gathered her clothes and sketch pad. Then she and Darius walked to their cars.

"Why did you take a swim without a towel?" he asked.

"Well, I hadn't been in Lake Elmore in so long, I couldn't resist. Besides," she said as she popped the trunk. "I was a Girl Scout, I'm always prepared." She pulled out a bath towel and dried her legs before slipping into her pants. Darius leaned in and kissed her on the cheek.

"All right, Girl Scout."

"Darius, I've been giving some more thought to your idea about an art gallery."

His heartbeat sped up. Was she going to stay in Elmore? "I like the idea," she continued. "I really like it and I think we should start planning it."

Darius wanted to scream at the top of lungs. She was staying. "Yeah, we can start scouting some places and everything."

Celina hugged Darius. "I love you," she said. "Thank you for doing this for me."

"I haven't done anything yet," he said.

Celina shook her head. "You have," she said, kissing him on the cheek. "I've got to get home and finish this painting. Maybe we can come back here tonight and do a little skinny-dipping."

Darius smirked. "You're a bad girl, aren't you? Under all that sugar, there's a lot of spice."

Celina winked at him as she got into the car. "Meet me here at nine and I'm going to redefine spicy," she said. "And if Tiffany's still watching us, she's going to get quite a show."

"How about I drive you here tonight?" Darius said, still a little wary about Tiffany stalking Celina.

"Fine," she said. "But Tiffany isn't going to be a problem for us. I won't let her."

"I hope you're right," he said as he watched the white bunny hop across the road.

When Celina got home, she dashed into the house to get her painting supplies before heading outside to start on her painting. Thomas and Velma were sitting on the sofa when she walked in. Thomas dropped his arm from around her shoulder when Celina walked in. "Don't mind me," she said as she headed for the bedroom. Celina wanted her father to be as happy as she was and since she knew her parents would never be a couple again, she didn't mind his budding romance with Velma. It was cute to see them together.

She changed out of her damp clothes and put on her paint-stained overalls, then grabbed her easel and headed outside with her canvas, her paint set, and her sketch pad. She set up her easel and then started painting. She began painting the powder-blue background to mimic the Carolina sky. She used a darker blue to paint Lake Elmore. Celina took out her felt-tip pen and began drawing the figures of the man and woman jutting from the middle of the lake. As she created the man's face, she couldn't help but think of Darius. She began drawing his features on the man, captured his eyes, including the twinkle in his eyes when he smiled, his dark wavy hair, thick eyebrows, luscious lips, and smooth skin. Celina decided to have the woman's face turned to the man's chest. Celina filled out her body and gave the woman long, flowing hair that looked wind-blown. At the last minute, she decided to turn the woman's legs into a fish tail. Celina began filling in the color of the man and the woman. She captured Darius's cocoa complexion by mixing burnt sienna oil paint with a hint of yellow to create his coloring. She colored the woman's hair midnight black and gave her a complexion about two shades lighter than Darius's. She then colored the fish tail blue-green. With a fine brush, she used a white paint to add the scales to the tail. Celina was so engrossed in her work that she didn't hear Darius walk up behind her. "Wow," he said. Celina turned around and dropped her paintbrush.

"Okay, you scared me," she said.

"I didn't mean to. This is awesome," he said staring at Celina's work. "I've never seen you at work before."

Celina turned her back to the painting. "I don't like people seeing my work before it's done," she said as she stretched her arms out.

"Why? Because you're drawing me again?" Darius said standing on his tiptoes to look over her shoulder.

Celina flung some paint on him. "Stop trying to look," she said.

Darius looked down at the paint stain on his shirt. "Oh, Miss Lady, you're going to pay for this," Darius said as he picked up a tube of paint and squeezed it on the front of Celina's overalls. She threw her hands up to stop the assault of blue paint. She walked toward Darius and grabbed his hands.

"You jerk!" she said as she turned the paint back on him. Darius wrapped his arms around her and lifted her off her feet, then flipped her onto the ground. Celina pulled Darius down on top of her.

"Once again, I will say it. You don't play fair, Darius McRae," she said.

"That's right," he replied before capturing her mouth with his. Celina wrapped her arms around his neck and pulled him closer to her. The cold paint seeped through their clothes and onto their skin. She slipped her hands underneath his T-shirt, kneading his skin as if it were wet clay. She rolled over so that she could be on top of Darius. She could feel his arousal through his jeans. Darius nibbled at her chin, causing her to melt against him like an ice cream cone on the hot sidewalk.

"Darius," she moaned. "It's broad daylight, what will the neighbors say?"

"Who cares?" he replied before raining kisses down her neck.

Celina mustered all the strength in her body to push away from Darius. "My father is in there," she said, her face flushing with excitement and embarrassment. She rose to her feet and returned to her painting. "Besides, we have a date tonight, remember?"

Darius walked up behind her and encircled her waist with his arms. "I can't wait until tonight," he said as his lips brushed across the back of her neck. Celina dropped her paintbrush in midstroke.

"Will you stop it?" she said as she turned around and painted a mustache across his face. Darius laughed and then kissed her, leaving a trail of brown paint across her face. "So, is this how you create all of your masterpieces?"

he asked. "We look like kindergarteners who just finished finger painting."

Celina rubbed in a spot of paint on his cheek. "You wear it well," she said, then kissed him on the forehead. "Do you want to have dinner before we head to the lake?"

Darius nodded. "I'm going to get cleaned up and I'll see you later," he said before playfully slapping her on the bottom. Celina smiled as Darius walked away, then returned to her painting. Before she knew it, the sun was setting in the distance and she was finished with her painting. She stood back and looked at her work. Calling it inspired was an understatement. Celina thought this was one of her best paintings. She was going to call it *H2Love.*

CHAPTER 16

Darius stared at Celina through his kitchen window. He watched the way she moved, the strokes she made on the canvas. No wonder her touch was so electrifying to him. Celina made broad strokes on the canvas, reminding him of the loving strokes that she lavished on him when they lay together in bed. Watching her at work showed him that Celina didn't do anything half way and when she threw her heart and soul into something, it was beautiful when it was finished.

That's going to be us. We're going to have a beautiful life and as soon as we get rid of Tiffany there will be nothing standing in our way, he thought with a sardonic smile. Why would that woman just go away? Darius didn't understand how a mind like Tiffany's worked. She was attractive enough to find someone else, but she had an unhealthy obsession with him and just as he'd told the police chief, she was out of control. Anyone who looked at him when he was with Celina knew that there was no other woman for him. Tiffany needed to learn that as well.

Darius continued watching Celina and as she stood back, admiring her work, he admired her. The way she filled out those denim overalls, the round shape of her derriere, her arms with their strong lines, and her striking face. She was the true work of art, not what she had put on the canvas. Darius didn't want anything to happen to her and he was going to do everything he could to keep her safe. He picked up the phone and called Chief Wayman.

"Chief," the man said when he picked up the phone.

"Chief Wayman, it's Darius."

"Oh, Mr. McRae, it's been a full week since I've heard from you. I was hoping this thing had blown over. What's happening now?" he said flatly.

Darius rolled his eyes upward at the chief's cavalier attitude. "Look, I know you think everything with Tiffany is a lover's quarrel, but she made a threat against Celina and you need to keep an eye on her."

The chief coughed into the phone. "Maybe it's just the talk of a scorned woman. Darius, I'm sick of you and Tiffany, all right. Buy that woman some flowers and let her down easily and leave me alone. This isn't a police matter."

"Chief, if she does something to Celina, I won't be responsible for what happens to her. She's resorted to stalking me and Celina and if I have to go above your head, I will. I'll call the feds, the state law enforcement division, anyone," Darius barked.

He heard what sounded like a fork clanking against a plate. "Fine, I'll keep an eye on her. But if this is more of y'all's shenanigans, I'm going to throw both of you in a holding cell and beat you with a rubber hose."

Darius hung up the phone and rolled his eyes. *Does he think this is a damned joke? That woman is unstable and if he doesn't do something soon, I'm going to take this matter into my own hands.* His new mission was going to be to know every step Celina made. It was one thing for Tiffany to come after him, but she'd crossed the line by threatening

Celina. He'd lay down his own life before he'd allow Tiffany to hurt Celina.

Darius decided that he'd have to hire a private eye, even if he had to get one from Columbia. Glancing out the window, he watched Celina make her way into her house with the painting. Thinking that someone was lurking in the shadows, he rushed out of his house, leapt over the fence and rushed to what he thought was a crouching figure in the bushes. It turned out to be a stray dog. Darius's heart was beating one thousand times per minute. He had to get back to his house before someone saw him. As he was leaving, the back door opened. "Darius McRae, what are you doing back here?" Velma Henderson, Thomas's nurse, asked.

"Hi, Ms. Henderson, I thought I saw someone lurking in the bushes."

The woman smiled and headed for her car. "You're protective of that girl, aren't you?" she said as she opened her car door. "Just make sure I'm invited to the wedding."

"All right, Ms. H.," he said as he headed back to his house and Velma got into her car and started it. Darius watched her from his porch as she backed out of the driveway. He sighed and headed inside. Before he could change his clothes, the phone rang.

"Yeah?"

"I see you didn't waste any time calling the police on me," Tiffany said. "Darius, I'm telling you, make them back off or you're going to regret it."

"Tiffany, you need help. You need to do something with your life and leave me alone. When's the last time you opened your store? You're really going to throw your life away over a man who doesn't want you?"

She laughed. "You treated me like trash and you need

to learn your lesson." The dial tone sounded in his ear. When he heard a knock at the front door, Darius nearly leapt out of his skin, expecting to see Tiffany standing there. To his surprise and joy, it was Celina.

"I thought you would have dinner waiting for me," she said. "You're still in your paint-stained clothes."

"Give me a second and we'll go grab something to eat. Why don't we go to Rudy's?"

"The rib joint?" Celina said, raising her right eyebrow. "Now, Darius you know, . . ."

"They have a great grilled vegetable platter and the potato salad is to die for," he said. "Just wait for me to shower." Darius dashed down the hall.

"Don't forget your swimming trunks," she said as she sat on the sofa. "Or on second thought leave them." Darius jumped in the shower and washed the dried paint from his body. He left the bathroom door open, secretly wishing Celina would come in the bathroom. He wanted to feel her arms wrapped around him, her lips on his neck, her breasts pressed against his chest.

"Are you drowning in there?" Celina called out.

"Why don't you come in and see?" he said. Darius listened out for the tapping of Celina's sandals on the tile. He looked up and saw her standing in the doorway of the bathroom.

"Trying to get me all wet, Darius?"

He pulled the curtain back and smiled at her reaction to his nakedness. Then he reached out and pulled her into the shower by the arm.

"Who needs the lake?" With his wet fingers, Darius unbuttoned the front of Celina's sundress, pushed it off her shoulders, and discovered that she wasn't wearing any underwear. A slow smile spread across his face. "I guess you were serious about skinny-dipping, huh?"

Celina returned his smile with a sly one of her own. "I'm always serious," she said as she shimmied out of her dress. Immediately, he pulled her against his body and the water from the shower poured on them, seeping through Celina's loose hair. Leaning in, he kissed her lips gently as he backed her against the wall. Wandering down the length of her body, he kissed every enticing inch of her, causing her to writhe underneath his lips. Intense feelings of pleasure and desire rippled through her body as Darius reversed his kisses and took her hardened nipples into his mouth. Each kiss and each stroke made her skin burn with desire.

"Darius," she moaned as his tongue lapped up the beads of water that pooled on her body. She shivered underneath his touch, Darius continued lashing her body with his tongue. Clutching his back to keep her footing as he lifted one of her legs across his shoulder, she inhaled sharply as he slid between her legs. His hardness throbbed against her and, in a swift motion, he was inside her. Their hips thrust against each other and heat enveloped them, making the cold water falling on them easy to ignore. Celina pushed him over the edge when she reached down and stroked his erection while he pumped in and out of her. She dropped her hand as she ground sensually against his body and bit down on his neck to muffle her screams of passion as she began to climax. She wasn't ready for the feeling to end and she lurched forward, urging him to go deeper, faster, and harder. Her muscles tightened around him, making him explode and growl like a lion leading the pride.

It wasn't until they'd pried themselves apart that it hit Darius that he hadn't protected them. Looking into her eyes, he could see that she was thinking the same thing. Stroking her cheek, he muttered his apology.

"We can't keep doing this," she said.

"I know," Darius said. "We don't have anything to worry about, we've discussed . . ."

"What about pregnancy?" she said.

"Would that be so bad? We love each other."

"We're not married and I'd never thought about marriage and babies until . . ." She stopped in midsentence and began squeezing excess water from her hair, not ready to open that much of herself to Darius.

"Until what?" he asked.

She cast her eyes upward, but didn't look directly into his dark ones.

"Until what?" he repeated.

"Until I fell in love with you. Now, I think about it all the time. But I have so much on me right now. Motherhood isn't in my immediate future," she said.

"So, what if we made a little one today?"

She turned her head away. "I don't want to talk about that. Let's just cross that threshold if we get to it."

Darius picked up his towel and wrapped it around Celina's shoulders, deciding not to press the issue. Even with the progress that they'd made, he knew parts of her were still afraid to surrender to love completely. He knew that he would have to give her all the time she needed to open herself to him. He dried her and pulled the towel around her body. An uncomfortable silence hung around them like dripping shower curtains.

She pushed away from him. "Darius, we'd better get dressed if we're going to make it to Rudy's."

"Yeah," he said, gently pulling her back into his arms.

"Come on," Celina said. "I'm starving."

Letting her go, Darius pulled his hormones under control as he headed across the hall to his bedroom, leaving Celina alone in the bathroom to get dressed.

The couple emerged from Darius' house a few moments later, still quiet, each one pondering the consequences of their lapse of judgment. As he drove, Darius stole a glance at Celina, "Are you all right?"

"I just keep wondering—never mind."

"Wondering what?" he asked.

"When this happiness is going to end," she said, then sighed. "Sometimes this doesn't seem real to me."

"It's not going to as long as we don't let it. Celina, I know you've seen the wrong side of love, the hurtful side. The difference between me and you is that I've lived it. I would never want to cause you a day of pain. I don't ever want to see you crying because of what I've done."

"I know that's what you say, now," she said with the vulnerability of a child.

Darius felt compelled to reach out and stroke her face. "Celina," he murmured. "I'm more than a man of my word." She closed her eyes and pulled away from Darius. He could only imagine what she was thinking. When they walked into Rudy's, neither of them noticed who was lurking behind them.

Celina hated being so cynical. Instead of reveling in the beauty of what they had, she kept looking for a way out. Yes, she loved him, but love didn't last and giving herself to Darius was scary. He had his heart in her hands and at any moment it could be crushed and she'd be just like her mother had been all those years ago. Celina felt breathless around him. It was as if she couldn't get enough of him—that scared her.

He had already pulled her out of her guarded comfort zone and changed the way she felt about being in love. Still, she struggled with believing love would last.

"Celina, talk to me," Darius said as they took a seat in the dim restaurant. A melting candle sat in the middle of the table, the flickering light bouncing off Celina's dark eyes.

"I think I've said all I need to," she said.

"Celina, I can't keep fighting the shadows. You're hot and cold. When we're in the moment, it's so good, then you sit back and borrow trouble. Have I given you a reason to believe that I'm going to act like your father?"

Shaking her head, she had to admit that Darius made her feel safe and if she were honest with herself, she'd realize that he was everything she needed and wanted. Celina couldn't bring herself to say that.

Darius continued, leaning against the table and fixing his full stare on her. "How many ways do I have to say it, show it, and prove it? I love you, Celina."

"And I love you, too, Darius. But . . ."

"Oh my word, do my eyes deceive me?" an older woman said as she waddled through the tables to get to Celina and Darius.

The couple looked at the woman and smiled. "Miss Rudy," Darius said as he stood up and kissed the woman on her meaty cheek. Celina smiled at Miss Rudy, who stared at her with a wide smile on her face.

"Baby, you look just like your Daddy. How's Thomas doin'?" the older woman asked.

"He's fine," she replied. "A lot better than when I arrived here."

Miss Rudy leaned in and kissed Celina on the cheek. "You're a good daughter," she said. "Not too many children come back here. Velma was in here talking about you the other day. She said that you're a painter or something like that and you live all the way in New York

City. I don't know who she was talking about more, you or Thomas."

"Oh really," Celina said as she and Miss Rudy exchanged a knowing glance.

"Well, your father will be well taken care of now," she said as she rubbed her hands together. "What can I get for you? Ribs and chicken, with a side of my potato salad and some slaw?"

"Well," Celina said, choosing her words carefully so as not to offend Miss Rudy. Turning down food in Elmore was equivalent to slapping the cook in the face. "I'm a vegetarian, so I would love the slaw and potato salad."

"I have something special for you, then," she said, not showing offense, to Celina's relief.

"Darius, chicken and ribs?"

He nodded and winked at her. "You know what I like."

Miss Rudy waddled down the hall to the kitchen. "It's like I never left here," Celina said. "Everybody remembers me. It's really comfortable here."

"It can be like that every day," Darius said. "Just think, once we get the gallery off the ground, you'll be able to see so many other people. They'll be so proud of your work and what you've accomplished."

"I know," she said, forcing herself to smile.

Darius grabbed her hand and kissed it gently. "Are you sure this is what you want to do?"

"Yes, Darius. This is what I want to do. Haven't you noticed that I don't do anything that I don't want to do?"

Darius kissed her hand again. "I know that you're terrible at hiding things, too. If you don't want to leave New York, you don't have to," he said.

Celina released a sigh of relief and squeezed Darius's hand. "I don't really know what I want right now. Part of me wants to stay here and get this gallery built and running, but I have so many other things that I want to do in New York. I want to go back to Paris and I want you to be a part of my life. It sounds like I want you to just put everything on hold for me while I chase my dreams and asking you to do that wouldn't be fair. Please tell me you understand."

Darius nodded, but his eyes showed his confusion.

"I just need some time to go back to the city to get some things together. Then I'll come back and we can look into starting the gallery. I did have a life there and I can't just leave it without making sure I'm making the right decision," she said.

"Are you talking about *us* or *your* life in New York?"

Both, she thought, but didn't say anything. Luckily, Miss Rudy returned to the table with a platter of roasted carrots, peppers, broccoli, and zucchini. She set the platter in front of Celina. A waiter followed her with grilled ribs, chicken, and potato salad.

"I'm sorry, we ran out of slaw. Celina, what do you think of the veggies?" Miss Rudy said.

"They look great," she said with a bright smile on her face. She was glad for the distraction. Darius forced a smile when he looked at Miss Rudy. Once she left the table, he turned to Celina.

"So, when are you leaving?" he asked struggling to keep his voice even.

"In a few days," she said quietly as she cut into a slice of zucchini.

Darius rubbed his chin and looked at her. "Were you going to tell me or was I just going to see you drive down the road while you waved good-bye?"

"Don't be like that. I just made this decision, but I was going to tell you before I left."

He nodded, then cut into a chicken breast. "I hope you find whatever it is that you're looking for," he said before taking the chicken into his mouth.

"Darius, I'm not looking for anything," she said. "I just need to . . ."

He put his hand up to silence her. "Celina, do what you have to do, all right? I'll be right here when you come back."

Her heart swelled when he said he would wait for her. Celina didn't feel as cynical about love anymore.

CHAPTER 17

Three days later, Celina was on a plane heading back to New York and, for the first time in a long time, she didn't feel as if she was going home. This trip felt like a formality because Elmore and Darius's arms felt like home now. She was finally beginning to fully open her heart to him, although she was still afraid.

"Excuse me," a woman, dressed in a floppy hat and sunglasses, said as she passed Celina's seat. "Is this 4-A?"

Celina looked up at the woman. She looked familiar, but Celina couldn't place her. "Yes, it is," she said as she stood up to let the woman pass.

"Thank you. I haven't been on a plane since September 11th, so I'm a little nervous," she said as she strapped into her seat.

Celina smiled politely, but silently prayed that the woman wasn't a Chatty Cathy. It wasn't as if she was a fan of flying herself, but once she got on the plane she was on it. There was nothing she could do to make the time go faster and conversations with strangers weren't something she liked to do. Her seatmate, however, seemed determined to talk to her.

"Haven't we met before?" the woman asked.

"Not that I'm aware of," Celina said as she reached into her backpack and pulled out her sketch pad.

"You're Celina Hart, aren't you? The artist."

"Guilty."

"Wow," she said. "You look a lot different up close. I've seen you around town."

Celina raised her eyebrow. "Around New York?"

The woman shook her head. "Elmore. I'm Tiffany Martin."

"What are you doing here?" Celina asked.

Tiffany smiled, removed her hat and glasses, and crossed her legs. "I'm here to warn you about that man who claims to love you. Darius McRae is a user and you're just his latest victim."

"I don't have to listen to this," Celina said as she reached up to press the stewardess button. Tiffany grabbed her hand and the strength of her grip surprised Celina. "Let go of me," Celina ordered.

"We're about to be thirty-thousand feet in the air, and you have nowhere to go, so just listen to what I have to say."

"Let go of my hand," Celina said again. This time, Tiffany let her go. "What do you have to say?"

"Celina, I'm not the bad person that Darius has made me out to be. He thinks I'm stalking him and that I've done some bad things at his store. I'm not that kind of person."

"Yeah, okay. What do you want? Because right now, you sound like a bitter, scorned woman who just wants to get in my head. Darius doesn't want you and you should just let it go."

"You don't know Darius and I'm just trying to warn you. He's going to throw you away like trash, just like he did me. He says all the right things, but he doesn't mean them. To him, women are interchangeable like socks and boxers."

"Why in the world would I listen to anything you have to say? If Darius is so horrible, why are you working over- time to get him back in your life?"

Shaking her head, Tiffany denied wanting Darius. "You think that you're special and he loves you more than anything. He said the same thing to me. You'll be crying over him before too long. Then you will under- stand. Darius is a user. Why didn't he come to New York with you? He has to make time for his other women since you've been taking up a lot of his time. I bet when you told him that you were coming to New York he didn't even put up a fight."

"You don't know what you're talking about and I tell you what, you'd better stay away from me and Darius when I return to Elmore," Celina said, struggling to keep her voice even.

Tiffany smiled devilishly. "You'd be better off if you stayed in New York. I'm trying to save you from a broken heart."

Celina shook her head. "What did you expect to ac- complish here? Did you think I was just going to believe what you had to say and tell Darius it was over so that you could have a clear shot at him? News flash, Tiffany. Darius doesn't want you. He's with me."

Tiffany turned her head away from Celina and looked out the window of the plane. "We'll see for how long," she snapped.

Celina pressed the button for the stewardess. The woman walked over to the seat.

"Yes ma'am?" she asked.

"I need a new seat, because I'm not sitting next to this woman," Celina said as she stood up and grabbed her backpack. The stewardess led her to a seat across the aisle from Tiffany. Luckily, Celina got a window seat and she didn't have to look at Tiffany anymore.

When the plane touched down at LaGuardia Airport, Celina didn't move from her seat until she saw Tiffany exit the plane. It was obvious that the woman was a stalker and the last thing she wanted was for her to know where she lived.

That woman is crazy, Celina thought as she stood at the boarding gate, watching Tiffany disappear in the crowd.

Darius sat in the office at the hardware store trying to stop thinking about Celina. What if she didn't come back from New York? Rising to his feet, he walked over to the window looking out over the town. *Why would she want to live in a town like this after all these years? I can't expect her to just drop everything she's worked for to be with me.* He wished desperately that she would. The silence in the shop was deafening; it seemed as if everything was on hold now that Celina was gone.

"Darius, got a second?" Richard said as he popped his head in the office.

Darius waved for the man to come inside. "What's going on?"

"That's what I came to ask you. How did things turn out with Celina?"

Darius turned away from the window and looked at Richard. "Well, she's in New York right now, so how do you think things went? I don't know if she's coming back or if she wants to come back."

Richard nodded. "I'm sure she's going to come back. She cares for you so much, Darius."

Then why did she leave? he thought as he looked at Richard, trying to absorb what the man was saying. He shrugged his shoulders.

"Why didn't you go to New York with her?" Richard asked.

"She didn't ask me to accompany her."

Richard rolled his eyes. "You know the problem with you young guys, no imagination. You should've hopped on the next plane and followed her. Women like stuff like that. It would prove to her that you are the man that's right for her. Ever heard that old Quincy Jones song, 'One Hundred Ways'? Take a hint from it, man."

"What if she has someone else in New York and she's going to end or reconcile things with him?" Darius said, voicing the fear that had been inside him since Celina said she was returning to New York. "How will I look just showing up?"

"He's a sorry man if she does have one in New York. He let her deal with her father's sickness all alone. Besides, if you don't show up, imagine how that will look. Go to her."

"Maybe her father has her address in New York. I could drive to Columbia and take the next flight to New York," Darius said, knowing that Celina didn't have someone else in the city. What was it about that place that made her want to go back to New York so badly?

"That sounds more like it. I'll hold the fort down here," Richard said as Darius picked up the phone to call Thomas Hart.

About an hour later, Darius was heading to Columbia with Celina's address and telephone number tucked in his pocket. He called the airline and booked a flight to New York. The last-minute flight was going to cost him over one thousand dollars, but the price didn't matter to him. He had to see Celina and make sure that she was going to return to him.

As Darius waited in line to board his flight, he wondered what he would find out about Celina once he got to New York. He'd been to the Big Apple several times but his visits never had as much meaning as this trip.

He moved through the security checkpoints without a lot of fanfare because, in his haste to leave, he hadn't packed a bag. One of the first things he would have to do when the plane touched down was to head to Macy's or Bloomingdale's to get some clothes.

Finally, he made it onto the plane. Darius buckled his seat belt and waited for the plane to take off. It seemed to take forever and he wished the plane would move at warp speed like in the Star Trek movies. Darius leaned back in the seat and closed his eyes. After what seemed like five hours, he heard the announcement telling the passengers that the plane would be landing at La-Guardia in five minutes. Sitting up, Darius couldn't hold back the smile spreading across his lips because it wouldn't be long before he held Celina in his arms and felt her lips against his. What if she had come back to New York to tie up loose ends with a man? Jealousy began to make his hair stand on end. Maybe her reservations about moving back to Elmore had something to do with her relationship with this New York man.

"Stop being paranoid," Darius told himself as he stood up to walk off the plane. Soon, he was enveloped in the sea of passengers who were exiting the plane. His thoughts turned from Celina to protecting his wallet from a thieving passenger. After all, he was in New York. Darius dashed through the airport and headed to the curb to hail a cab.

"Where you headed, guy?" the Iranian driver asked as Darius climbed into the backseat.

"118th Street," Darius said as he pulled out his cell phone and dialed Celina's number. Before he hit send, he asked the driver how long it would be before they reached their destination. Darius eased back in the seat and exhaled an exasperated breath. He didn't want to call Celina until he was outside of her apartment. Placing his phone on the seat beside him he stared out the window at the congestion ahead of them. Darius had forgotten the last time he'd been stuck in a traffic jam. In Elmore, everything was less than five minutes from everything.

Though he didn't want to, if Celina wanted to stay in New York, then we would move here to be with her.

"Hey," the cabbie said, "it might be a little more than twenty minutes. Hope you're not trying to make a reservation some where."

Darius shook his head. "I'll be fine. If you could let me know when we get close to my stop, I'd appreciate it."

The driver grunted and traffic began to move at a snail's pace. Darius felt like a child waiting for Christmas day as they crawled along in the near gridlocked traffic.

"How much farther?" Darius asked.

"We haven't even moved a mile," the cabbie said, his voice displaying his annoyance.

Darius leaned forward and handed the man a twenty dollar bill. "If you can find a way around all of this traffic and get me where I need to be, I'll make it worth your while."

The man took the money and smiled. "I know a great short cut. But you need to hold on to your seat." He took a sharp turn down a side street and pressed hard on the gas. Darius bounced around the back seat before wising up and putting his seat belt on. The scenery whizzed by so quickly, Darius had no idea where he was. After what seemed like the longest taxi ride in history, the driver told Darius that they were near their destination.

He retrieved his phone, which was now underneath the seat, and dialed Celina's number.

"Hello," Celina said. Her voice was like a sweet jazz song.

"It's me," he said. "I was thinking about you."

"Really?" Celina said. "Just what were you thinking?"

"How much I miss you, hearing your voice, touching your bushy hair."

"Darius, I've only been gone a few hours. Not even a full day."

"That's a few hours too long," Darius replied. He could feel Celina's smile through the phone.

"How are you going to make it these next three days? If a few hours are this taxing on you, you're not going to make it."

"I'll make it," he said. "Or you could cut your trip short."

"Hey, guy, here's ya stop," the cabbie said.

"Who was that?" Celina asked.

Darius ignored her question as he pulled his wallet out of his pocket and handed the driver three twenty dollar bills for the ride.

"You know what I've always wondered," he said as he closed the door to the cab. "Does your apartment face the street?"

Celina sounded confused as she told him her place faced 118th Street. "Why does that matter?" she asked.

"Look out the window," he said.

"What?" Celina said. "You're not making any sense right now."

"Just humor me," he said as he looked up at the brownstone, shielding his eyes from the sun. He saw a lace curtain move on the third floor.

"Darius, is that you down there?" she asked excitedly.

"It's me." The phone went dead and Darius looked at the small silver phone to see if his signal had dropped. A few seconds later, the front door to the building opened and Celina marched down the steps. She was looking like New York again, not the same woman who stood before him on the back steps of Thomas Hart's house in Elmore. She was dressed in a black Prada minidress that was tailored to her exquisite frame, a pair of black stiletto boots that left a sliver of skin showing. Her afro was pulled up in a ponytail with a pair of designer sunglasses stuck on her head. "I can't believe you're here," she said as she rushed into his arms. Celina's lips brushed across his neck.

Darius let her go and held her at arm's length so that he could look into her eyes. "I thought about stepping back and giving you time to do whatever you needed to do, but I know that you've been known to sabotage a relationship. Besides, I missed you."

"And, you don't play fair," she said with a laugh.

Darius smiled. "That's true. So, are you going to invite me up?"

"Of course," she said as she grabbed his hand and led him up the steps as if she were excited to show him her place. Celina's loft was everything he expected it to be. The walls were painted bright yellow, with green ivy stenciled on them. The colors reminded him of a bright summer day. Several prints of her work sat on the floor. The ceiling was painted powder blue like the sky. "Wow," Darius said as he looked around the place.

Celina smiled. "I can't believe you, Darius."

"What?"

"You're here."

"That is a good thing, isn't it?" he inquired. Celina nodded.

"It is."

"I mean, if I'm crowding you, let me know, because I don't want to scare you away."

Celina kissed him on the cheek. "I don't think I have a reason to be afraid."

Progress, Darius thought as he fought to keep his expression unchanged.

"Are you hungry?" Celina asked as they walked into the kitchen. Darius followed her and wrapped his arms around her waist.

"Yes, but not for anything in your icebox." Darius captured Celina's lips with his, kissing her with an unbridled passion that made her head spin. He let her go. "But, I'm willing to wait for that. This dress means that you have somewhere to go, doesn't it?"

Celina cleared her throat several times and rubbed the front of her head. "Um," she said. "I was about to head into midtown and drop off some prints at the Barbara Mathes Gallery. Why don't you come with me and we can make a day of it?"

"I'd love to," Darius said, although, he really wanted a day of making love to his woman. The woman he wanted to love, cherish, and honor for the rest of his life. The thought of waking up to Celina every day made him smile. "All right, would you grab this for me?" Celina asked as she picked up the prints from beside the door and handed them to Darius.

"You're taking a cab, right?" he asked as he placed the prints under his arm.

"Cabs are a luxury," Celina said as she reached into the ivory and yellow jar sitting by the door on a wrought iron table and pulled out a Metro card. Darius shook his head, not looking forward to lugging Celina's art collection through New York's underground.

"I'll get the cab and you can cook me a steak for dinner," he said.

Celina giggled. "What, are you afraid of the subway?"

"No, just the hernia I'll get from lugging your masterpieces," he said.

Celina tapped him on the shoulder. "All right, Darius, we'll take a taxi, but let P. Diddy take care of your steak."

"Justin's for dinner, huh? I'll settle for that, as long as you provide the dessert," he said as he headed out the front door.

"You're so bad," she said as she locked the door behind them. The couple walked about three blocks before a yellow cab passed them. Darius soaked up the city atmosphere, the hustle and bustle of the crowd, the mix of Spanish, hip-hop, and old soul music blaring from the various brownstones. Trucks, cars, and SUVs sped down the road as if they were rushing to a fire or the crash of the stock market. Celina seemed to flourish in the busyness of it all. He wondered how she could walk so comfortably in those killer shoes. Darius was sure this was why she always walked around barefoot at home. He watched her as she stuck her arm out to hail a cab. Her profile was big-city chic. How could he ask her to give this up for Elmore? She was in her element and nothing in Elmore could compare to New York.

"Celina," Darius said as they got into a cab that finally stopped for them. "Are you sure you're ready to give this up?"

She smiled and shrugged her shoulders. "Maybe. Right now, I just want to be wherever you are."

Darius touched her face. "You don't know how that makes me feel to hear you say that," he said as he kissed her lips gently.

The Jamaican taxi driver cleared his throat. "Where you two heading? Weddin' chapel?"

Darius laughed.

"No," Celina said. "Not right yet. East 57th Street."

The driver put the pedal to the medal and headed for midtown. When Darius and Celina got to the gallery, he was surprised to see a banner heralding Celina's exhibit.

"Wow, I didn't know you had a showing here," he said in awe.

"The gallery director heard a rumor that I'd left Paris and she made it her mission to get me here. It's a short showing, just a few pieces for a few weeks. I told her I have to go back south, so she put this together really quickly. I didn't know about it until I got off the plane."

Darius nodded, thinking that he was asking Celina to give up a lot to be with him. When they walked into the gallery, a tall, wispy, blond woman dressed in the Manhattan uniform—all black—greeted them. She rushed toward Celina. "Oh my goodness, you look divine. Is that Prada? Did you pick this up in Paris?" Then she turned to Darius. "Wow, did you pick him up in Paris, too?"

Celina shook her head, looking as if she was about to die of embarrassment. Darius had forgotten how brash city women could be. Celina turned to Darius and smiled. Then she looked at the woman. "No, Millicent, this one is homegrown."

"Really?" Millicent asked. "Maybe I need to take a trip down south. Are there any more like you at home?"

"No," Darius said. "I'm one of a kind."

"Pity," Millicent replied. "So, Celina, get on with the introductions."

"This is Darius McRae, my boyfriend."

Millicent raised her perfectly manicured eyebrow. "Celina Hart has a boyfriend." She linked her arm around Celina's and said in a loud whisper. "I see where the inspiration for these paintings comes from."

Darius cleared his throat, "Are you ladies going to take these paintings or does my arm have to fall off?"

Millicent raised her arm and snapped her fingers. "Where is William? I swear these interns are getting lazier and lazier. Darius, dahling, will you just bring these paintings over here." She led Celina and Darius to a dim area off the main floor. Darius leaned the paintings against the wall. "What do we have here?" Millicent said as she pulled the white cloth covering the paintings back. She eyed the paintings with wide-eyed wonderment. "I love them all, but this one." She pointed to Celina's latest work, *H2Love.* "This has got to go on the Web site. This will start people talking."

"Yes, it will," Darius commented, remembering the day Celina painted it. He stole a glance at her. She had a bright smile plastered on her face as if they shared the same thought.

"Well," Millicent said as she looked from Darius to the painting. "You must be the model."

"No, just the inspiration," Celina said. "So, when does the show open?"

"Tomorrow night and I have so much to do," Millicent said as she placed her hand to her forehead, reminding Darius of a drama queen. "But the buzz is there. Fresh from Paris, New York's own Celina Hart. The *Times* is coming, as well as *InStyle,* and all of the TV stations. Word is you have a famous former president as a fan, so please don't wear a blue dress."

Darius and Celina broke out laughing. "I don't have a blue dress," Celina replied once she gained her composure.

Millicent looked at Darius. "You will be here, right? I'm sure you have an haute couture tuxedo for Celina's big night."

Millicent was starting to grate on Darius's nerves. "Actually," he said ironically. "I'm happy with what I'm wearing."

She visibly blanched. "You can't be serious. This is New York, the press, you're Celina's best accessory," she said.

"Millicent," Celina said. "Calm down. Darius is more than an arm piece, okay? We're going to go grab some-

thing to eat. I'll be back later to check out the space.
Thank you so much for this."

Millicent nodded. Celina and Darius turned to walk
out the door. Celina squeezed Darius's arm once they
got outside. "And you wonder why I want to give this all
up," she said.

He shook his head and kissed Celina on the cheek.
"Miss Millie just doesn't have any manners, now, does
she?" Darius said as he held his arm up to hail a cab.

CHAPTER 18

Celina talked Darius into taking the subway to Justin's and as soon as they got on the crowded subway, she wished they had taken a cab. She grabbed the only empty seat in the car and Darius stood above her.

"So," he said as he held on to the bar above her seat. "Do I really need a tux?"

"Maybe a nice suit, but not a tux. Don't pay Millie any attention. She thinks that anyone not from New York or not an artist has no sense of fashion. After lunch, we can go shopping, if you want to," she said.

Darius grinned. "You don't trust my judgment?"

Celina snorted. "Well," she said stroking the fabric of his jeans. "Not in everything. And I didn't see you with any bags when you appeared on my doorstep."

"Are you trying to say I don't have model quality?" he joked.

"Well, when you're naked you do," she said, then grew serious. "Guess who followed me to New York."

"Don't tell me it was Tiffany," he said.

Celina nodded and replayed the scene on the flight.

"Did she follow you from the plane?" Darius asked.

"No," Celina said. "I made sure she left before I did."

Darius banged his hand against his thigh. "I told Wayman she was dangerous, but he wouldn't listen."

Celina shuddered, not wanting to believe that Tiffany would do something to hurt her or Darius. She placed her hand on Darius's leg. "Your love does all of this to women?"

"Tiffany never loved me, she loved what she thought I could do for her. We were supposed to be Elmore's answer to Ben and J-Lo."

Celina laughed. "We all saw how their relationship turned out. What are we supposed to be?"

He leaned down and kissed her lips softly. "Celina and Darius."

When the train came to a stop, they got off, holding hands and smiling at each other. Even to the most cynical New Yorker, the love between them was undeniable. Some people passing them on the street smiled at the young couple. "So, what are the well-dressed arm pieces wearing these days?" Darius asked as they passed a new men's boutique about three blocks from Justin's. Celina looked up at the store's marquee and squealed. "That's my painting," she said. "Lou used it." Celina pulled Darius by the arm and they walked in the store.

"Welcome to Legacy," a tall, dark-skinned sales clerk said when Celina and Darius walked in. "What can I help you find, today?"

"Is Lou here?" Celina asked excitedly. Darius raised his eyebrow, wondering just who in the hell was Lou.

"I'll go check," he said as he headed to the back of the store. Darius walked over to a rack of Italian suits, holding his breath and waiting to see "Lou." Celina walked toward the back of the store. "Celina Hart!" a big voice boomed. Celina hugged Lou tightly, nearly being smothered by the woman's huge breasts. "Louise Parker. I can't believe you finally opened this place."

"Well, I had to find something to do with that painting," she said as she looked around the store and spotted Darius. "Um, who is that? He is a prime piece of . . ."

"That's my boyfriend," Celina said.

Lou's mouth dropped open. "Your what? I can't believe it. You've actually let a man get close to you."

Celina shook her head. Lou was one of the first people Celina had met when she moved to Harlem. The two women had moved into the same brownstone. Louise, who was twenty years Celina's senior, stopped her and told her how much she loved her hair. Celina thanked the woman and proceeded to pick up one of her paintings. Lou stopped dead in her tracks and offered Celina five hundred dollars for it. Celina, at the time, was strapped for cash, and sold the painting. "I'm going to make this painting famous," Lou had said as she held up the canvas that depicted a man standing at the edge of a lake, looking into the water at the reflection of his ancestors. "I'm going to put this up at my shop."

Celina had nodded and continued lugging her things up the steps. Lou had reached out and given Celina a hand, telling her that she reminded her of her daughter and, if she ever needed anything, to let her know. Celina had been touched by the older woman's kindness and the two became fast friends. Over the years, Celina and Lou had lost contact with each other because Celina was off doing her art shows and Lou had opened Legacy in Chelsea, but their bond remained unchanged.

"So," Lou said, breaking Celina out of her thoughts about their friendship. "This guy, what's his name?"

"Darius." Celina smiled when she said his name.

Lou was shocked at Celina and the way she was acting. She clearly remembered Celina saying that she'd never fall in love and that she didn't need the hassle of it.

"Well, well, the artist has found love. Is he from New York?"

Celina shook her head. "We actually grew up together."

Lou smiled. "Ah, Southern Comfort. Have you guys moved to New York?"

"I don't think that's in the plans," she said. "Oh, I forgot to tell you! I have a showing tomorrow at Barbara Mathes's Gallery."

Lou clasped her hands together and smiled. "I can't believe this. I'm there," she said. "So, that's why you're here? Mr. Darius needs a suit." Lou looked at him and smiled. "I must say, you have good taste."

Darius walked over to the two women, relieved that Lou was a woman and carrying an olive-green Sean John suit with a quarter-length jacket.

Celina reached out and touched the suit. "I like it," she said.

"Hello, Darius," Lou said extending her hand to him. "I'm Louise, also known as Lou."

"She's my New York mom," Celina said as the two shook hands.

"It's nice to meet you," he said. "Just need to try this on."

Lou looked at him, then the suit. "Make sure you get a crisp white shirt to go with this. It is going to look great with your skin tone. I know men's fashion. The fitting room is right through there," she said, pointing to a pair of ivory curtains. Darius disappeared behind the curtains. A few minutes later he came out, modeling the suit. "What do you think?" he asked as he pulled the jacket open and turned from side to side.

Lou clapped for him as if he were a runway model. "That looks good. It's yours. If the press talks to you, mention Legacy," she said with a laugh.

Darius looked at the price tag on the suit. "I can't buy this," he said.

"You're not, I'm giving it to you," she said. "Alan, get Darius one of those white dress shirts for the suit." Alan nodded and walked over to a display of shirts, where he picked one.

After Darius got his suit, and Celina and Lou had caught up with one another, the couple headed to Justin's for lunch. As usual, the trendy restaurant was packed. There was an hour wait for a table. "I'm starving," Darius said. "Why don't we go there?" He pointed down the street to an outdoor café. Celina smiled because the place reminded her of Paris. Since The French Bistro had just opened up, there wasn't a crowd. Celina and Darius took a seat at one of the tables closest to the street.

"I used to eat at a place like this in Paris," she said as she picked up the colorful menu.

"Are you going back to Paris?" he asked. "I know that was a great opportunity for you. Thomas is doing better . . . you could go back and finish that project and . . ."

"Darius, I'm where I want to be. I thought I made that clear?"

He reached across the table and grabbed her hand. "I just don't want you to feel like you're giving up your life to be with me. Watching you and how you move through this city, seeing your name plastered across buildings, I know you're meant for more than just being in Elmore."

Celina kissed his hand. "There are planes, trains, and automobiles that can take me anywhere I need to go. Darius, I'm an artist, a free spirit, remember. I love you and I don't want you to think that I'm doing anything that I don't want to do."

"And you're sure about this?"

Celina nodded. "I've never been more sure about anything." Though she still had her insecurities, she knew that loving Darius was the best thing that had happened to her in a long time. His love was better than Paris, more important than an art gallery opening, and the one thing that had been missing from her life.

They ate their authentic French entrées in silence, only commenting on the taste of the food between bites. After lunch, Celina decided to take Darius back to her place so they could go sightseeing in Harlem. They hopped on the subway, heading back uptown. The ride back was less crowded and Celina and Darius sat side by side. She leaned against him. "I like this," she said.

"What? Riding the subway?"

"Sharing New York with you."

Darius fell silent, but finally built up enough courage to ask, "Are you going to move back here?"

"No, we have to open our gallery," she said. "Darius, I love New York, but it doesn't compare to you."

When they returned to Harlem, the last thing Darius wanted to do was walk around sightseeing. His time on the plane and their nonstop movement was catching up with him.

"I need a nap," he told Celina as they walked up the steps to her brownstone. "I've been going all day."

"All right, well, I need to get some things together for tomorrow. So, you nap and I'll work." Celina opened the door to her loft and walked in. Once she and Darius were inside, she pointed him in the direction of the bedroom. He kissed her on the cheek. "Feel free to wake me up," he said as he walked into the bedroom. Before Darius could take his shirt off, his cell phone rang.

"Yeah," he said.

"I see your girlfriend has a gallery opening tomorrow. Wouldn't it be a shame if something ruined her big night?" Tiffany said.

"Listen to me, Tiffany, leave Celina alone." Darius tightened his grip around the phone.

"Maybe I will. Darius, how long do you think she's going to stay with a one-trick pony like you? She has a life in New York that you can't compare to and when I'm done, she's not going to want to hear your name," she said before hanging up the phone. Darius looked up and saw Celina standing in the doorway.

"That was her, wasn't it?"

Darius nodded. "Celina, don't worry about Tiffany. I have it under control," he said as he motioned for Celina to come over to the bed. She sat down beside him.

"Everything would be perfect if she wasn't sticking her nose where it didn't belong," she said angrily. Celina rose to her feet and paced back and forth. "Something has to be done about her. If she's unstable enough to follow me here, then there's no telling what she might do."

Darius reached out to her and wrapped his arms around her waist. "Calm down, baby. Why don't you join me in bed, I just want to feel you against me," he said.

Celina kissed his cheek. "I wish I could, but I have so much to do before tomorrow. So, you sleep and I'll work." Celina stood up and headed into the living room.

Darius silently prayed that Tiffany wouldn't make good on her threat and ruin Celina's opening.

CHAPTER 19

Darius was on edge as the hours before Celina's showing ticked away. Was Tiffany going to make good on her threat to cause trouble? *Why can't that woman just fall off a subway platform?* he thought as he sat on the edge of the bed, watching Celina slip on her Roberto Cavalli gown. The powder-blue and pink gown clung to her body as if she was the inspiration for the design. Darius's eyes followed her as she walked over to the closet and opened the door. He was surprised at how stylish Celina was. She had names like Prada, Cavalli, Donna Karan, and Dolce in her closet. She had three pairs of Jimmy Choo shoes and a pair of Manolo Blahnik sandals. Those Manolos were the shoes she decided to wear. Celina bent over and picked up the pink sandals. Then she turned to Darius.

"Are you going to watch me or are you going to get dressed?" she asked.

Darius shrugged his shoulders and smiled. "I was enjoying the show and," he said as he stood up, "trying to figure out how to take this dress off without ripping it." He encircled her waist and kissed her on the back of her neck.

Celina hit him on the shoulder. "Stop it," she said. "You're going to make me late."

Darius let her go and smiled wickedly. "I'm going to the bathroom," he said as he headed out of the bedroom. Darius showered and shaved quickly. When he walked out of the bathroom, Celina was adorning her hair with a pink ribbon that matched the pink in her dress. She looked more like a model than an artist.

"Wow," Darius said.

Celina turned around, getting a full view of him in nothing but a towel. Suddenly, she wasn't worried about being late. "You'd better get dressed or we're never going to get out of here," she said as she picked up her makeup case and headed to the bathroom.

"I bet I'll be dressed before you put your face on," he called out as the bathroom door closed behind her. Darius dressed quickly, slipping into his new suit. As he buttoned his shirt, Celina walked out of the bathroom, radiant. "I'm ready," she announced.

Darius could hardly breathe as he looked at her. "Beautiful," he said, giving her a long, lingering look. Celina had on a light dusting of foundation and a clear gloss on her lips. The only thing that was missing was a halo.

"Are you ready, Ms. Lady?" Darius asked as he grabbed his jacket. Celina smiled and headed out the door. Darius walked behind her, admiring the view of her shapely behind in her haute couture gown. Once they got outside, they walked a couple of blocks to hail a cab.

"No subway tonight?" Darius ribbed.

Celina raised her eyebrow. "In this dress? I think not," she said as she raised her arm to hail a cab. A taxi pulled up to the corner immediately and Darius knew why the driver stopped; Celina had power over traffic in that dress. Darius grabbed her hand and kissed it after they were seated in the cab. "How are you feeling?" he asked.

"Nervous. Does it show?"

Darius shook his head. "All I see is beauty." About fifteen minutes later, the taxi was stopping in front of the gallery. Darius stepped out of the cab, not expecting the sudden flash of cameras. Instinctively, he threw his hand up to shield his eyes from the bright blue flashes. Celina stepped out of the car camera-ready, with a smile plastered on her face. Darius watched her nervousness evaporate under the watchful eye of the media. Reporters swirled around her, asking her questions about the show, her latest work, Paris, and her dress. Celina linked arms with Darius after answering the reporters' questions and walked into the gallery. "So, this is your life?" Darius whispered through his smile.

"Some days," she said. "Millicent knows how to create a buzz." Another flash of light bulbs went off, capturing Celina and Darius on film. Millicent walked over to them, looking like a peacock, in Darius's opinion, with blue, gold, and green feathers in her hair. Her sequined black dress hugged her reed-thin body so tightly Darius wondered if she could breathe.

She leaned in and kissed Celina on the cheek. "You look amazing," she said breathlessly. "That dress and this exhibit are going to launch you into the stratosphere."

"Lofty goals," Celina said, keeping a plastic smile on her face for the photographers. "Let's just get through the night and see what happens."

Millicent led Celina and Darius into the main gallery where all of the paintings were. While a group of reporters cornered Celina and Millicent, Darius wandered around the gallery, looking at his girlfriend's body of work. He looked up and saw that the main focus of the showing was *H2Love*. Smiling, he couldn't help but think about the creation of the painting and how it changed everything between them. That was the day he knew he had to have her in his life and not just for a moment, but forever. Crossing over to it, he smiled as he stared at the image.

"Beautiful, isn't it?" a woman asked. Darius turned and faced her. "Liza Damien." She extended her hand to him.

Darius shook her hand and nodded. "Celina is a great artist."

"And you're the perfect model," she said, looking from Darius to the painting. "Ellian, get this shot. Do you have a few minutes to answer some questions?" The cameraman focused his lens on Darius. He looked around for Celina, hoping that she would save him from the reporter and the glare of the spotlight, but she was in another corner with a group of reporters.

"Why not?" Darius said.

Liza smiled and stuck a microphone in his face. "Your name?"

"Darius McRae."

Liza nodded and told him what station she worked for and to relax and be natural.

"We're here with Darius McRae, who looks just like the image in Hart's new painting, *H2Love.* Darius, are you a model?"

"No, Celina and I are old friends and she asked me to pose for a painting. I had no idea that it would be this popular."

"Old friends? Well, how does it feel to be immortalized on canvas like this?"

Darius turned his head and looked at the painting again. "Right now, it hasn't sunk in. Maybe when I'm seventy-five years old with a potbelly, it will."

"Thank you," Liza said as she signaled for Ellian to

turn the camera off. She shook hands with Darius, then headed over to the other reporters who were interviewing Celina. Darius walked around the showroom looking at the other paintings. When someone tapped him on the shoulder, he thought it was another reporter. Darius turned around and looked into Tiffany's face.

"She does have some talent," she said as she flung her hair back. "Not much, but I guess there isn't anything else going on tonight and these people will do anything to get free booze and food."

"Why are you here?" Darius asked.

Tiffany smiled. "I'm here to support a fellow Elmore native. I mean, isn't that why you posed for this picture?" She pointed to the painting.

"You're not welcome here and if you don't leave, I'll have the police escort you out."

Tiffany placed her hands on her round hips. "And cause a scene at your beloved's showing? Darius, you wouldn't."

The last thing he wanted to do was mar Celina's evening, but Tiffany had to go.

"What do you want?" he asked acquiescing.

She turned toward Celina and then back to Darius. "Why her? What does she have that I don't have?"

"Me. Tiffany, I never promised you anything and I never loved you. I'm sorry that you thought there was something between us when there wasn't."

She folded her arms underneath her breasts. "Darius, I was there for you when you were whining about your ex and she comes into town for five minutes and all of a sudden she is the love of your life? That's not fair."

"There for me?" he said trying to keep his voice low and even. "Tiffany, you were a rebound screw. I had no intentions of having anything serious with a money-grubbing gold digger like you."

Tiffany's eyes narrowed into tight slits, then she hauled off and slapped him with all the fury inside her. A few people standing near them peered in their direction.

"You will not talk to me like that. I loved you."

Darius took a step back and exhaled. "Leave," he snapped.

A gallery security guard walked over to Darius and Tiffany. "Is there a problem over here?" he asked as he looked at the angry scowls on their faces.

Tiffany turned to him and smiled. "No, sir. I was just leaving. I have a plane to catch," she said, then turned to Darius. "You have to come home and I won't forget this."

The guard followed Tiffany out the front door as Darius looked for Celina in the crowd. He hoped she hadn't seen what happened. Darius knew that when they returned to Elmore, things were going to get a lot worse.

By the end of the night, Celina's cheeks burned from all the smiling and all she wanted to do was head home and fall asleep in Darius's arms. As the party started to wind down, she found him sitting in a corner hiding from reporters, something she wished that she could do. The reporters and gallery patrons kept her busy all night, which was a good thing, since everyone loved her work and she sold more than half of her paintings. Celina wouldn't allow anyone to buy *H2Love*. That one belonged to her and Darius. She walked up behind him and wrapped her arms around his waist. "Where have you been all my life?" she asked.

Darius pointed to the painting. "Sitting right here on the wall." He turned around and kissed Celina gently on the lips.

"Did you have fun?" she asked.

"It was an experience. Do you think it's going to be like this when we open the Celina Hart Gallery of Fine Art in Elmore?" he asked.

"Wow, you really have been giving this some thought." Celina looked up at *H2Love*. "This has to come with us. When the showing is over, I'll have Millicent ship it home." Celina was shocked that she called Elmore home, given that she hadn't lived there in more than twenty years, but being with Darius was home, whether it was Elmore, Harlem, or a tent in the woods. "Are you ready to go?" she asked. "Maybe we can go grab a bite to eat."

"I want to grab something, but not a bite to eat," Darius whispered huskily.

Playfully she punched him in the arm, "But I'm hungry. Trust me, it's worth the wait," she said with a smile.

Darius nodded. "All right, my lady, lead the way."

As they headed out the door, Millicent stopped them. "Celina, Celina, this was a fabulous showing and we have so many orders. You know I got an offer for $50,000 for *H2Love*."

Celina shook her head. "It's not for sale. We're going to hang it in our gallery in South Carolina."

Millicent nodded. "Let me know when it opens. I would love to see it. Are you going to have exclusively new art or all of your work?"

"A mix," Darius said. "We'll make sure you get an invite to the opening. I'm sorry but we have to go."

Millicent waved good-bye to the couple as they walked out the door. "Great save," Celina said once they made it outside. "Millicent would have kept us in there for hours."

Darius nodded. "I could tell."

Celina hailed a cab. The wind had picked up outside.

Even though it was still summer, the nights were growing cooler, announcing that fall wasn't too far away. She'd never paid much attention to the weather before, always carrying a jacket with her to keep the winds at bay. Tonight she had something better and when Darius wrapped his arms around her, she knew she never had to worry about a jacket again. This was right and finally she knew it.

"Where are we headed?" Darius asked as he and Celina slipped into the cab.

"You'll like it," she said. Celina leaned over the seat and gave the driver the address to The Blue Smoke Jazz Standard on East 27th Street. Then she eased into Darius's arms as the cab took off.

"Nights like this make me miss living in a city," Darius said, gently stroking her arm. "What would we be doing if we were in Elmore?"

Celina smiled. "Maybe at the lake, watching the stars. Listening to some Coltrane on the stereo. Taking each other's clothes off." She gently bit his bottom lip.

"Damn, do we need to get on a plane? That sounds better than wherever we're headed."

"What did I do to deserve you? Darius, you've opened my eyes to so much and you've opened my heart. I'll love you forever, I know it."

Darius smiled and kissed her. "And I'm not going to let you forget you said that, Ms. Hart."

When the cab pulled up in front of the jazz club, Celina's cell phone rang. She pulled the phone out of her purse. "Hello?"

"Celina, it's Velma. Your father took a turn for the worse. We're rushing him to Columbia."

"Oh, my God," Celina said as all the color rushed from her face.

Darius looked at her with concern in his eyes.

"Is this the stop or what?" the cab driver asked. "The meter is still running."

"Wait a minute," Darius said gruffly.

"Miss Velma, I'll get on the next flight and meet you at the hospital. Call me if there's a change."

"Celina, I will, and I'm so sorry," Velma said.

Celina closed the phone, then turned to the driver. "Turn the car around. We have to get to Harlem, now."

"I don't go to Harlem at night, lady. You'd better take the train or the bus."

Celina reached across the seat and grabbed the driver by the collar. "Take me there right now or the least of your worries is going to be driving into Harlem."

Darius pulled Celina around her hips. "Calm down, baby," he said. "Look, guy, we'll make it worth your while." Darius reached into his wallet and pulled out two hundred-dollar bills. "Come on, it's an emergency."

The driver took the money and put it in his pocket. "What's the address?" Celina rattled off her address and the driver took off.

When the driver got to Celina's brownstone, she and Darius hopped out of the cab and ran inside. She stuffed clothes into a bag, not caring if her outfits matched. She grabbed her shoes and tossed them in the bag. Celina took off her dress and threw it in the corner of her bedroom, not caring about its price, then scrambled to pull on a grey sweat suit and white tank top.

Darius watched her as she moved with the swiftness of a maniac. He walked over to her and grabbed her arm. "Celina, slow down," he said. "Breathe. I want you to sit down and I'll call the airline and get us two tickets."

Celina nodded. She was trembling like a leaf, tears threatening to fall from her eyes. Darius walked over to the side of the bed and picked up the phone. Celina watched his mouth move, but she couldn't hear what he was saying. *What if we don't make it in time? I can't lose my father, not now. We've just made our way back to each other.*

"Celina," Darius said as he handed her a pair of tennis shoes. "Do you want me to call your mother?"

She nodded as she took the shoes from his hands. "She would want to know," Celina said in a quiet tone as she tied her shoes. "But maybe we should just wait until we get to Columbia and find out what's going on."

Darius nodded. "The only flight they had was one to Charlotte, NC, that leaves tonight. We can get to Charlotte, rent a car, and drive to Columbia."

Celina nodded. "What time do we leave?"

"We'd better get a taxi to the airport now," he said. "Are you ready?"

Celina stood up and walked over to Darius. He wrapped his arms around her. "I'm so scared," she whispered against his ear.

"It's all right. Let's just get to Columbia." Darius grabbed Celina's bag and led her to the door. As if in a trance, she followed Darius outside. In the span of two hours, she went from celebrating the most successful show of her career to hopping on a plane to check on her father. It was like Paris all over again. Celina was beginning to wish that she'd never come back to New York. She'd gone to Elmore to take care of her father and she wasn't supposed to do anything but take care of him and now that he needed her, she was nowhere to be found.

"If something happens before we get there, I will never forgive myself," she whispered.

"What did you say?" Darius asked as they slid into the cab. She leaned against him, afraid to repeat herself.

The traffic was thin and the cab driver got to La-Guardia in twenty minutes, giving them plenty of time to go through security to make their flight. Celina walked through the airport slowly, leaning on Darius as she dragged along. It would be an hour before they'd be up in the air and time seemed to be standing still.

"Do you want to eat something before we get on the plane?" he asked her.

"I can't eat," she said, running her hand over her face. "I just want to get to my father." As they sat down, she buried her face in Darius's arms, fighting the tears that burned in her eyes.

When the boarding announcement for their flight blasted through the PA system, Celina caught a second wind and dashed to the boarding gate, leaving her bag at Darius' feet. He snatched it up and followed her to the gate, bumping into a few seated passengers mumbling his apologies along the way. Catching up to her, he grabbed Celina's shoulder.

"You can't go anywhere without these," he said as he handed her the boarding pass she'd left in the side of her carry-on bag.

"I'm sorry, my head is just all over the place," she said as she accepted it. "I just want to fly out of here and make it to my father before it's . . ." Her voice trailed off and she got a faraway look in her eyes.

Darius pulled her closer. "Come on, baby, I'm here for you." They walked through the gate and got on the plane. Celina didn't know what to expect once they made it to South Carolina and she saw her father again.

CHAPTER 20

Celina and Darius pulled into the Columbia city limits about 8 AM. Celina slept for most of the ride, but she would wake up abruptly scared by thoughts of Thomas dying. Darius would grab her knee and offer her words of encouragement, but she didn't hear much of what he said because she was so focused on seeing her father.

Darius turned the car into the hospital's parking lot and looked over at Celina as he put the car in park. Celina hopped out of the car before it fully stopped and bolted to the entrance of the hospital. Darius had to sprint behind her to catch up. Reaching her, he grabbed her shoulder, "Are you going to call your mother?" he asked.

She shook her head. "Not until I know what's going on," she said, then reached out to open the door. Suddenly she dropped her hand and sobbed.

"You're not going to know until you go inside," he said softly. "I'm with you."

Celina squeezed his hand. "Why is this happening? I thought that he was getting better and I was going to be able to tell him how much I love him and how I understand why he and my mother got a divorce and that it didn't have anything to do with his love for me. I wanted him to share in my life, I wanted to paint for him." Tears spilled down her cheeks as she spoke. "If I walk in there and he's gone, it's going to remind me how much time I wasted being mad at him and now it might be too late to . . ."

"Shh, you can't think like that when you don't know what's going on. Let's go," he said as he reached around her and opened the door. As they walked inside, she clung to him as if she hoped to draw strength from him.

They headed to the nurses' station. "Excuse me," Darius said, "We'are looking for Thomas Hart."

"One moment," the nurse replied as she typed Thomas's name into the computer. She looked up at Celina and Darius. "Are you family?"

"Yes," Celina replied. "I'm his daughter. Now where is he?"

The woman turned back to the computer. "He's in the intensive care unit. Only family can go up there. Take the elevator to the fifth floor and turn right." Celina was pressing the button on the elevator before the woman could finish giving her directions. Darius thanked the woman for her help, then walked into the elevator car with Celina.

"Breathe," he whispered putting his arms around her shoulders. She threw her head back and licked her lips. Her throat felt as if it had been packed with cotton, like the top of an aspirin bottle. She swallowed hard, hoping the feeling would go away. Her nerves made her stomach bubble as if a million butterflies had been released in it. Darius stroked her back, sensing her discomfort. When the elevator pinged, signaling that they had reached their destination, Celina stepped off and looked for the intensive care unit. After finding it, she walked until she saw her father's bed, covered with a plastic tent and tubes all over the place. The machines around his bed beeped, whizzed, and pushed out air. Thomas's eyes were closed and he was so still that it didn't seem as if he was alive. Celina's knees buckled and Darius reached out to hold her up. Looking at her father's ashen face, she knew that it was only a matter of time before he was gone forever, and there was so much that she wanted to say.

A doctor walked in and tapped Celina on the shoulder. "Ms. Hart?" he asked. Celina turned around and faced the man. "I'm Dr. Samuel Fisher. I've been taking care of your father."

"H-how is he?" she stammered.

"Ms. Hart, we've done all that we can do for your father. His cancer has rapidly advanced. He can't breathe without the respirator and he's in a lot of pain."

Celina waved her hands and shook her head. "No, but he was doing so much better," she said. "The breathing treatments and all of his other treatments were supposed to be working."

Dr. Fisher nodded. "They were working. However, with cancer cells, you can't be too sure that anything is going to work forever. Without these machines, your father's lungs aren't functioning. His cancer never went into remission, so the threat of this happening was always a possibility."

Celina looked at him. "We have to do something," she said, as tears streamed down her face.

The doctor stroked Celina's arm. "I'm sorry to say that we've done all that we can. He wanted us to keep him on the machines until his family could get here," Dr. Fisher said solemnly. "Your father wants to be removed from the ventilator."

Celina shook her head furiously. "No, I don't want my father taken off the machine. Where is Dr. Russell? He can help my father."

"Ms. Hart, I'm sorry. He has a living will and we have to follow his wishes."

More tears fell from her eyes as she looked down at her father. "Can I touch him?" she asked. The doctor nodded. Celina stuck her hand through the plastic and felt her father's skin. He felt so cold and clammy. Thomas opened his eyes and looked at Celina. When he smiled it looked as if his lips cracked.

"Oh, Daddy," she said. "I can't lose you, not now. I love you so much."

Thomas blinked his eyes rapidly. "Daddy, we lost so much time together. But these last few months have been just what we needed. I'm glad we got a chance to know each other again. I know you loved me and I want you to know that I love you, too." Celina leaned in and kissed Thomas on the forehead.

He closed his eyes and the machines went wild. Alarms began blaring and lights started flashing. Celina backed away, holding back a loud sob. "Wh-what's going on?"

The doctor rushed to Thomas's side. "Ms. Hart, I need you to step outside," he said as three nurses and two doctors stormed into the ICU.

Slowly, she backed to the door, watching the doctors rip away the plastic tent. They started chest compressions. Darius walked up behind Celina as she backed into the hallway. "Celina," he said. "What's happening?"

"He's gone," she whispered as he pulled her into his arms. "It was like he was waiting for me to come home and now he's gone."

Darius stroked her hair as he held her. "I'll call your mother," he whispered.

Celina watched through the window as the doctors worked on Thomas, fighting to save his life. The scene reminded her of a bad hospital drama, only this was real.

She pressed her hand against the window as one of the doctors looked at his watch. Celina knew that her father had slipped away. Backing away from the door, she irrationally hoped that if the doctor didn't find her that she wouldn't have to hear and believe that Thomas was gone.

The door opened quicker than her feet could move and the doctor made his way over to her. "Ms. Hart, I'm sorry." He placed his hand on her shoulder.

Celina shook her head from side to side as if she were trying to block the words. "Please, no," she whispered.

"We did all that we could," he said.

Tears poured from Celina's eyes like a rushing river and her knees threatened to sink from underneath her. She leaned against the wall, shaking, trembling, and shivering. The doctor waved for a nurse and Darius ran over to Celina.

"Baby," he said as he put his arms around her. She passed out in his arms.

"Let's get her into a bed," the doctor said. "She's in shock."

Hours passed as Darius stood by Celina's hospital bed. *You have so much on you right now and I know you need a break, but you can't leave me right now,* he thought as he stroked her hand.

A nurse walked into the room. "Has she come to yet?"

Darius shook his head. "Is there anything you can give her?" he asked, his voice filled with worry and concern. "Is this normal?"

"The doctor wants to wait a few more minutes before we try anything. She just lost her father and that has to be quite a shock. She's lucky to have some support.

Her mother's waiting outside. Do you want me to send her in?"

"Sure," Darius said.

A few seconds later, Rena rushed through the door with John in tow. She flung herself into Darius's arms. "What's wrong with my baby?" she asked.

"She's in shock. We thought Thomas was getting better and that's the only reason she went back to New York for that gallery opening. She thought she had time and just finding out that she didn't and losing him so suddenly was too much."

Rena rubbed Darius's back. "I'm glad that you're here for her. Celina would never have gotten through this alone."

John reached out and grabbed Celina's hand. "She's opening her eyes," he said excitedly. "Celina, baby, can you hear me?"

She moaned softly. "Wh-where am I?" Celina said as she attempted to sit up in the bed. Darius rushed to her side. "Celina, you're in the hospital, remember?" She began to cry as if the reason they were in the hospital came rushing back. Darius hugged and held her close to his chest as she sobbed. Rena sat on the side of the bed and stroked Celina's back.

"I want to go home," Celina said. "I have to get out of here."

Darius helped Celina to her feet. "I'll take you home," he said.

Rena nodded. "Take her home and we'll take care of any paperwork and arrangements that need to be made," she said.

"Darius, take care of our girl," John said as they left the room. Once they were in the hallway, Darius took note of her condition. She was an emotional wreck, with red puffy eyes and dried tear stains on her cheeks.

Darius didn't know what to say to her. He didn't know how to comfort her because he'd never lost anyone close to him before.

"Do you want something to eat?" he asked. Celina shook her head. They walked out of the hospital and got into the rental car. Celina snapped her seat belt in place and stared out of the window listlessly. Darius drove slowly out of the parking lot. He wondered if he should have taken her out of the hospital. Did Celina need to go home to her father's house today? He glanced at her as he made his way to the interstate junction.

"Celina, are you sure you want to go home?" he asked.

"I have to," she said. Her voice was weak. "I have to start making plans for him."

"Your mother can help you with that. You don't have to do this alone," he said.

Celina kept her head turned toward the window, pressing her hand against the glass and falling silent.

"I should've been here. Been by his side every minute. That's why he wanted me to come home. I should've taken him to the hospital, not Ms. Velma," she said. "Was this my way of paying him back for what happened twenty years ago? How could I have been so selfish?" Celina slammed her hand against the window. "That show in New York could've waited."

"Celina, you can't beat yourself up about this. You didn't do anything wrong. You couldn't have known that your father was going to die tonight. What would've been different if you'd been here?"

She turned and looked at him. "That's just it, I would've been here. He would've had my arms around him. He wouldn't have been surrounded by strangers."

Darius took her hand in his. "Celina, you and your father made peace with each other and that's all that matters. He made you understand what happened those many years ago and you got a chance to forgive him."

"Did I?" she asked as she took her hand from underneath his. "Maybe that's why I left. I knew my dad didn't have a cold. No matter how well he seemed to be doing, I knew there was no cure for cancer. I knew he could've relapsed, but the first thing I did was hop on an airplane and go to New York for a stupid show."

"Celina, your father seemed as if he was doing well. You can't blame yourself for what happened. You were here in the end and you were here when he called you," he said.

Celina didn't reply. She just leaned back in the seat and closed her eyes. Darius watched as tears fell from her eyes.

For the rest of the trip, Celina slept and wept, leaving Darius feeling helpless. He wanted to do something to help Celina, but what? When he pulled into Thomas's driveway, he half expected his old friend to come to the door. Thomas would always wave to Darius as he cut the lawn. The two men didn't talk much, but since he and Celina had started seeing each other, he saw a glimmer of respect in her father's eyes anytime they saw one another. Darius wanted Thomas to be around and to watch him fall in love with his daughter. He wanted Thomas to give him his blessing to marry Celina if and when he asked her.

"Celina," he said, as he tapped her on the shoulder. "We're home."

Sitting up, she sighed as she looked at the house. Her hand was poised to open the car door, but she didn't.

"Are you sure you want to go inside?" he asked as he opened the door for her when he saw that she wasn't going to.

Slowly, she emerged from the car, obviously not

wanting to enter the house. Darius walked a few inches back from her. Celina turned around. "I want to be alone right now," she said.

"No," Darius said. "You don't need to be alone. Celina, let me take care of you, okay?"

She ran her hand across her face and turned away from Darius. "I don't want to argue with you, but I need to be alone. Please, just go away."

"Celina, are you . . ."

She turned to him and yelled, "Just go, Darius! just leave."

He backed down the steps. "Celina, if you need me, I'm right next door." Darius headed to his house, keeping his eyes on Celina as she walked inside. He wanted to do something to help her through this tough time in her life, but if she didn't want his help, there was nothing he could do. And that made his heart hurt like hell.

CHAPTER 21

Celina sat in her father's favorite chair with his robe draped over her shoulders. She inhaled deeply and released a sigh. She wished she had been there with her father when he needed her most. *I never should've done that stupid show,* she thought as she hugged herself. Celina felt a breeze against her cheek. "Celina," she heard a voice say. She furrowed her brows.

"Who's there?" she said as she stood up. She followed the voice that continued calling her name. The calls grew louder as she reached her childhood bedroom. It was funny because she hadn't spent a night there since she'd been back.

"Celina, I know you love me."

She looked around, but didn't see anyone. "Daddy," she called out. "Oh, Daddy, I'm sorry I wasn't here for you." Celina felt his presence around her, pulling her against his chest.

"But you were. You gave me what I needed, your forgiveness. Live your life, baby, you have a right to do that."

Celina looked up to the sky. "I wanted you in my life."

"I had my chance to be in your life and I blew it. You

don't owe me anything. I let you down, not the other way around. Live your life."

Celina dropped to her knees. "Daddy, please, don't leave me, not now. I need you."

"Celina?" She turned and looked to the door and saw a figure there that she'd expected to be Thomas, but Darius walked into the room and took her into his arms.

"Are you all right?"

She held on to Darius. "He was here. He said-said that I was there for him when he needed me."

Darius looked into Celina's eyes. "Who was here?" He stroked her cheek gently.

"My dad." She leaned her head against Darius's shoulder. Darius scooped her up into his arms.

"I think you need some rest," he said. "Have you eaten anything? Do you want me to fix you some soup or something?"

Celina shook her head. Darius carried her into the living room and laid her on the sofa. He covered her with the afghan from the back of the sofa. "Darius, you don't have to do this," she said.

"I know," he said before kissing her forehead. "Stay here and I'll fix you a cup of soup or something."

Celina grabbed his arm. "I just want you to hold me. Sit here with me for a little while." Darius eased down on the sofa beside her, pressing her head against his firm chest. He stroked her hair gently as she cried silently. Though she was sad, she felt at peace and found comfort in his arms and the fact that her father didn't blame her for not being there. The front door of the house opened and Rena and John walked in.

"Celina," Rena said softly as she approached the sofa. "Are you all right?"

She looked up at her mother and smiled through her tears. Rena walked over to her daughter and sat beside her. "When do you want to have the funeral for Thomas?" she asked.

Celina shook her head. "I don't want to think about that right now," she said, burying her head in Darius's chest.

"I know this is unpleasant, but we have to make these arrangements and you're his daughter. You have to do this," Rena said.

Celina leapt to her feet. "I don't have to do it today."

Rena stood up in Celina's face. "You're right," she said. "But you can't hide away in this house. Thomas is gone. You made your peace with him and he got a chance to tell you what happened all of those years ago. He told me that he could go peacefully because he knew you didn't hate him."

"You talked to him?" Celina asked. Rena nodded. She took Celina's hand in hers.

"When you went to New York, Thomas called me. He told me that you two had repaired your relationship. He said you didn't cringe every time he said my name. You laughed at old memories that the two of you shared. Then, Thomas asked for my forgiveness. I told him he didn't have to ask for what he already had."

Celina stifled a sob with her hand. "That's why we have to put him to rest," Rena continued. "We have to put him to rest and honor that new relationship you two had."

Celina nodded. "I just can't right now," she said.

Rena clasped her hands together. "Well, I'll cook dinner and we can sit down and talk later." She gave Celina a sideways glance. "Because I know you haven't eaten today and I don't want to hear any back talk, young lady."

"Yes, ma'am," Celina said, feeling like a child again.

Darius smiled at her. "Mrs. Malcolm, why don't I help you in the kitchen?"

Rena waved her hands. "No, I'll take care of it. Come on, John," she said as she turned toward the kitchen. Celina sat down and leaned against Darius.

"Somehow she always does that," she said.

"What?"

"Makes me feel like a twelve-year-old." Then Celina smiled for the first time since her father passed away. Darius smiled too, then the couple broke into a fit of laughter. Celina looked at Darius and kissed him gently on the lips. "Thank you for being here for me," she said. "I don't think I could've made it today without you."

"That's why I'm here," he said. "And if the shoe was on the other foot, I know you would have done the same thing for me."

"I love you so much," she said, then wrapped her arms around his neck and hugged him.

A few hours passed, with Celina and Darius sitting in the living room silently. Rena walked into the living room and cleared her throat.

"All right love birds, dinner is ready," she said from the doorway. Celina and Darius followed Rena into the kitchen and sat at the table. She had cooked fried chicken, mashed potatoes, and macaroni and cheese. Rena sliced a tomato and a cucumber for Celina and the four of them sat down.

"Let's all pray," John said as everyone held hands around the oak table. "Lord, we come to you today with a heavy heart and praise in our mouths. We thank you for the life of Thomas Hart. Lord, we know you have taken our brother to a better place and we pray for the strength to deal with the loss of this man. We ask you to protect and guide this family and keep us in your loving arms. Amen."

Celina looked up at her stepfather. She'd never heard such words of comfort. She knew that she would make it through this time because she had her family and Darius to help her. Celina was learning that she could lean on people and she didn't have to run anymore. She smiled as she looked around the table and at the people who were there to support her. Celina reached out and grabbed Darius's hand and offered him a silent thank-you. Rena looked at the couple, then turned to John.

In a loud whisper, she said, "Looks like we'll be celebrating a wedding soon."

"Mom, I heard that," Celina said, embarrassment creeping up on her cheeks, turning her face a shade of pink.

"I know you did," Rena said. "Did you hear it too, Darius?"

He coughed, nearly choking on his chicken leg. "Uh, yes ma'am, I heard you loud and clear," he said as Celina patted him on his back to dislodge the meat in his throat.

"Rena," John said in a stern voice, "let's eat dinner in peace. Leave these kids alone."

She rolled her eyes, then smiled. "All right, I'll leave it alone, for now," she said as she picked up the platter of fried chicken from the middle of the table. "Maybe tomorrow we can go down to Norris Funeral Home and start making plans for Thomas's celebration, because you know your father would've wanted a party." Rena laughed, but it didn't reach her eyes, which were glistening with unshed tears.

Celina smiled. "I think you're right," she said quietly.

Rena nodded. "I know your father," she said. A knock at the door interrupted their dinner.

Celina stood up. "I'll get it," she said. Celina walked over to the door and opened it. She smiled when she saw

Velma standing there. The older woman hugged her tightly.

"I'm so sorry about Thomas," she said when the two women broke their embrace. "I wish you two would've been able to spend more time together."

Rena walked to the front door to see what was taking Celina so long to come back to the table. "Baby, what's going on?" Rena asked. Then she looked at Velma. "Hello."

"Hi, I was Thomas's nurse," she said, extending her hand to Rena. "I was with him when he got sick."

Celina noticed a nervous vibe from Velma. She could've sworn the older woman's hand trembled when she shook hands with Rena.

Rena nodded, indicating that she knew who Velma was. "We were just about to have dinner. Why don't you come in?"

"Well, I don't want to interrupt your family dinner. I just wanted to pay my respects," she said. "I didn't realize you were going to be here, Rena."

"Velma, that's all water under the bridge. What happened with you and Thomas was years ago. I've moved on," she replied.

Celina looked from her mother to Velma. "What's going on?"

Rena raised her hand. "Ancient history. Velma, come in and join us for dinner. You and Thomas had something special."

Velma nodded and walked in the house. Celina shook her head in disbelief. Velma was the woman who had broken up her parents' marriage twenty some years ago. *I just can't believe this,* Celina thought as John brought an extra chair for Velma. Darius looked at the strange expression on Celina's face.

"You okay, babe?" he asked.

She nodded, but gave him a "we'll talk later" look.

"So," Rena said, breaking the uncomfortable silence that fell over them. "Velma, how did you and Thomas link up again?"

Velma looked tense as she bit into her piece of chicken. "Well, Thomas needed a nurse and when I heard that he was sick, I wanted to help." She turned to Celina. "I had no idea that you didn't . . ."

"I was eight years old. How would I have known?" Celina snapped.

Rena shot her daughter a cautionary look. "Celina."

"I'm sorry, but is this the woman who broke up our family?" Celina said sharply as she leaped to her feet, knocking her chair over.

Velma placed her napkin in her plate. "I'd better go. The last thing you all need is me fanning the flames of the past."

"No, Velma. Now, part of the reason Celina came here was to make peace with her father. Celina, Velma and your father fell in love. And maybe I pushed him into her arms, but Velma is not the reason I left your father. So, there's no reason for you to disrespect her. Now, both of you sit down. Velma should've been your step-mother. Out of respect for me, she never married your father. I moved on with my life and your father and Velma never got a chance to be together," Rena said.

Celina shook her head from side to side. "I don't understand."

Rena slammed her hand against the table. "There's nothing for you to understand because this had nothing to do with you. Velma had a relationship with your father. That's all you need to know. I came to grips with it years ago."

"Let me say something," Velma said. "Celina, I loved Thomas and he loved me. But after you and your mother left, I was branded a home-wrecker. In a small town like this, you have to deal with the stares and whispers and I couldn't do it, so I left town, leaving the man I loved behind. I came back a few months ago when I heard Thomas was ill. That is why I took the job as his nurse. I never meant to scratch an old wound. I just wanted to be with the man I loved before he died."

Celina couldn't harbor any ill will toward Velma. She would've done the same thing if it had been Darius. She understood why Velma did what she did.

"Let's just finish dinner," Rena said firmly.

The rest of the meal went by in silence. Celina stole glances at her mother and Velma. Darius stroked her leg.

"Do you want to take a walk?" he whispered when they'd finished eating.

Celina nodded and the two stood up and excused themselves from the table. Once Darius and Celina got outside, he looked at her.

"That was a lot to digest, huh?" he said as he took her hand.

Celina shook her head and rubbed her face. "This is just too much," she said. "I mean, Velma and my father had a relationship and I hired her to be his nurse."

"Celina, that doesn't have anything to do with you. If your mother is okay with it, then just let it go. Your father is gone," Darius said. "All of that stuff happened a long time ago."

Celina nodded. "I know, but maybe I just didn't need to know about their affair."

"Now you know. Does it change how you feel about your father?"

Celina squeezed Darius's arm. "Let's not talk about that," she said. "I knew my father was unfaithful to my mother, but I just didn't expect to come face-to-face with it, today."

Darius kissed Celina on the cheek as they headed down the block. "Don't worry about it," he said. "Just remember the memories you have of your father. It doesn't matter what happened between your parents. Your father loved you and you know that."

She rubbed her hand across her face. "I know. I just wish I didn't know what I know now."

"There's nothing you can do to change what happened twenty years ago. You don't have to like it, but you have to deal with it and move on."

Celina felt like a little child being chastised by a teacher. She glared at Darius. "I'm going home, alone," she said.

"Celina," he said as she sprinted down the street. "Celina."

She turned around and looked at him. "You know what, I don't need you telling me how to feel or how to think." She waved her hands in the air. "Just leave me alone."

"I'm not going to do that, because I love you."

"So what," she snapped. "That doesn't give you the right to dictate how I am supposed to mourn my father."

Darius grabbed Celina's arms. "That's not what I'm trying to do. I want to support you, but you have to let me."

She pushed away from him. "No, I don't," she said, then stormed away.

CHAPTER 22

Three days had passed since Celina and Darius had their argument. He tried calling her, but she wouldn't answer the phone. Rena told Darius to give her daughter some time to come to terms with everything, but he was tired of waiting.

Darius called Richard at the store and told him he wouldn't be in.

"I guess you're going to Thomas Hart's funeral?" Richard said.

"Yeah," Darius said, even though he wasn't aware when the funeral was. "Call me if there's an emergency."

"All right, boss. Send my condolences to the family," Richard said before hanging up.

Darius looked out the window at the Hart house. A stream of visitors had been pouring in and out of the house all morning. Darius walked onto the porch and stared next door, hoping to see Celina. Rena walked outside and looked at Darius.

"Darius McRae, stop staring and come over here. She may not admit it, but she needs you."

"Mrs. Malcolm, Celina needs her space."

"No, she needs a swift kick in the . . . Darius, I love my

daughter, but ever since she found out about Velma and Thomas, she has been trying to push you out of her life. Don't let her do that."

Darius shrugged his shoulders. "What can I do? She won't talk to me."

Rena placed her hands on her hips. "Put your black suit on and get over here. Don't make me come over there and get you, son. I know what my daughter needs and it's you."

Darius laughed. "Yes ma'am," he said as he headed into the house to put on his black suit.

Moments later, Darius walked over to the Hart house, holding his breath as he walked in the front door. He knew things were going to be hard for Celina today and he didn't want to add to it. A few other well-wishers were sitting on the sofa, and he nodded toward them and headed for the kitchen to find Celina.

She was standing next to the refrigerator with a carton of juice in her shaky hands. Striding over to her, he took it from her hand and set it on the counter. "Good morning," he said.

"What are you doing here?" she asked, her voice wavering as she spoke.

"I came here because I don't want you going through today alone," he said. "You have a tendency to shut people out and you don't need to do that today."

Celina fell into his arms. "I'm sorry about these last few days," she said against his ear. "Thank you for being here."

"Don't worry about it. I'm where I want to be. Celina, I love you and I know you need someone to lean on right now. I'm not holding you responsible for anything that you've said."

She looked into his eyes and smiled though her tears.

"Still, I had no reason to be rude to you when all you've tried to do is help me."

Darius brought his finger to Celina's lips. "None of that is important right now. Have you eaten?"

Celina shook her head. "No, I don't have the stomach to eat anything right now."

"Sit down and let me fix you that juice you were about to drink," he said.

She took a seat at the end of the table and watched Darius as he poured orange juice in a glass and even though she'd told him that she wasn't hungry, he grabbed her a cheese Danish.

Watching her, Darius thought she reminded him of a child, although she was elegantly dressed in a long black dress with matching gloves, and her hair pulled back in a bun. Her eyes had sadness in them, and she looked as if she would cry at any moment. Darius came over to her and placed the food and drink in front of her.

"Thank you," she said. "I hate this."

"What?" He asked as he stroked her hand.

Celina rolled her eyes as a neighbor walked into the kitchen and grabbed a pastry.

"All of these people here. Where were they when my dad was sick? He needed help and none of them were around. Now look at them, like vultures."

"Celina," he said. "Maybe they didn't know. I didn't even know that Mr. H. was as sick as he was."

She pushed her breakfast aside and nodded. "You're right."

Rena walked into the kitchen, dressed in a black and white dress that stopped below her knees. "Darius, did you get her to eat?" she asked.

"I'm trying," he replied.

Rena patted Darius on his shoulder. "There are some

blueberry muffins on the counter. Why don't you and Celina share one?"

"I'm fine," Celina said, picking at the Danish that she had pushed away.

"I'll force-feed you if I have to. We have a long day ahead of us and I don't want you to pass out on me," Rena said.

Celina rolled her eyes, then broke off a piece of the pastry and popped it in her mouth. "Happy?"

Rena shook her head and then turned to Darius. "Please talk to her and make her eat," she said as she headed into the living room to greet the guests.

Darius slid his chair closer to Celina's and held her close. "That wasn't nice. You know your mother is only concerned about you," he said.

"I know, and I'll apologize later." She groaned and pushed her plate away. "I just want this day to be over."

Darius held her tighter. "It will be," he said. "But you can't rush it."

She leaned her head on his shoulder and cried. He stroked her back and whispered in her ear that everything would be all right.

Pushing back from him, she looked at him as she wiped her eyes. "You know, I think the gallery should be named after my father."

"You still want to do that?" Darius was taken aback. He knew Celina was going to move back to New York after the funeral. "Are you going to stay here?"

She nodded. "I don't want to go back to New York. This is home now and if you'll still have me, I want to be here with you."

"You don't even have to question that," he said. "I want you in my life forever, but this isn't the time for that discussion."

Celina nodded in agreement.

"The limo is waiting. We'd better go," Rena said as she stood in the doorway of the kitchen. The guests were filing out of the house ready to follow the family to the funeral home. Celina and Darius walked out of the house and got into the family limo, followed by John and Rena. Celina pulled a pair of dark sunglasses out of her purse and put them on as the driver started the car. Rena reached out and patted Celina's knee.

"Are you OK?" she asked.

Celina shook her head somberly as Darius caressed her arm. She closed her eyes as her tears fell. Pulling a handkerchief from his pocket, Darius gently wiped her wet cheeks and put his arms around her.

When the car pulled up to the church, a small crowd had already gathered. Darius looked out at the mourners and saw that half of the town was there. When he saw Velma walk up the steps of the church, he blanched and prayed that her presence there wouldn't upset Celina more. Stealing a glance at Celina, he saw that she wasn't bothered. He hoped that she'd come to terms with what Thomas and Velma shared.

Rena stretched her legs and grabbed John's hand. "Are we all ready?" she asked.

"Yes," Celina said, then knocked on the glass separating them from the driver.

He walked to the back of the car and opened the door. John and Rena got out first. Celina closed her eyes, took a deep breath, and then let Darius help her out of the car.

"It's going to be all right, baby," he whispered as they walked up to the doors of the church.

"Promise?" she whispered.

Darius pulled her tightly against him as they entered the church and took a seat in the front row reserved for the family. Spirited gospel music filled the air. Thomas's favorite choir from St. Luke's Baptist church sang his most cherished hymn, "Wade in the Water." The people in the church swayed from side to side as the soulful voices of the singers penetrated the air. Celina leaned against Darius, fighting back the tears as the choir sang. Thomas's casket sat in the front of the church, surrounded by lush green potted plants and white, yellow, and red rose wreaths. The marble coffin was covered with an American flag, because he had served in the Vietnam War.

The pastor stood up in the pulpit as the choir finished their song. "What a beautiful selection. I'm sure Thomas is smiling down at us. Now let us pray."

Everyone bowed their heads and the pastor began a prayer for Thomas's soul. As he spoke, Celina gasped and released Darius's hand. In the blink of an eye, she bolted from the church.

Once she made it outside, she held the edge of the limo and vomited. Her body shook as she tried to steady herself against the car.

What is wrong with me? she thought as she wiped her mouth with the back of her glove. Celina's head ached. She didn't know if it was seeing her father in the casket, the heat in the church, or could it be something else? Celina stood up and a chill ran through her body. What if she was pregnant? *I can't be, I can't be,* she thought as she paced back and forth. Then another wave of nausea washed over her.

Darius walked over to her. "Celina, are you all right?" he asked, stepping closer to her.

"I'm fine," she said. "I'm fine." Celina brought her hand to his chest and pushed him away. "I think I got too hot in there."

"Are you sure that's all it was?"

"Let's go back inside," she said as she grabbed his hand. He led her into the church and back to her seat.

Rena peered at Celina as Darius helped her sit down. "Are you all right?" she asked quietly.

Celina nodded, then turned her attention to the pastor as he spoke. As hard as she tried to focus, she couldn't. The only thing she could think about was the possibility that she was carrying Darius's child. *I can't tell him until I know for sure. Then we'll figure out what to do,* she thought. Celina felt a cool breeze against her cheek.

"Death is rebirth." She whirled around to see who said that and her gaze collided with Darius's. He placed his hand on top of hers and she relaxed against him as the choir began to sing another hymn.

After the funeral, it seemed, to Celina's dismay, that the whole town descended on the house. People brought in casseroles of pasta, potato salad, fried chicken, baked chicken, barbecued chicken, and tons of desserts. Celina walked into the house, pushing past the guests who offered their condolences, and headed for her father's bedroom. Darius followed her into the room and stood at the door, watching her as she kicked off her shoes.

"Celina, are you sure everything is all right? You've been acting strange since you ran out of the church." he asked as she flung herself on the bed.

"Darius, I'm just tired. Come in and close the door," she said.

He closed the door and came over to her. She opened her arms to him. "I need you to hold me." He held her in his arms and rocked her back and forth.

"Is there something you want to tell me?" he asked. "What really made you run out of your father's funeral?"

"Nothing. I told you, I was hot and . . . I don't want to talk right now," she said as she stroked his neck.

"Do you want something to eat?" Darius asked.

Celina shook her head. "Why do people always want you to eat after a funeral? I mean, fried chicken isn't going to bring my father back." She ran her hand over her face. "I just need to lie here for a minute, because I can't deal with those people telling me how sorry they are and shoving food in my face. Will you lie here with me?"

Darius nodded and kicked his shoes off. He lay back on the bed, positioning himself so that Celina could lie on his chest.

"Celina, I love you," he said. "Anything you want or need I'll do it for you."

"Thank you," she replied. "Darius, I wouldn't have gotten through this without you."

"Marry me."

She propped herself up on her elbows. "What?"

"Celina, I want to go to sleep with you in my arms and wake up the same way. I've never felt this way about anyone before and I know I'll never love anyone as much as I love you. If this is too much, right now, we can talk about it later, but I want you to be my wife."

Celina was speechless. She didn't know what to say, so she just leaned her head against his chest and closed her eyes, pretending to go to sleep.

CHAPTER 23

Days after Thomas's funeral, Rena and John returned to Chicago. Rena asked Celina if she wanted to return with them for a few days to clear her head.

"This is my home now," Celina said. "Darius and I have a lot of work to do."

"So, my next visit is going to be for your gallery opening, huh?" Rena asked. "Well, at least you've decided to put some roots down somewhere. And thank God you have gotten out of New York. I never liked you living there. That place is so dangerous and you were all alone and . . ."

"Ma, why don't you get in the car before you miss your flight?" Celina said, then kissed her mother on the cheek.

Rena hugged Celina, then stepped back and took a good look at her daughter. "You've been eating pretty good? You're getting thick."

Celina looked down at her midsection. Was her mother right? She had been eating more lately, and she hadn't been working out as much as she did in New York. She wouldn't admit it, but she was beginning to think that she really was pregnant, though she knew she wouldn't be showing so soon. Still, something told her she needed to be sure.

After Rena and John left, Celina headed for the drugstore. "Good morning," the clerk said when she walked in. Waving, Celina quickly ducked toward the back of the store where the pregnancy tests were. Before picking up an EPT test, she looked around to make sure she didn't see anyone because the last thing she wanted was to be the talk of the town or have someone tell Darius what she'd been buying. Celina grabbed two rapid response tests, then sped to the register. After checking out, she headed back to her house, desperately praying that the tests would be negative. She was more than a little thankful that Darius had returned to work that day so she could take the tests in private. It wasn't that she was trying to hide her suspicions from him, but she didn't want to get his hopes up.

Opening the box and reading the instructions, Celina was poised to take the test, when there was a knock at the door. Shoving the tests underneath the sink, she dashed to the front door and found Darius standing there.

"Hi," she said when she opened the door. Darius picked her up and spun her around. "What's going on?" she asked, totally confused and flustered.

"We got it." Darius's eyes sparkled with excitement.

"Got what?"

"Space for the gallery. Celina, you're going to love it."

"So, when am I going to see this great place?" she asked, clasping her hands together. Though she put on an excited face, part of her wanted to take the pregnancy test and find out if her suspicions were correct.

"What are you doing now?" he asked.

"What-what do you mean?" Nervousness crept up her back. Did he know?

"Hiding something, Ms. Hart? You seem a little nervous."

Celina smiled brightly and stroked his forearm. "Why would you say something silly like that? Everything is fine."

Darius stepped back and looked at Celina as if he were asking, "are you sure?" "Come on, let's go, then."

Celina grabbed her keys from the coffee table and followed Darius out the front door. When they got in the car, Celina considered telling him about her pregnancy suspicions.

"What?"

"Nothing," she replied. "I'm just amazed that you had time to do this."

"I work for myself, remember? I can do what I want to do."

Celina smiled. "That's right. You're the boss, at least at the hardware store."

Darius took Celina's hand in his and kissed it. "Have you been working on some masterpieces to hang in the gallery?" he asked.

Celina shrugged her shoulders. "I haven't really felt like painting. You know, maybe we should have some classes for kids in the summer and on Saturdays. Or maybe we should come up with a summer camp to expose the kids to art."

"What's with all the talk about kids?" Darius asked as he pulled up to a warehouse.

"You know how it was growing up here. There was never anything to do in the summer. If we did something like a summer program, the kids would have something constructive to do." Celina got out of the car and looked up at the building as she shielded her eyes from the sun. "Wow," she said.

Darius walked up behind her, brushing his lips against her neck. "You like it?"

Celina turned around and wrapped her arms around Darius and squealed with delight. "I love it."

Suddenly, Darius reached into his pocket and pulled out a burgundy velvet box. He dropped down on one knee and looked up at Celina, whose mouth had dropped open.

"I know you have a lot on you right now. Your life is changing and I want to be here for you. I need you in my life, today, tomorrow, and forever." Darius opened he box, revealing a princess-cut diamond ring in a white gold setting. "I want to be your husband and I need you to be my wife."

She blinked her eyes rapidly to hold back her tears. "Darius, I don't know what to say."

He stood up and caressed her face. "All you have to do is say 'yes,'" he said. "I know you didn't answer me before and my timing was probably off when I asked after your father's funeral."

Celina chewed thoughtfully on her bottom lip, out of nervous habit. He stared into her eyes as he held the ring out to her.

"Yes," she whispered. "Darius, I love you so much. I never felt this way about a man before. You've brought something into my life that I never wanted to give myself—a chance to fall in love. Then I came home and found you."

Darius slid the three-carat diamond ring on her finger, then pulled her into his arms and kissed her long, hard, and passionately. Neither of them heard the footsteps creeping up behind them.

"Well, isn't this a postcard," Tiffany said, causing the couple to break off their kiss.

Celina shot a contemptuous glance her way. "Why don't you go stalk someone else?"

Tiffany laughed. "I'm not stalking anyone. You and your boyfriend think too highly of yourselves. You're on a public street; anyone could have passed by and seen such a nasty public display. What would your poor dead father think of making a spectacle of yourself like this? Then again, from what I've heard, Thomas Hart wasn't much better."

Darius held Celina back as she lunged for Tiffany. "Why don't you just leave us alone," Darius said as he struggled to hold his fiancée. She wiggled in his arms like a minx, itching to rip Tiffany apart.

"That's your specialty, leaving people alone. Remember all of the promises that you made to me about us being together?" Tiffany snapped. "Don't get too comfortable with Darius. As soon as you step out of his box, he's gone."

"That's the difference between me and you, Tiffany," Celina flashed her hand in her face. "Darius is committed to me. He never made a commitment to you."

Tiffany shuddered as she looked at the ring. "You're marrying her?"

"Yes, Darius made a commitment to me and there's nothing you can do to change it, because he doesn't want you," Celina snapped.

Tiffany narrowed her eyes into tiny slits. "You will not make it down the aisle, mark my words," she threatened.

Celina reached out and grabbed Tiffany by the collar. "You're not a threat to me, but I have a warning for you. Stay away from us, or you're going to regret the day you met me."

Darius whispered for Celina to calm down. She released Tiffany and gave her a little push. Tiffany's nostrils flared as she turned to walk away.

Celina turned to Darius. "Do you believe her? She follows me to New York and then she comes here with these lies. She's lucky that I didn't deck her for that crack about my father."

"Remind me not to get on your bad side, Ms. New York," Darius joked. "And to think I wondered how you made it in the city."

Celina gave Darius a playful shove and laughed. "You know what, I'm not going to let her steal my joy."

Darius wrapped his arms around her. "So, where were we before we were so rudely interrupted?" His breath tickled her neck.

Looking into his eyes, she never realized that love could feel this good, this right, and this special. She kissed him gently on the lips, then boldly grabbed his hands and slipped them inside her shorts.

"I want you," she whispered against his ear. Darius reached into his pocket and pulled out a set of keys.

"Let's go inside," he moaned as he stroked her upper thigh with his thumb. "We don't want to give the town a show."

Celina stepped back, allowing Darius to open the door. "How did you get the keys?" she asked.

Darius smiled, then pushed the door open. "I'm full of surprises." Celina walked in and smiled at the scene. The place was decorated with white and yellow roses, and a pink and blue blanket was spread in the middle of the floor with a bucket of ice holding a bottle of champagne, a plate of strawberries beside the bucket. Celina didn't care about the blank walls or the hard slate floor. All she saw was the beauty in what Darius had done for her to make this day special. "Darius," she murmured. He turned around and handed her the keys.

"It's all yours," he said.

"What?"

"This is yours, for you and our future," he said as he waved his hand.

"Darius, I can't accept this. It's too much." He shook his head as he reached down and picked up a succulent strawberry and placed it between her lips.

"It isn't," he said as she bit into the berry. "There's nothing I won't do for you and our future. You're the most important thing to me."

Celina unbuttoned her blouse and slid it from her shoulders. In the back of her mind, she wondered how long it would be before she started showing the world she was carrying Darius' child. Grabbing her hands, he took over undressing her. Darius pulled her shorts down, slipping the denim garment over her long legs, then he scooped her up in his arms and laid her down on the blanket. She looked up at him as he slowly took off his golf shirt. Every time Celina saw his body, she felt inspired to paint. Darius was definitely her muse. She wondered if their child would look like her or Darius. Maybe the child would look like his or her grandparents. Darius leaned down on top of Celina, gently kissing her collarbone, nibbling on her as if she were a tasty treat. Celina's body was wrought with desire, hot with yearning, and she clutched his back, pulling him down on top of her to let him know she was ready.

"Slow down, baby," Darius said. "We have all day, all night, and all our lives." She relaxed and let him take control of her body. Unsnapping the front clasp of her satin bra, he took her full breasts into his mouth, moving from left to right. His tongue teased her nipples, making them hard as rocks. Celina moaned in delight as he slowly slid down her body, blazing a trail to her hot center. She arched her back, pressing her supple body against his mouth. Darius ran his hand down the valley of her breasts as he kissed the tender skin between her legs. Celina was on fire and near explosion as his tongue darted in and out of her, lashing against her tender bud.

She closed her eyes as he dove deeper, lapping up her womanly juice. "Oh," she moaned as she reached back, grabbing the blanket as Darius led her to the edge of ecstasy. Pulling back, he reached for the bottle of champagne, then made quick work of opening it. Next, he poured it down her stomach and drank from her body, making her nerves stand on end. Celina closed her eyes, lost in the sensations Darius's tongue elicited as it touched her most sensitive spot. She stroked the back of his neck as the waves of an orgasm attacked her senses.

Darius looked up at her. "How do you feel?" he asked as he spread her legs and eased between them.

"Good, really good," she replied breathlessly. His manhood throbbed against her thighs and she took his burgeoning erection in her hand, stroking him back and forth. Darius threw his head back as she moved her hand faster and faster. Darius reached into his discarded pants and pulled a condom from his pocket. She took the red packet from his hand, opened it, then slid the latex sheet on Darius before guiding him to the hot folds of flesh between her thighs. Pressing her body closer to him, Celina felt every inch of him inside her and she tightened herself around him. She tried to lose herself inside him. Their bodies were intertwined like ribbon. Celina clasped her lips against Darius's neck, muffling moans of passion, as he played her body like a skilled musician, finding every erogenous zone and pleasure point that she had.

When Darius rolled over on his back, it was Celina's turn to play conductor. With her legs locked around him, Celina threw her body backwards, grinding against him as sweat beaded on their bodies. She held his face in her hands as she began to shiver and Darius ran his hands up and down her spine, as if he knew she was near climax. Falling against his chest, she gave in to the eruption between her legs. Darius held her tightly as the same feeling washed over him. Clinging to each other, they settled on the blanket in a spoon shape as the aftershocks of their lovemaking rippled through their senses.

"Let's make a toast," he said as he released her from his arms and grabbed two glasses and what was left of the champagne.

Taking the glass, Celina thought that it was best if she didn't drink because she wasn't sure if she was pregnant or not.

Darius turned to Celina. "To love. Finding it, keeping it, and making it grow."

Celina clanked her glass against his. She watched him as he sipped his champagne. "What's wrong?" he asked when he noticed Celina wasn't drinking.

"I—I don't think I should drink this."

Darius furrowed his brows. "Why not? We are still celebrating, aren't we?"

Should I tell him? she thought, looking into his eyes with a plastic smile plastered on her face. What if I'm not pregnant?

"Celina," Darius said. "What's wrong?"

"I-I think I might be pregnant," she blurted out, then quickly stood and walked over to one of the boarded-up windows. Darius followed her and wrapped his arms around her, holding her close.

"Are you telling me that I'm going to be a father?" he asked. His voice was peppered with excitement.

Celina covered her bare breasts with her arm. "I'm not really sure. Earlier, when you came by, I was in the bathroom about to take a pregnancy test."

Darius planted a sloppy wet kiss on her forehead. "Why didn't you tell me?"

Her eyes met his and she said, "Because I'm not sure that I am pregnant and I wanted to be sure before I said anything. I'm not even sure I'm ready to be a mother."

"What do you mean?"

Celina ran her hand up and down her throat. "Darius, I don't even know if I'm pregnant, so please, let's not turn this into an argument."

He looked away from her as she walked over to the blanket and picked up her clothes. "You know," Darius began, "I'm not trying to argue with you, but Celina, this child, if there is one, is mine, too, and any decision that you make . . ."

She pulled on her shorts and put on her bra. "I know that, Darius, but it is still my body. Besides, we're not even sure if there is a baby."

"I don't want to hear that BS. If we created a child, then we need to make a decision together about what happens next."

Celina bristled at Darius's harsh tone. "Did you think I was saying I wanted to have an abortion? Darius, I would never do that. You know what, just take me home."

Darius walked over to her as she buttoned her blouse. "Baby, I'm sorry," he said. "It's just . . . I've been here before, but it isn't fair for me to take this out on you."

"You're right it isn't, especially when I don't even know if I'm pregnant or not. And what do you mean, you've been here before?"

"It doesn't matter. Let's just go," he said as he pulled up his shorts. Celina grabbed his arm.

"You listen to me, now it's my turn," she said. "We're not leaving until you talk to me."

Darius sighed and looked at Celina. "All right, when I was in DC, you know I was involved with someone. Renita and I were going to get married. Not only did she cheat on me, she robbed me of my child."

Celina gasped and placed her hand on his shoulder as if she was urging him to continue with the story.

Darius sighed and grabbed her hand. "The day I decided to come back to Elmore was when she and I had this confrontation. After nine-eleven, I wanted to put my life in order. I knew Renita was with another man that day, but I had to know why. So, I went to her to see if we could salvage our relationship. That's when she told me," Darius said. His voice trailed off. Celina held on to him. She had never seen Darius like this before, so quiet and introspective. "She had an abortion because she said a child would get in the way of her career."

"Darius," Celina murmured.

"I can't go through that twice," he said. "Celina, if you are pregnant, you have to know that I want you and our child. You won't be doing this alone. Family means everything to me. Even when I was working eighty hours a week, I still wanted a family, children, and a wife."

"I know that, and if I am pregnant, I want this child. I would never do something that drastic, not with all that's happened," she said referring to her father's death.

Darius seemed to brighten. "So, let's go take the test," he said.

Celina exhaled and took his hand. "All right," she said as they headed out the door.

CHAPTER 24

Darius paced back and forth waiting for the bathroom door to open. When they arrived at the house, Celina had dashed into the bathroom and told him to wait outside. As he waited, he questioned if he was actually ready for fatherhood.

Is anyone ever ready for fatherhood? It happens and you deal with it. I love her and I will love this child, he thought.

The door to the bathroom opened and Darius held his breath as she came over to him with the white plastic test in her hand.

"I guess I was wrong. I'm not pregnant," she said. Darius looked at the test; only one stripe had turned pink.

"Well," he said. "Maybe this is for the best. We're going to have the rest of our lives to have a family." Darius pulled Celina into his arms and hugged her tightly.

"Are you disappointed?" she asked.

"I don't know," he replied. "You know what, it's okay. Now we should really talk about children and our future."

Celina kissed Darius gently and led him into the living

room to the sofa. "You're right. I do want children and all of that, but I will not be a stay-at-home mother."

Darius nodded and kissed Celina's dainty hand. "I never thought you would be. My son will eat meat, though."

Celina pinched the meaty part of his arm. "I don't think so, carnivore. And don't try to sneak chopped steak into our daughter's applesauce."

Laughing, he pulled Celina down on his lap. "Let's talk about the gallery. Maybe we should have a big opening around the same time as the azalea festival. There will be a lot of people in town and you could do some paintings of these famed bushes."

"Well, I need to call Millicent and get her to ship *H2Love* here. I have some other paintings in New York I want to go in the gallery and I need to do something as a tribute to my father."

Darius nodded. "That would be good," he said. "Listen, I need to go and check on the store. Dinner, tonight?" he said.

"Sure, I'll cook."

"Why don't we just go to Rudy's? Remember, I'm a carnivore." Darius said, then kissed Celina on the forehead. "I'll see you in a couple of hours."

As Darius walked out of the house, he tried not to think about the fact that Celina wasn't pregnant. He didn't know why he was so upset that she wasn't going to have a child. They had years to start a family and it wasn't as if she had deceived him about the pregnancy; she just simply wasn't pregnant. Darius got into his car and headed downtown. He looked at his watch and saw that it was almost time for the store to close. Richard had been there all day and the least Darius could do was close up for him. Darius pulled up to the front of the store and parked his car. He walked into the empty store. "Richard," he called out.

"In the back," the man called out. Darius walked to the storage room where Richard was stacking boxes of fertilizer. He leaned against the wall and looked at the man who was more like a second father than an employee.

"Why don't you clear out of here?" he said, as he began to stack the other boxes.

Richard furrowed his brows. "She turned you down?" he asked as he stopped stacking the boxes.

Darius smiled. "No, she didn't. We're going to Rudy's for dinner tonight."

Richard looked at him shook his head. "So what's with the sour face? I know that I'm old, but when most people get engaged, the last thing they normally do is come to work and load manure."

"I found out something today and I just need a little time to clear my head," Darius said as he moved a few boxes. "Celina thought she was pregnant, but it turned out to be a false alarm."

"Well, Darius, you should be thankful. I know your generation thinks it's okay to have kids and not be married, but maybe it is just best that you two tie the knot first, then start a family."

"I know that and that's what I'm trying to tell myself, but I wanted her to be pregnant. I'm just not so sure she wanted to be. She said all the right things about wanting a family, but when that test was negative, I could see the relief on her face."

"That's why you shouldn't rush into having a family. You and Celina have time to start a family. What's the rush? Marriage is hard enough without starting off with kids in tow."

Darius shrugged his shoulders. "I was robbed of the

chance to be a father before and I just didn't want history to repeat itself. I thought that, I don't know, that she was trying to hide it from me."

"Do you really think Celina is the kind of woman who would do that to you?" Richard asked as he patted Darius on the shoulder. "When it's time to have a family, you both will know it. I think I'm going to take you up on that offer to go home early."

Darius smiled. "All right, I'll see you tomorrow."

Once Darius was alone in the store, Richard's words began to sink in. He and Celina did have time to start a family and she would include him in any decision that would deal with their child.

What am I worried about? he thought as he closed the door to the storage room. Darius was about to lock up the store when the door chime went off, signaling that someone had walked into the store. He looked up and saw Celina standing there.

"I didn't like the way we left things at the house," she said as she closed the door behind her and flipped the lock.

"Celina, I'm sorry. This wasn't even about you. I know what kind of woman you are and you would never do what Renita did."

Celina reached out to Darius. "You're right. I wouldn't do that. And when I said that I wasn't ready to be a mother, it didn't mean I would go out and have an abortion. I'm not that cold. To be honest, I don't think anyone is ready to become a mother until the doctor places her baby in her arms."

He squeezed her tightly. "I know, baby," he whispered in her ear. "I didn't mean to dump all of that on you. I guess I didn't realize that I was still carrying those demons with me."

"I'm glad you told me. I do want to have your baby,

but I can't say that I'm devastated that I'm not pregnant. I'd like to be Mrs. McRae before we bring any babies into the world."

Darius tweaked her nose. "I'm going to hold you to that," he said. "Because I want lots of babies."

"Why don't we get out of here and have dinner, then we can have some dessert in bed," she said seductively.

Darius smiled. "I like the sound of that. Let me shut off the lights and we're out of here."

A short time later, Darius and Celina were settling into a booth at Rudy's.

"Hey there, you two," Miss Rudy said when she spotted Darius and Celina. "I got something special cooking for you."

"Thank you so much," Darius said as she placed silverware on their table.

"You all look so cute together," she commented. "It's like you were planted here at the same time just so you could fall in love. I'll send a waiter over here with menus."

Darius stared into Celina's eyes as Miss Rudy strolled away. "She's right, you know."

"I know we look cute together."

"No, we have been all over looking for something that grew right here," he said.

Darius took her hand in his.

"I never thought I would feel this way, I never thought I would fall in love and not be hurt," she said. "Darius, I thank God for you coming into my life."

He kissed her hand gently. "I'm really not hungry for food right now," he said. "I want to skip straight to dessert."

Celina blushed. "You are so bad, although I was thinking the same thing," she whispered as the waiter walked over to the table. Darius told the waiter that he and Celina would be taking their food to go.

They couldn't get out of the restaurant fast enough. Darius wanted to be with Celina in the worst way. They sped to his house, ignoring the posted speed limits. When they got to his place, they both hopped out of the car, leaving their dinner on the backseat, and were all over each other. Darius fumbled with his keys as the two of them kissed the whole way to the steps leading to the front door. She pulled at the buttons on his shirt as he unlocked the door. He pushed the door open and they tumbled to the floor. Darius pulled Celina's tank top over her head, then unsnapped her bra, causing her breasts to spill forward. Darius took her succulent breasts into his mouth, kissing and sucking on her nipples, making her moan in delight.

Celina unbuttoned his jeans, sliding them off his body. His arousal was evident as she slid her hands inside his satin boxers. Darius grabbed her hands and held them above her head as he peered at her, drinking in the image of her perfect body. Despite himself, he pictured her swelled with their child. He was sure that she'd glow like pregnant women do and her beauty would be even more radiant.

"I love you," Darius said before uniting her mouth with his. Celina melted against him as he peeled her linen shorts off. Heat radiated from his body as her skin touched his. She buried her face in his neck and her lips grazed his skin slightly, unleashing an inferno inside him.

When she wrapped her legs around his waist, he felt how hot and wet she was and he was ready to take her instantly, but not on the floor. Instead, he scooped her into his arms and rushed into the bedroom, gently laying her on the bed. He kicked out of his boxers and reached over on the nightstand to grab a condom. Celina watched him as he placed the protection on his hard penis. He then turned to her with a smile on his face, one that she returned as she wrapped her arms around his neck and whispered, "Je t'aime," which means "I love you" in French, in his ear. Darius was unable to resist her anymore. He buried himself deep inside of her, finding every spot that made her moan and shiver. Her muscles tightened around him, making him quake. Burying his face in her breasts, he suckled on her tender nipples, making her whimper in delight. Darius felt her trembling and he knew she was on the brink of an orgasm. He pressed deeper into her, wanting to make her feel the deep passion he'd been holding back. As she called out his name, he captured her mouth with his, muffling her expressions of desire, which were a mix of primal groans and declarations of love. Darius sucked in her tongue, pulling the words out of her mouth. His body felt like a rocket about to explode. He tried in vain to hold back his own orgasm until he was certain that she'd been pleased. But when she pressed her hips into his, he gave in to the feeling.

"Oh Celina," he called out as he exploded in her valley, then collapsed on top of her. Pushing her hair back from her forehead, he kissed her gently. Celina smiled and ran her finger up and down his spine and he pulled her closer as electric jolts ran through his body. "You have to stop," he whispered.

She responded by gently biting him on the earlobe. Darius groaned with pleasure and was instantly aroused as her tongue darted in and out of his ear. She positioned her body to receive his love and Darius rotated his hips to give her what she desired. Celina inhaled sharply as he entered her and continued his sensual dance, making her call out his name as he stroked her up and down. She clutched his back and placed her mouth against his neck. The heat from her breath sent chills up and down his spine. Darius felt his hardness constrict and he was ready to explode again.

Once they were spent from hours of lovemaking, Darius and Celina fell asleep in each other's arms. Darius snuggled his face in his favorite spot, Celina's bushy hair.

Celina woke up smiling, though it was the middle of the night. She stroked the side of his face, trying not to wake him and wished she had her sketch pad so that she could draw his sleeping frame. He looked angelic as he slumbered. Slipping out of the bed, she headed for the bathroom to take a shower. Quietly, she stepped in the shower and turned the spray on. She hadn't felt this at peace since her father died, she thought, as she closed her eyes and let the water seep through her hair, down to her scalp. It reminded her of Darius's touch, the feel of his tongue against her skin. She closed her eyes and smiled as she relived the passion they'd just shared hours ago. It was so real, it was as if Darius was right there in the shower with her. She turned around and there he was. "I just thought you needed some help washing your back," he whispered as he rubbed her back with a bar of soap.

"And here I thought I was in the middle of a fantasy," she said as she turned around and wrapped her arms around his neck. "I was hoping I could sneak out of here and catch you sleeping."

Darius kissed her collarbone. "Why is that?"

"I wanted to draw you. You inspired me."

Darius raised his eyebrow. "How did I do that?"

"Just by being you," she said, then splashed some water in his face.

Darius laughed. "Oh, you're going to pay for that," he said as he grabbed her and held her under the shower spray. Celina squealed like a little girl as the water ran down her back. She threw her hands up to protect herself from the shower spray.

"Stop it!" she exclaimed.

Darius let her go and kissed her on the cheek. "You're so sexy when you're wet," Darius growled in a low voice as he ran his finger down the valley of her breasts. Celina pushed her wet ringlets out of her eyes and her body began to sizzle under Darius's touch. He reached out and grabbed her hand, placing it on his desire. "See what you do to me," he said.

She felt him grow underneath her fingertips and reached back and turned the water off as Darius backed her against the wall.

"Celina," he murmured as he kissed her lips. She happily accepted his penetrating kiss. He pulled her closer to him as if he were trying to mesh his body with hers. She moaned as he stroked her inner thighs.

"We'd better stop," she said breathlessly. "Before we get carried away without the proper protection."

Darius smiled devilishly. "Too late." He pulled her mouth up to his, kissing her with a fiery passion that turned her knees to jelly. Darius lifted Celina's leg around his waist. She curved to his body like an artist's clay. She thrust her hips into his, allowing him to glide into her hot and awaiting body. Darius pressed deep into Celina, making her hot body light up like a firecracker. He struggled to keep his footing in the slick tub. Celina clutched him as she bounced up and down, stimulating herself as Darius was on the brink of an orgasm. He held her tightly as he slid down the wall, keeping Celina on his lap. She wrapped her legs around his waist, arching her back like a cat. Darius moaned as she tightened herself around his manhood. Celina looked into his eyes. "I love you," she whimpered. "I love you. I love you."

She'd never felt so free, so alive. She didn't care that she and Darius weren't protected, because she knew their child would be loved, protected, and wanted. Celina wrapped her arms around his neck, pulling him close to her as she felt herself release. Darius rained kisses across her face. "I love you, too," he said breathlessly. They clung to each other in the damp tub, seemingly breathing one breath.

It was nearly dawn when Darius and Celina fell asleep again, giving Darius only a few hours before he had to head to the hardware store. When they woke up, Celina went next door to start a new painting. The man in her painting looked like Darius, which was becoming a standard for her. She drew his frame sleeping on a fluffy white cloud. Golden sun rays encircled his head. Celina decided to use watercolors to add a whimsical feel to the painting. For the landscape, she used a brown oil-based paint to add dimension to the piece. Celina was engrossed in her work and didn't hear the door open behind her.

"Nice painting." The voice startled Celina. She whirled around and locked eyes with Tiffany. "You know," she continued. "If you and Darius think I am so dangerous, why don't you lock your doors?"

Celina stood up and glared at Tiffany. "Get out before I call the police."

Tiffany reached out and grabbed Celina's arm tightly. "Why don't you just go back to New York? Darius is mine."

Celina looked up at Tiffany and snatched her arm away from her. "You need help, seriously. These delusions that you're having about you and Darius being together shows how crazy you are. We're getting married and he's made it clear that he wants nothing to do with you."

Tiffany ran her hand over her face. "Because you messed up everything. I love him and I'm not going away because you're here. I'm coming to you as a woman . . ."

"You're coming as a burglar. You broke into my house, issuing threats. Darius doesn't want you. Move on with your life," Celina exclaimed.

Tiffany pushed her backwards, knocking her into the easel. Celina's painting crashed to the floor, along with her brushes, paint, and water cup. Celina fought to keep her balance. She grabbed Tiffany's arm and ended up pulling her down on the floor. Out of anger, Celina kicked her in her midsection. Tiffany countered with a slap to the face. Celina pushed Tiffany off her to stop a further assault. "I'm not going to fight you," Celina said, rising from the floor. "Now, get out of here."

Tiffany lunged for Celina's legs, knocking her down. Celina hit her head on the overturned canvas. She swung her legs wildly, catching Tiffany on the chin, forcing her head back. Celina crawled away from Tiffany, desperately trying to reach the phone to call 9-1-1. Before she could reach the phone, Tiffany grabbed the back of her hair. Celina yelped in pain. Tiffany tried to drive her head into the floor, but Celina lifted her leg and kicked Tiffany in the stomach, knocking her backwards into the kitchen table. Celina leapt to her feet and grabbed the phone. She dialed 9-1-1, but as the operator answered, Tiffany knocked her out with a chair from the table. Unconscious, Celina fell to the floor. Startled, Tiffany ran out the back door.

Celina came to in a hospital bed. She focused her eyes and saw Darius standing in the doorway talking to a man in what looked to be a police uniform. Celina's vision was blurry, but the images slowly came into focus. She struggled to hear what they were saying, but she could tell they were arguing.

"I warned you, Chief," she heard Darius say in an angry whisper. "If Celina doesn't pull through . . ."

"She will," Chief Wayman said. "I spoke to the doctors."

"What about Tiffany? You know she did this."

"We won't know anything until Ms. Hart wakes up."

Darius pounded his hand against the door frame. "Damn it," he snapped. "Wayman, you know Tiffany is behind this. She has been stalking us and she showed up in New York, outside of our building. I've been telling you for months that this woman is unstable and dangerous. Did you listen to me? Now look what's happened."

"None of what you reported before was illegal, but if she assaulted Celina, then we can bring charges against her."

Celina cleared her throat, causing Darius and the chief to turn around and look at her. "All of this for me?" she said in a hoarse voice.

Darius rushed to her bedside. "You're awake," he said as he stroked her hand gently.

She smiled weakly. "How can a girl sleep with you two standing there arguing like cavemen?"

Chief Wayman walked over to Celina's bed. "Ms. Hart, how are you?"

Celina groaned. "A little sore, but I'll be fine," she replied.

He pulled out a small notepad and a pencil that looked as if it had been gnawed on by a mouse. "Can you tell me what happened to you?" he asked.

Celina tried to sit up in the bed, but a sharp pain in her back forced her to lie flat. She nodded. "I was in the house, working on a painting for the gallery. Then she walked in," she said. "I should've locked the door; I mean, I've lived in New York too long to sit in a house with the door unlocked."

"She who?" Chief Wayman asked.

"Tiffany Martin. She walked in the house and started making threats and telling me to leave town. Then she grabbed my arm and we fought and I got away from her, then I called 9-1-1 and the last thing I remember was a sharp pain to my back. Then I woke up here."

Darius raised his eyebrow at the chief. "Is that enough now? Can you go out and arrest her?" he demanded.

The chief nodded his head and pulled out his cell phone. He barked into the phone and told an officer to head over to Tiffany's and bring her in for questioning. "I'll let you two know when we have the suspect in custody," he said as he headed out the door.

Darius turned to Celina once the chief was gone. "Babe, are you all right?" he asked as he kissed her hand.

"Yeah, I guess. I had no idea that she was this crazy," Celina said.

"Neither did I," he said. "I'm sorry that I got you involved in all of this. Had I known that she was like this, we could've stayed in New York."

Celina stroked his cheek. "And let her think she ran us out of town? Besides, it's not your fault you're so irresistible," she said. Celina closed her eyes and groaned as a wave of pain washed over her.

Panicked, Darius pressed the button for the nurse several times in rapid succession. Within minutes, two nurses rushed into the room and stood on either side of Celina's bed.

"Ms. Hart, are you feeling any discomfort?" one of the nurses asked.

"My back, it's killing me," she said. The other nurse stroked her hand, while the senior nurse checked Celina's pain medicine.

"This is good," she said as she punched numbers into the computer. "Your spine is probably just bruised.

You're going to be fine, Ms. Hart. Let me get the doctor."

"Hurry," Darius said, worry peppering his tone.

Celina whimpered as the pain became more intense and sharper. Seconds later the doctor walked into the room.

"Sir, if you could give me a moment with Ms. Hart," he said.

Nodding, Darius walked outside and paced back and forth as the doctor worked on Celina. His anger grew with each moment he stood outside. Tiffany was going to pay for this and if the police didn't get her, he damned sure would.

CHAPTER 25

Darius drove slowly from the hospital because he wasn't sure if he should go to Tiffany's, but he had the feeling that if he didn't get her, the police wouldn't. Tiffany was going to answer for what she'd done to Celina.

Celina.

Yes, he'd lied to her when he said he was going to check on the hardware store, but he hadn't wanted her to worry about his safety since they now knew how unstable Tiffany was.

He said that he was going to let the police handle everything and kissed his fiancée before dashing away. Honestly, he had about as much faith in the Elmore Police Department as he had in finding the Easter Bunny leaving chocolate eggs on his doorstep.

If only the police had taken reports from all the other times Darius had called them and coupled those with Tiffany's assault, the district attorney wouldn't have had a problem bringing charges against Tiffany. He simply couldn't wrap his mind around why Tiffany couldn't deal with rejection and move on. She was an attractive woman and shouldn't have a problem finding another lover. Her fixation on Darius was unhealthy and now that she'd become violent, she had to be stopped.

He slowed down as he pulled up to the intersection leading into Tiffany's neighborhood and scanned the driveway for her car. It wasn't there. Darius had only visited her once and hindsight told him that it was the biggest mistake of his life. Had he known that his one night of tipsy sex with her would've led to this, he would never have talked to her at the small business meeting or accepted her invitation to dinner two weeks later.

But he did, and now Celina was paying the price. After spotting an Elmore Police squad car parked near Tiffany's house, Darius decided to turn around. The last thing he needed was to get arrested himself.

They must not have her, he thought as he wheeled his car around and headed for the hardware store. When he arrived, there was a police car parked near the store. At least the chief was finally taking him seriously. But Darius knew he and Celina weren't going to be safe until that woman was in jail.

Where is she? he thought as he headed toward his house. Darius knew Tiffany wouldn't be crazy enough to return to the scene of the crime. Though he couldn't be sure that she wouldn't go to the hospital and try something there. She had to know that Celina had fingered her in the assault and she would probably try to silence her. Darius pulled out his cell phone and called the police chief to make sure someone was watching Celina's room.

"Chief Wayman," the massive man said. Darius could almost see him chewing on the end of a cigar.

"It's Darius. Have you picked up Tiffany?"

"Not yet. She seems to have disappeared," the chief said. "We have a car at her house and I placed an APB out for her."

"Are you going to place a guard at Celina's hospital room?"

"Yes, Darius. Don't worry, we'll find her."

Darius sighed heavily, wanting to give the chief a piece of his mind, because this wouldn't have happened if Wayman had taken him more seriously when he told him that Tiffany was stalking him. Instead, he said, "Fine."

"If you see her, call the police. I know you might be tempted to take the law into your own hands, but the best thing you can do is take care of Ms. Hart."

"I got it," Darius said with a sigh. "Just call me if you find her."

"I will, Darius, now you go back to the hospital and let us find Tiffany," the chief said, then hung up the phone.

Before heading to the hospital, Darius took one more swing by Tiffany's place. The police car was still there and the house was dark and still—too quiet for his taste because he knew that she was out there somewhere. He just wondered how long it would be before she made an appearance.

Celina stretched her legs in the bed and looked out the door. Why was a police officer standing outside? Where was Darius? The pain in her back had subsided because of the medication, but the doctor didn't want her to get out of bed yet. Pressing the button that raised the bed into an upright position, she reached over her shoulder for the phone, then stopped short of grabbing it. She needed to call her mother and tell her that she was engaged, but she didn't want Rena to know she was in the hospital. *I'll just wait*, she thought.

A few seconds later, Darius walked into the room. "Hey, babe," he said as he kissed her on the cheek.

"How are things at the store?" she asked.

"Don't worry about the store," he replied as he took a seat in the chair beside her bed. "Have the doctors said anything?"

"Dr. Lewis was in here earlier and he said he wants me to rest my back for a few days, and then I should be able to go home. I'm pretty lucky, according to the doctor. There was no serious damage to my spine."

"I'm sorry about all of this," he said. "I feel like it's my fault that you're in here."

Celina reached out and grabbed his hand. "You're not the one who hit me with the chair. You had no idea that this woman was obsessed with you. Have they caught her yet?"

Darius shook his head. "That's why the officer is outside your door."

Fear gripped Celina. "Do they think I'm in danger?" she asked, her voice low and quiet.

"Don't worry about that. With me and the police here, she would be crazy to show her face around here. She'd be arrested on the spot," Darius said.

Though his words were meant to reassure her, they didn't. Celina shivered inwardly as she thought about facing Tiffany in her hospital bed, where she lay totally helpless.

Darius looked in her eyes, seemingly reading her mind. "I'm going to be right here for you," he said. "She's never going to hurt you again."

She wanted to ask how he knew that was true. Was he going to hold a vigil at her bedside twenty-four hours a day? What was going to happen when he had to go to the hardware store? The officer would have to take a break at some point and then she'd be vulnerable to another attack from that madwoman. Celina closed her eyes.

"Do you need anything?" Darius asked as he looked at Celina. "Are you in pain?"

She shook her head. "I'm just scared," she whispered. "What happens if she does come here?"

Darius kneeled beside the bed and gently stroked her hair. "You don't have to be. Celina, I swear to God, I'm going to protect you."

"I know you're going to try," she whispered. "Maybe I should go to Columbia to recover, just until the police get her."

"Is that what you want to do? You don't have to run from her," Darius whispered.

Celina closed her eyes and held on to Darius tightly. "I don't want to run, but I don't want to be afraid either. This is crazy," she said, "I never had to deal with anything like this, even when I was in New York. This isn't supposed to happen in Elmore; it's supposed to be safe here."

"Celina, if you want to leave, we can. But you're going to be safe, I promise you that, no matter where you are. I'm not going to let anything happen to you ever again." Darius kissed her on the forehead and Celina felt comforted.

"My mother can't find out about this," she said.

Darius blanched. "Well, uh, I called your mother on the way over here," he said.

Celina's eyes stretched to the size of quarters. "Why would you do something like that? She's going to be on the next plane from Chicago and she doesn't need to be here."

"Because my future mother-in-law would kill me if I didn't. You're right, though. She and John are on their way here."

Celina groaned, then smiled at Darius. "You did the

right thing," she said. "I just didn't want her to worry about me. Nor do I want her hovering over me."

"It won't hurt to have some extra eyes," he said. "I know your mother will help us keep you safe."

Celina closed her eyes as her back began to spasm, but the pain subsided as quickly as it attacked her senses. For a moment, she wondered if everything she was going through was worth it. Her life had been turned upside down and now it seemed to be spinning out of control. She looked at Darius and flashed him a smile that didn't fully reach her eyes. She did believe that Darius was going to protect her, but the "what ifs" nagged at her. What if he turned his back and Tiffany got to her again? He was going to do everything that he could to protect her and she had to believe that. She couldn't let Tiffany win. Looking up at her fiancé, she realized that he would keep her safe.

A few hours later, Rena and John burst through the door of Celina's hospital room. "Oh my God," Rena exclaimed.

Celina put her finger to her lips, pointing to Darius, who was sleeping in the chair. "I look a lot worse than I feel," she said in a hushed whisper.

Rena sat on the edge of the bed, rubbing the back of Celina's hand. "If I find the little tramp who did this—" she said.

Celina shook her head and looked up at John, who's face was stoic. "You're spending more time in the south than you ever expected, right?" Celina said.

John chuckled. "Baby girl, I wouldn't be any other place." He planted a wet kiss on her forehead. "Celina, how are you, really?"

"Guys, I'm fine and you didn't have to rush back down here. I know this last-minute trip had to be expensive."

Rena rolled her eyes, not buying for a minute that she

was all right. Darius sat up in the chair and looked at his future in-laws. "Hi," he said.

Rena smiled at him, then hugged him tightly. "I'm so glad you are here for my baby," she said. She glanced over at Celina. "I never thought I would say this, but I believe you were safer in New York. So, what happened? This woman just broke into the house and assaulted you? Do you know her?"

Celina glanced over at Darius. "I know her, she's . . ."

"A crazy woman who has been stalking me and Celina for months," Darius said.

"But why?" Rena asked. "I mean, before Thomas got sick, you hadn't been here since you were eight years old. Was she a crazed fan that followed you from the city or something?"

Celina closed her eyes. She knew she was going to have to tell her mother the truth. "She had a relationship with Darius," she said.

Rena's mouth dropped open, then she finally came out with, "Oh, really."

Darius stood up so that Rena could sit down, but she stood toe-to-toe with him. "Darius, what kind of woman is this? I mean, why would she hurt Celina? Are you still seeing her or sleeping with her behind Celina's back?"

"No, there is nothing going on between me and Tiffany. She's crazy," he said. "But the police are looking for her. That's why the guard is at the door."

"That settles it," Rena snapped. "You're going back to Chicago with us."

"Wait, no," Celina said. "I'm not going anywhere."

John placed his hand on his step-daughter's shoulder. "Maybe you should hear your mother out," he said quietly.

Darius waved his hand in the air. "I can take care of Celina," he said.

Rena glared at him. "You're the reason my baby is in this hospital."

Celina rolled her eyes and shook her head. "Can all of you just stop? I'm not some damned China doll that's broken and needs to be put back together. I'm not going to Chicago, I'm not running from the psycho and I'm not going to blame Darius for something she did. No one else is going to do that, either," she snapped. Despite her doctor's warning to stay in the bed, Celina swung her legs over the side of the bed and gingerly stood up. She pushed Darius and her mother's hands away as they tried to help her walk to the bathroom. Each step she took hurt her and the short trip to the bathroom made her feel as if she had run a marathon. Sitting in the bathroom to clear her head, she ignored the hushed whispers she heard on the other side of the door because she'd made her decision. She wasn't running.

CHAPTER 26

After a week and a half in the hospital, Celina was released. The doctors were extra cautious about her bruised spine at her mother's request—much to Celina's dismay.

Adding to that, on the day Celina was released, Rena announced that she and John weren't leaving Elmore until Tiffany was carted off in handcuffs. She felt as if her mother blamed Darius for what happened and that wasn't fair. She didn't know what had been going on while she'd been cooped up in the hospital, but it was taking its toll on Darius.

"You're quiet this morning," she said as he drove her home.

"I'm just tired," he replied.

She figured that to be true because he hadn't left her bedside for more than five minutes over the last week and a half. She didn't see him sleeping much between taking calls about the store and calling the police to check on the status of the case.

"You haven't been sleeping much," she said. "Darius, you see I'm fine. Now you're going to have to take care of yourself." She rubbed his cheek gently. "Heard anything from the police today?"

Darius shook his head and yawned.

Celina exhaled loudly. "You know what," she began. "We have a gallery to open and I'm sick of worrying about that psycho."

Darius smiled. "That's what I love about you. You have this fighting spirit, but if you think I'm going to let you start working your first day out of the hospital, you're wrong. I'm taking you home, planting you in your bed and putting your mother on guard duty."

Celina pouted like a little girl. She was tired of being cooped up and she wanted to paint, draw, go look at her gallery space, or do anything else but be tied down.

Darius continued. "Besides, your mother is already a little miffed with me and if I don't hurry and get you home, she's going to give me one of those talks. She speaks softly, but her words have a punch." He visibly shuddered, then smiled.

Celina nodded, "That's Rena Malcolm for you," she said. "I'm sure she's in the house cooking a welcome home meal."

Darius pulled his car into Celina's driveway. John was sitting on the porch with a glass of lemonade and a copy of the local paper. When her stepfather saw her getting out of the car, he bounced off the porch and met her at the edge of the gravel sidewalk. "Baby girl," he said as hugged her. "How do you feel?"

"Just a little sore."

He nodded then looked at Darius. "Son, why don't you take her bags inside? Rena wants to talk to you," John said as he walked Celina up the steps.

"What does Mom want with Darius?" Celina asked

nervously, as John helped her into one of the rocking chairs on the porch.

"To eat some crow, as they say in the south. She knows what happened isn't his fault, but she has been treating him like it was." John held his stepdaughter's hand. "This has been really hard for your mother, you know. First, your father passed, then we get a call about you being in the hospital. She reacted the way she usually does and that's to overreact."

"I know, and the last thing I wanted to do was worry you two," she said. "I didn't even want Darius to call you."

"We're parents, we're going to worry and this wasn't your fault or Darius's. Life just happens sometimes and there isn't much you can do about it. Had he not called, you know Rena would've hated him forever."

Celina leaned on John's shoulder, fighting back tears.

"What's wrong?" he asked when he saw the look on her face.

"I'm really missing my father right now," she whispered. "I'm glad I've always had you in my corner."

John kissed her on the top of her head. "And I always will be. Celina, everything is going to be all right."

"I know that, but I just don't like feeling afraid."

"Don't be, then. Don't tell your mother, but I went down to the pawn shop on Main Street and bought you a handgun. It's in your nightstand drawer. Promise me you will take a class and learn how to use it properly."

"John, I don't need a gun," she said. "Because if I run into Tiffany again I might use it."

"Keep it anyway. Once she's behind bars, throw it away or sell it. I don't like the idea of someone thinking that they can do this to you and get away with it," John said.

She nodded. When Tiffany was arrested and things calmed down, she would turn the gun over to the police.

"Come on, let's go inside before your mother comes out here," John said.

When Celina and John walked in, Rena and Darius were setting the table. "I was starting to wonder if the two of you were actually going to come in and eat. Celina, why don't you go to your room and rest? Darius will bring you a plate."

"Yes ma'am," she said, then stole a glance at Darius as she walked away. Celina stopped in the hallway watching her family. Darius winked at her, then turned to Rena as she told him to get some silverware. John walked over to Rena and kissed her on the cheek.

"You're not being too hard on the boy are you?"

Rena smiled. "Would I do that?" John shot her a "yeah, right" look.

"Darius," John said. "Why don't you go check on Celina and let me and my wife have lunch in here."

Celina smiled as she watched them, then she headed up the hall to her room. There was no way she was going to let Tiffany rob her of this.

Darius walked into the bedroom with a tray of roasted bell peppers smothered in cheese, with mushrooms, onions, and roasted tomatoes and a bowl of brown rice.

"How are you holding up?" he asked as he put the tray on the side of the bed and sat down.

"Maybe I should ask you that," she said. "Why did my mother want you to come in here?"

Darius smiled as he cut into the veggies and held the fork out to Celina. "Just enjoy your meal."

She pushed his hand away. "Not until you tell me what happened."

"She apologized for what she said at the hospital. Now, eat."

Celina took the fork and nibbled on the vegetables and he took her bare feet into his hand and massaged them as she ate.

"Why don't you stay with me tonight?" Darius suggested.

Celina laughed. "My mother isn't going to like that. Even though I'm an adult and fully capable of making my own decisions, she makes me feel like a twelve-year-old whenever we're together."

"We're going to be married soon," he said focusing his stare on Celina's face. Her eyes were closed and she gently bit her bottom lip. Darius boldly inched up her calf, past her knee, his fingers grazing her thighs. He could tell she was suppressing a satisfied moan. Darius smiled, but stopped before he took things too far.

Celina opened her eyes. "Why did you stop? That was the best medicine I've had all week."

Darius raised his eyebrow. "I stopped because you need to eat," he said. Celina frowned.

"Thanks to you, food is the last thing on my mind." Darius stifled a laugh as Rena walked into the room.

"Celina, are you all right? You haven't touched your lunch."

"Um, I'm getting to it. I just don't have much of an appetite," she said then looked pointedly at Darius.

Rena followed Celina's gaze and shook her head. "Carry on," she said. "Darius, do you want something to eat?"

"No, thank you," he replied. "I'm going to go check in at the store." He leaned over Celina and kissed her on the forehead. "I'll see you later." Darius headed out the door and blew a kiss at Celina as he walked outside. He

knew she had a support system at home for now, but
Tiffany was still at large and he hadn't heard anything
from the police. Darius got into his car and headed to
the police station because someone was going to give
him answers.

The first thing he saw when he arrived was Chief
Wayman heading to his car. "Chief," Darius called out.

Wayman dropped his head, then walked over to
Darius. "I know what you want and no, we haven't found
her yet."

"Elmore is only so big. Celina's out of the hospital and
I don't want Tiffany to take another run at hurting her."

"I know and trust me, we're going to find her. I have
my officers keeping an eye on Ms. Hart's house and your
store."

"I hope that's good enough," Darius snapped.

"What's that supposed to mean?" Wayman bellowed.

"It means if something happens to Celina, it's on your
hands. You didn't listen to me when I came to you and
look at how this has escalated."

Wayman placed his hand on Darius's shoulder. "As
you've said many times. I'm not going to let you bully me
into doing my job. I know what needs to be done and
we're going to do it." Darius fought back a sarcastic response as he moved the chief's hand from his shoulder.
"I know you love her," Wayman said. "But the police have
to do our job without your interference."

Darius nodded, pretending to understand, but he was
going to interfere, as the chief called it, because he was
going to find Tiffany before she did something else.

Arriving in her neighborhood, Darius decided to park
his car a half a block away because if either the police or
Tiffany saw him, it would complicate his amateur
sleuthing.

Moving stealthily, he cut through the bushes behind a row of houses and prayed no one had motion-activated lights on the side of their homes. He stood across from Tiffany's backyard, watching for any movement around the evergreen shrubs near her back porch. Darius wondered how she just disappeared without raising an eyebrow from the police.

I bet she is hiding in plain sight, he thought. *No one just disappears.*

He knew he needed to get inside her house because if there were any answers to be found, they would be in there. Getting inside her house would be easier said than done—especially with two police officers staked outside of the place. Part of him said, *let the police handle it.* "They've done such a good job so far," he mumbled as he headed back to his car.

Celina woke up with a jolt of pain. She had gotten out of bed to watch TV, but her pain medicine knocked her out and she'd fallen asleep on the couch. She faintly remembered her mother asking her if she wanted to get in her bed, but Celina had been waiting for Darius to come back. Where was he, she wondered, as she gingerly sat up on the sofa.

"Ma, John," she called out.

Rena walked into the living room. "Are you okay?" she asked as she helped Celina to her feet. "I told you to get in your own bed."

"Did Darius call while I was sleeping?" she asked as she stretched her back.

Rena shook her head. "He does have a store to run, Celina. Don't worry about Darius so much. You need to focus on feeling better," she said. "Have you read over the information that the doctor gave you about exercising your back and everything?"

"No."

"What are you waiting for?" she asked. "We need to get you back on your feet. I know what John did."

"Huh?" Celina asked, pretending she didn't know where the conversation was going.

Rena put her hand on her hip and looked up at her daughter. "Celina, I cleaned up your room and opened your nightstand drawer. Surprise, surprise, what did I find? You don't need a gun."

"I know that," she said. "John was just trying to help. I had no intention of using it."

Rena shook her head. "I don't want you to get in trouble with that thing. Do you even know how to use a gun?"

"No, but it's not even going to come to that. I doubt Tiffany will be back. Every policeman in Elmore is looking for her."

Rena pulled Celina to her and hugged her tightly. "I worry about that woman. She seems crazy. I know Darius isn't going to let anything happen to you. He loves you so much. That's why I had to apologize to him. I was wrong for what I said at the hospital. There's no way he could've known that this woman was nutty as a fruitcake."

Celina smiled at her mother. "He told me that you apologized. I just didn't believe it," she said.

Rena pinched Celina's cheek. "You and John act like I'm the wicked witch of the Midwest and I'm not. Anyway, you and Darius are going to have a beautiful family one day. I just don't understand why you two haven't told me that you're getting married."

"What? How did you know?" Celina asked.

Rena raised her eyebrow. "I told you, I cleaned up

your room. I saw that rock in your jewelry box. Things have been difficult lately, but we know that's going to change," she said as she gently stroked her daughter's arm. "We're going to plan the best wedding Elmore has ever seen."

Celina laughed. "All right, Mom," she said, then kissed her mother on the cheek. Rena helped her walk around the living room, then led her to the bedroom. Celina changed into her satin nightgown, but she wasn't tired.

Where is Darius? she thought as she sat on the bed and looked out the window.

CHAPTER 27

Darius walked up the back steps of Tiffany's house since it was just dark enough for him to creep in unnoticed. He jiggled the cheap lock to see if it was open. It wasn't, but, luckily for him, the locks were flimsy and he could jimmy it open with his credit card.

Where do I start? he thought as he walked through the kitchen. He headed for the living room, wishing he could turn on a light and take a closer look at the papers that were thrown all over the oak coffee table. He scooped most of them up, rolling them up like a paper towel tube and stuck them in his jacket pocket. Next, he moved to the bedroom, which was down the hall on the left. He could see the closet was open and most of Tiffany's clothes were gone. He walked over to her nightstand and looked at the notepad sitting on top of the alarm clock. There was faint handwriting on it, but he couldn't read it in the dark. Darius took the pad and put it in his other pocket. Satisfied that some of the things he had taken would give him a lead on where Tiffany was, Darius headed out the back door, leaving undetected. He headed to Celina's.

"Hello, son," Rena said after opening the door and

hugging him tightly. "Celina finally told me about your engagement."

Darius smiled. "With everything that was going on, we just didn't get a chance to tell you, but we were going to."

She nodded. "I understand. She's in her room pretending to be asleep, but she's waiting for you."

Darius kissed his future mother-in-law on her cheek before heading down the hall. He knocked on Celina's bedroom door, then walked in.

"Where have you been?" she asked as he sat on the side of the bed.

"Doing some research," he said as he pulled out the papers he had taken from Tiffany's house and placed them on the bed.

"What is this?" she asked. "Darius, where did you get all of this?"

"I got into Tiffany's house tonight. We have to find her so the police can arrest her."

Celina smacked his arm. "You could have gotten arrested. What were you thinking?"

Darius looked away from the papers, which were printouts from various travel sights. "Celina, I didn't get arrested and if we don't hurry up and find her, we will be looking over our shoulders for the rest of our lives and I won't live like that."

Celina dropped her head, then turned back to him. "I know you're right, but I don't want you taking these kinds of risks, Darius. The police are on this. Let them do their job."

"Do you see what kind of job they're doing? I got into her house without anyone seeing me. Tiffany could be hiding right here in this town."

Celina looked at the papers, which held information on several areas, including New York, New Orleans, Dallas, and Beaumont, Texas. "Or she could be in any of these cities," she said exasperatedly. "Darius, we can't do this. Neither of us is an investigator. The police will find her. We have a gallery to open and I'll be damned if I will let her take more from me than she already has." She wrapped her arms around his shoulders. "I won't be afraid of her and I won't let her make us paranoid."

Darius squeezed Celina's shoulder. "How are you doing? Is your back all right?"

"Great subject change," she said with a laugh. "I'm fine, though. What about you?"

Darius pulled Celina's face to his and kissed her lips gently. "Better now. You think your mom will mind if I sleep over?"

Celina blushed. "Darius," she whispered.

He kissed her hand. "I really just want to sleep," he said. "You're still recovering and I know I won't get much sleep next door without feeling you next to me."

"Stay," she whispered. Darius smiled as he kicked off his shoes and hung his jacket on the wooden bedpost. He positioned himself so that she could lie against his chest, then they both drifted off to sleep.

The next morning, Rena knocked on Celina's door. "Hello," she said, then walked in. "Do you two want breakfast?"

Darius and Celina sat up in the bed. "Ma," she said, flustered.

Rena walked into the room with a smile on her face. "Good morning. John is cooking breakfast. Should we set a place for the two of you?" she asked.

"Sure," Darius said. "Thanks."

Rena winked at the couple as she walked out of the bedroom.

Celina exhaled loudly. "That was not my mother."

"You're a grown woman," he said. "We're getting married and I'm practically fully clothed. She knows why I was here."

"Yeah, you're madly in love with me and you can't sleep without me beside you."

Darius held her tightly and kissed her on the cheek. "Come on, let's go and get something to eat," he said as he stood up. Darius reached out and helped Celina out of bed. He could tell she was still experiencing a little bit of pain. They walked into the kitchen and sat down with Rena and John. "Good morning," John said in between sips of hot coffee. "How are you feeling, Celina?"

She looked at Darius and smiled. "Better. I'm not in as much pain."

John smiled as he caught the look between Celina and Darius. "That's good to know." Rena set two plates in front of Darius and Celina. She had grits and eggs on Celina's plate with a side of strawberries and blueberries. For Darius she had a side of bacon with his grits and eggs.

"Celina, how are you going to cook meat for your husband?" she asked with a laugh.

Before she could reply to her mother, there was a knock at the door. "I'll get it," John said as he pushed away from the table.

Darius turned his head to see who was at the door. When he saw Chief Wayman standing in the doorway, his stomach fluttered a bit. Maybe he had been seen leaving Tiffany's.

"Good morning," the chief said. "Is Mr. McRae here?"

"Yes, come in. I hope you're here to tell us that you've found the woman who assaulted my daughter," John said.

"Sir, we are still working on finding her. I just need to speak with Darius."

Celina looked at her fiancé as if to say, "I told you

there would be trouble." Darius stood up and walked into the living room.

"Chief," he said. Wayman cocked his head to the side, motioning for Darius to go outside. He followed the chief to the front porch. When Darius and Wayman stepped onto the porch, Darius took a deep breath. Was he going to jail? Wayman looked at Darius, suspicion clouding his eyes.

"Darius, someone broke into Tiffany's house last night," the chief said as he rocked back on his heels. "Know anything about it?"

Darius shook his head and looked directly into Wayman's eyes. "Nope."

"Darius, consider this your first and final warning— stay away from this case. If I find out you were the one who broke into her home, you will be charged with obstruction of justice."

Darius smirked. "You're threatening me with charges? That woman disappeared from town and you're harassing me because someone snuck past your Keystone cops and got inside her house?"

"Cut the bull, Darius. I know you were the one who broke in," Wayman snapped. "I'm givin' you rope; don't hang yourself." Wayman turned and headed down the steps.

"Chief," Darius called out. "I'm going to step back and let you all handle this case, but you'd better be sure nothing happens to Celina."

"You better make sure you don't give me cause to arrest you," Wayman said, then walked to his car.

Darius released a sigh of relief as the police chief left. Then he turned to walk into the house but John stopped him.

"Son," John said. "You're not going to do baby girl any good on the other side of the law."

Darius nodded respectfully and remained silent.

"You've been chastised enough. Let's finish breakfast," John said as he held the door open for Darius.

"Yes, sir," Darius said.

When they returned to the table, Celina focused her questioning stare on the two men.

"What happened?" Rena asked.

"Nothing, the chief just wanted to ask Darius some questions. They still haven't caught Tiffany," John replied.

Darius smiled, happy that John had only told half of the story. However, from the look on Celina's face, he knew that she wasn't buying it. The family ate in silence for a few minutes, then Rena stood up and took her dishes to the sink.

"I hate this," she said as she dropped the plate and fork in the sink. "We're just sitting around here waiting for the other shoe to drop. What you two should be doing is concentrating on the gallery and your wedding."

"Mom," Celina said. "We're going to do that."

"That's right," Darius said. "We can't spend the rest of our lives looking in shadows and I'm sure you two want to get back to your lives in Chicago."

Rena shook her head. "Not until that madwoman is caught."

Despite himself, he was glad that Rena and John were staying around. The extra set of eyes meant that Celina would never be alone and he didn't mind having his mother-in-law feeding him every day. He was marrying into a great family, one with a foundation of love and support. "Darius, why don't you and Celina go out and do something. Celina, I haven't seen you painting, drawing, or anything since I've been here," Rena said as she wiped her hands on a dish towel.

Celina stood up and slowly walked over to her mother.

"Mommy, I love you," Celina said, then kissed her. "I'm going to take your advice—shower, change, and paint."

Darius smiled at the mother–daughter moment. "I'm going to head next door and change," he said.

"Stay out of trouble," John mumbled as he passed Darius.

About an hour later, Darius and Celina were at the warehouse, planning their future. He watched Celina as she drew the designs for the interior of the gallery. She wanted a Parisian motif for the gallery. Darius watched as she sat in the chair, balancing her sketch pad on her knees, making broad strokes with her charcoal pencil. Her hair fell into her eyes as she concentrated on the image. He wished he was an artist too so that he could capture her essence. She was the real work of art. Celina pushed her hair back and looked at him.

"What?" she asked.

"Nothing, I was just looking," he said breaking out into a wide grin.

Celina stuck her pencil behind her ear, then held the pad up. "What do you think?"

There were no words that could describe what he thought of her sketch. Her rendition of the gallery was breathtaking. There were rounded archways and the walls were covered with ivy and violets. Two Romanlike columns were drawn in the middle of the space, adding depth to the room. "Wow," was all Darius could say. "This is beautiful. I would do most of the work myself. We should make the carpet and the flowers on the wall match."

Celina smiled brightly. "That is a great idea," she exclaimed, clasping her hands together. Darius was thrilled to see the excited gleam in her eyes, which had replaced fear and anger. She stood up slowly, clutching her back. Reality sank in; things were still topsy-turvy in their lives.

Darius grabbed Celina's arm, helping her to her feet. "Are you all right?"

"Just a little stiff," she said. "I'm fine."

He shook his head. "This shouldn't be happening," he said. "Things shouldn't be this complicated." Celina caressed his face.

"It really isn't that complicated. We just have to watch our backs until Tiffany is caught. It doesn't change anything for us. If anything, we get to spend more time together, so maybe we should thank her for that once she's behind bars," Celina said, then smiled devilishly. "And, you need to stop playing junior policeman."

"I know," Darius replied. "I had to do something. Tiffany didn't just fall off the face of the earth." As he wondered when she was going to return, neither of them noticed the shadowy figure watching their every move.

Later that evening, Celina and Darius stole away to his place for a quiet dinner. Darius ordered Celina to sit down and put her feet up. He didn't have to tell her twice; she lounged on his sofa with her feet on the coffee table. Part of her felt sorry for Darius as he rushed around the kitchen putting their meal together, but he was the one who ordered her to sit. Glancing down at her sketch, she felt hopeful for the first time in a long time. She wished she had her colored pencils so she could bring the piece to life and color the floor blue like the lake in her *H2Love* painting. Maybe moss on the walls would be better than ivy, she mused, then began erasing the delicate drawings. Darius walked into the living room, glancing over her shoulder.

"What's wrong with the design?" he asked.

Celina looked up at the tray of food he was holding in

his hands. He had fresh strawberries, blueberries, and apple chunks, along with two steaming bowls of fried rice. The smell of ginger and onions wafted through the air.

"This smells good," she said, abandoning her sketch pad. Darius set the tray on the table. Celina grabbed her bowl of rice. "I could get used to this, Mr. McRae."

"Don't. Do you know how hard it is to cook without meat?" he asked as he picked up the discarded sketch pad. "Why did you change this?"

"I don't want it to look too much like the Garden of Eden. I think we should base the design of the interior around *H2Love*," she said in between bites of rice. Darius nodded and wiped a stray grain of rice from her chin. "So, moss will work better than ivy."

"You're the artist," Darius said as he pulled a piece of fruit from the bowl.

"Do you like the idea, though? I need some feedback," she said. "We're in this together, remember?"

Darius rubbed her arm gently. "I totally trust your judgment. Whatever you want to do is fine. All I need to know is what materials you need," he said as he stuck his fork into his rice. "You're a genius and you know that."

"Flattery will get you everywhere," she said as she set down her empty bowl. A calm hush fell over them. For the first time in what felt like forever, it was okay to be still. She wasn't worried about Tiffany for the moment; she was with the man she loved. Everything was going to work out just fine because they had love, something Tiffany wouldn't understand if it bit her on the nose. Celina looked at Darius as he ate. She couldn't help but think of the turn her life had taken. His love had awakened a dormant part of her that she didn't realize existed. She knew every day with Darius wasn't going to be paradise, but she was willing to take the bitter along with the sweet. She'd given up the notion that love only brought hurt and pain, knowing that it wasn't love that hurt, but people with misplaced emotions. As she looked at him, she knew he would never hurt her. He would be her partner, her skilled lover, and her supporter. She would offer him the same devotion and dedication.

Darius caught Celina's stare. "What's wrong?" he asked.

"For a change, nothing," she replied, then lovingly embraced his smooth brown face. Darius grasped her hand and held it against his heart.

"Baby," he whispered. Celina leaned against his chest, feeling more connected to him than she had ever felt to anyone. Soon, Darius and Celina were sleeping in each other's arms, totally at peace.

CHAPTER 28

She moved like a black cat, blending in with the night. At first, she was afraid that she'd be caught, since the cops had been hot on her trail, but no one would expect her to camp out in the warehouse where Darius and Celina were going to create their future—a future that should've been hers.

Tiffany had gotten bold again, following Darius and Celina as they moved through Elmore. At first she was sorry about what had happened in Celina's house—she had lost control and attacked her when she only wanted to scare her into leaving but now she simply didn't care.

Any dreams Tiffany had of being with Darius were gone and it was the bushy-haired witch's fault. She knew attacking Celina was wrong and a better woman would have just let Darius walk away, but Tiffany didn't lose easily. Rejection was as foreign to her as a third-world country. She knew—at least a part of her did—that she had gone too far to turn back.

Before she completely vanished into the shadows, she was going to make her presence felt. Flicking her lighter as she entered the warehouse, she was giddy at the thought of watching the place burn. A car passed on the street, causing Tiffany to fall to her knees, so that she wouldn't be seen in the bright headlights. She knew it was one of the police officers that had been trying to find her these past few weeks. She knew these men and knew that they'd never had a manhunt before. These were the same men who would come into her shop while they were supposed to be patrolling the city and buy gifts for their wives, girlfriends, and other family members. She was more than confident that she wasn't going to be caught.

Celina sat straight up in the bed, waking from her sleep with a feeling of dread inching up her spine, followed by a feeling of nausea. Running into the bathroom, she vomited the contents of her dinner into the toilet bowl.

Darius followed her into the bathroom. "Sweetie, are you all right?"

Celina stood up and clutched the edge of the bathroom sink as she turned the water on to rinse her face off. "The strangest feeling just came over me," she said. "I don't know what it was or what to make of it."

"Are you sure you aren't . . ."

"Darius, I just got out of the hospital. I think they would have told me. I had every test imaginable run on me."

Darius folded his arms across his chest. "Then what do you think it is?"

Celina shrugged her shoulders, then headed for the bedroom. "Maybe something I ate," she said giggling.

"Hey," he said, following her into the bedroom. "You ate what I cooked."

"I rest my case," she replied as she crawled into bed.

He slid in behind her, encircling her waist with his arms and she leaned against him feeling totally relaxed.

"Maybe," he began, "you should go see the doctor in the morning just to make sure you don't have mad carrot disease or something."

She laughed and sucked her teeth, making a clucking sound. "You are so funny."

He kissed her on the back of her neck. "Go back to sleep," he said. "Did you tell your mother where you are?"

"Trust me, she knows," Celina said as she closed her eyes.

The next morning, Celina and Darius were awakened by a knock at the door. Celina looked at the clock. It was only five minutes after 6 AM. She nudged Darius. "Someone is at the door," she said.

He slowly rolled over. "What time is it?" he asked as he stretched and looked at the clock. "It's too early. They can come back."

The knocking continued. Celina nudged him again. "It might be an emergency," she said. Reluctantly, Darius got out of the bed and headed for the front door, with Celina on his heels, wondering if it was the police with news about Tiffany. He opened the door and saw Rena standing there with a scowl on her face.

"I told her to call you," he said as he stepped aside and let her walk in.

"That's not why I'm here," she said. "The police called. Someone broke into the gallery."

"What?" Celina said. "When?"

Rena shook her head angrily and then sat down on the sofa. "I know that woman did it," she said. "She's still here in Elmore and the police can't find her, but she can break into the gallery."

Celina shook her head side to side. "I can't believe this."

"I'm just glad that you were here with Darius," she said. "The police said they don't know if it was Tiffany for sure, but they're investigating that."

Darius rolled his eyes. "Sure they are. They're always investigating something but they never do anything."

"Don't you get into trouble," Rena said as she watched Darius pace the floor back and forth. "The police want you two to come over and look at the space and make sure nothing was taken and survey the damage."

Celina folded her arms under her breasts. "Fine. We'll go, but not until later."

Rena smiled tensely. "Okay. Are you all coming over for breakfast? You know John was worried about you when he didn't find you in your bedroom."

Celina laughed and hugged her mother. "All right, we'll be there for breakfast," she said. Darius smiled and waved good-bye to Rena. "We'd better get dressed and go next door," he said as he headed to the bathroom.

Celina watched him as he walked away and shivered as she thought about Tiffany being back. Maybe that was the reason she had suddenly woken up; and maybe she was sick because she knew Tiffany was back.

Darius watched Celina as she dressed and the only thought he had was that he must keep her safe. There was no doubt that Tiffany was the one who'd broken into the gallery space.

"What's wrong?" Celina asked when she caught Darius's stare.

"You know it was Tiffany who broke into the warehouse."

Celina picked at her hair with her fingers. "I'm sure it was her, but what can we do about it?" she asked as

Darius pulled a T-shirt over his head. "All we can do is hope Chief Wayman will do his job."

Darius rolled his eyes. "They've done a great job so far. Celina, I don't want you out of my sight, because if she hurts you again, I don't know what I would do."

She walked over to him. "Let's not think about that. We just have to be cautious until that lunatic is locked up. When we talk to the police, we'll find out what is going on. Now, let's get next door before my mother comes back in a panic."

When Darius and Celina arrived next door, Rena and John were sitting at the kitchen table drinking coffee. "Good morning, love birds," John said as he sipped his coffee. Rena smiled at the two of them. Darius joined John at the table while Rena and Celina got breakfast. John turned to Darius. "You haven't gotten into any more trouble with the law, have you?" John asked. "Rena said the police called here looking for Celina."

"No, sir. Someone broke into our warehouse," Darius explained.

John shook his head and lay his hand flat on the table. "It was that woman, wasn't it?"

Darius nodded. "I'm sure it was," he replied.

John rubbed his forehead thoughtfully, then rocked back in his seat. "We have to do something," he whispered. "I know I told you to stay aboveboard, but if the police can't find this woman, someone has to."

Rena and Celina walked over to the table with two plates of grits, scrambled eggs with cheese, and waffles. "What are you two plotting over here?" Celina asked, causing Rena to raise her eyebrow suspiciously.

"Nothing," John said with a smile. "I was just telling Darius how I'm getting fat with all of this southern comfort. My beautiful wife doesn't cook like this in Chicago."

Rena rolled her eyes. "And don't get used to it,

either," she said. "Darius, do you want some bacon or sausage?"

"No, ma'am," he replied. "This is more than enough."

Celina sat beside Darius and leaned over to whisper in his ear. "You know I don't believe a word you and John just said."

Darius feigned a look of astonishment, but he didn't say anything. *This woman knows me too well.*

Watching Darius as he ate, Celina knew that he and John were planning something. As they sat at the table, John and Darius laughed like old friends, but there was something underneath those smiles. Celina cut into her waffle, never taking her eyes off Darius and John as they whispered to one another.

"When are you two going to talk to the police about the break-in?" Rena asked.

John cleared his throat. "Why don't you let me and Darius handle this? Before you start, I know you can take care of yourself, but I have some choice words for the chief."

Celina raised her eyebrow. "Okay, John, but both of you need to stay out of jail."

John and Darius rose to their feet quickly and headed for the door. "We'll be back," John said before the door closed behind them.

"Those two are up to something," Rena said as she started clearing the dishes.

Celina nodded in agreement.

"So," Rena began. "Do you think you're going to like living here again?"

Celina smiled and shrugged her shoulders as she thought about her mother's question. This place that she'd never wanted to come back to as a child was the place where her life had changed, where she fell in love, made peace with her father, and came to grips with her hang-ups about love.

"Yeah," she replied with a smile. "Despite what has happened lately, this is a good place."

Rena had a far-off look in her eyes as she glanced at her daughter. Finally, she said, "You and Darius remind me of me and Thomas, before the infidelities. Your father and I were so in love, we couldn't bear to be apart. Maybe we were married too young. I mean, we were only nineteen and neither of us had experienced the world. At least you and Darius have been around enough to know that you've found what you're looking for." Rena stroked Celina's hair and beamed. "I'm so happy for you, baby girl. This is what you needed, someone who would show you just how good love is. Now, if this woman would go away, you and Darius could concentrate on each other, the gallery, and your wedding without having to look over your shoulders every day."

Celina nodded in agreement as she helped her mother wash the dishes. "This is going to be over soon. The police are going to get their act together and find Tiffany. Then Darius and I can have the life we deserve."

"I hope you're right and I hope those men aren't going to spend the night in a jail cell. Who do they think they're fooling? I know the two of them have linked up to form their own search party for Tiffany. They're probably nowhere near that police station."

She dried her hands on a dish towel. "I think I'd better go to the police department and check on Darius and John."

"Celina, be careful," Rena said as she watched her daughter walk out the door.

Zooming down the street, Celina headed for the police department, hoping John and Darius hadn't gotten arrested. But Celina had her suspicions about where her stepfather and her fiancé were. All their whispering at breakfast told her that they were going to do a lot more than just talk to the police. *Those men are not slick, I know that they're up to something.*

Despite the fact that she should've been on her guard about Tiffany, Celina headed to the warehouse. This woman wasn't going to destroy her dream. Celina and Darius had worked too hard to allow Tiffany to terrorize them. Celina circled around the warehouse before she stopped. The place looked as if it was secure. She was a little surprised to see that Darius and John weren't there. *Where are they,* she thought as she stopped the car and got out.

Walking to the front door, Celina kept looking over her shoulder, expecting Tiffany to leap out of the shadows. As she suspected, she knew they weren't there because she didn't see Darius's vehicle parked in the small lot.

As she unlocked the door to the warehouse and walked in, Celina was happy to see that nothing had been damaged on the inside. But she did notice that the rear door lock had been damaged.

"Tiffany!" she called out. "If you are in here, just give it up. I'm tired of this and I'm not going to hide from you or run from you ever again. If you're in here, come out!" Standing in the middle of the warehouse in a karate stance, she waited for Tiffany to make an appearance. After a few moments where nothing happened, Celina walked out of the warehouse, but she was sure Tiffany was somewhere close by.

Crouching in John's rental car, Darius and the older man kept an eye on Tiffany's house. Darius and John had taken the rental car because it would be easier for them to fly under the police's radar than if they'd gone in Darius's. More than two hours had passed and there was no sign of Tiffany at her house.

"Do you think she'd actually come here?" John asked.

Darius nodded. "If she was bold enough to break into the gallery, I think so. There's something she's going to need from this house."

"When we see her, what are we going to do?"

"Call the chief so the police can finally do their job."

John nodded. "I'll be glad when this is over and you and Celina can focus on what's important."

Darius smiled. He couldn't wait for the day when the only thing he and Celina would have to worry about was planning their wedding.

John looked at Darius intently. "Celina is like a daughter to me and I don't want to see her hurt. So, you'd better protect her heart with the same fury you're protecting her with now."

"I will," Darius replied. "I know how hard it was for Celina to give her heart to me and I would never do anything to make her regret that decision."

"You'd better not," John warned. "Because I would have to come back here and hurt you. Baby girl needs happiness in her life and I know you can give it to her."

Nodding, Darius shook hands with John before they turned their attention to the house.

After a few more hours of watching the house and seeing nothing, they headed for the police station. Once they arrived, Darius boldly walked into the chief's office without even letting his secretary announce him.

"Darius," the chief said in an exasperated tone. "You're here about the break-in, aren't you?"

Darius nodded. "This is Celina's stepfather, John Malcolm," Darius said. The chief stood up and extended his hand to John, but his gesture was not returned.

"When are you going to find the woman who hurt my

stepdaughter?" he snapped. "You know she broke into the warehouse."

Chief Wayman ran his hand over his face and sighed. "We don't have any proof that it was Tiffany, but she is a suspect. Mr. Malcolm, what happened to Celina was tragic and we will bring Tiffany to justice, but you have to let us do our job," he said.

"And what are we supposed to do in the meantime? Live in fear?" John boomed. "I won't do it. If you all don't hurry up and find this woman, you're going to bring the south side of Chicago out of me."

Darius and John stormed out of the office and headed back to the house. Darius knew this mess was far from over.

CHAPTER 29

As the days passed, Celina and Darius spent more time planning their wedding and the gallery opening than worrying about Tiffany, though she still loomed over them like a dark cloud.

Celina toyed with a strand of hair as she watched the workers place the columns in the middle of the gallery. The place was starting to come together nicely. The walls had been painted sea green so that they would contrast with the ocean-blue carpet that would be installed later that afternoon. Celina had about three hours to turn the wall into a moss-covered forest before the carpet installers came. Dipping her brush into the green paint, she used quick strokes to finish the painting. A pair of hands roamed up and down her back.

Celina's lips curved into a smile. "Darius, I'm working," she said without turning around.

"And you look so good doing it," he said.

Celina turned around, wrapping her arms around his neck. "What a nice thing to say, but I don't have time to take a break."

Darius pulled Celina against his body and stared into her eyes. "There's always time for a break," he said, then playfully smacked her on the behind. "But you're right, we have a lot of work to do." He let her go, then turned to the workers, asking if they needed any help.

Celina headed outside to grab more painting supplies from her car. She looked toward the woods, wondering if someone was out there waiting to ruin everything she and Darius had worked for. *Don't worry about that woman,* she told herself as she opened the trunk of the car and headed back inside. With all of the people in the warehouse, she knew she was safe. When she walked inside, the columns were in place and she returned to her work and pretended not to notice when Darius sent the crew away for a break. After the five men left, he closed the door and slid the bar lock in place.

"Darius, I needed that light to paint this wall," she said as she dropped her brush.

He walked over to her with a smile on his face. "But I need something else," he said as he ran his index finger across her collarbone, traveling down the front of her overalls. Darius quickly kissed her before she could muster a protest. When her body responded to his touch, he knew that sending the crew away was the best decision he'd made all day. He unsnapped the hooks on her denim overall set, allowing the oversized jeans to fall from her petite body. Underneath, she wore a simple pair of black lace panties and a cropped T-shirt. As Darius lifted the shirt over her head, he was thrilled to see that her breasts were bare and ripe for his lips. Her nipples were erect, reminding him of juicy berries ready to be sucked, licked, and devoured.

Celina pressed her lips against his ear. "We're never going to get this place up and running like this." Then she reached down and pulled at the waistband of his nylon basketball shorts.

"If we're behind because of this—" He slipped his

hands between her legs, stroking her inner core with his thumb. "—I really won't care."

The tarp covering the floor became their love nest as Celina eased back, trying not to get the paint on her body, but not really caring whether or not she did, for it had been weeks since she and Darius had been intimate, because of her injuries. Now that she was healed, she yearned for him, hungered for his kiss and craved his touch.

"Is your back all right?" Darius asked as he covered her body with his.

Celina's reply was to suck on his bottom lip then flick her tongue across his top lip. "I'm fine," she replied. "I want you. I need you."

Those words made the nerves in his body sizzle, and he kissed her softly and then more aggressively, as he felt her arch her back against him. He reached between her thighs and felt her desire and Celina ached as she felt him throbbing against her thighs. Neither of them thought about the protection they needed as she stroked and caressed his manhood, guiding him to her center. Her body screamed "make love to me now" and Darius answered, thrusting his hips into hers, drowning in the warm wetness that was his woman. She shivered with burning desire, wrapping her legs around his waist, pulling him into her as if she wanted to make him disappear inside of her. That would've been fine with him because he could live inside her love forever. Being with Celina opened his heart to so much and made him want things that he'd ignored in the past.

Making love to her, he thought about a family, their son or daughter and growing old with Celina by his side. Feeling her against his body, her round hips against his, drove him mad with desire. She did things to his body and made him feel pleasure that he'd never known.

With his head thrown back in ecstasy, he cried out, "Oh, I love you."

She arched her back, wanting to say the same thing back to him, but the words died in the back of her throat, as she reached her climax and every emotion that she felt seemed to spill out of her. Darius had become more than a lover—he was her protector, her friend, and she couldn't wait for him to be her husband. They lay on the floor wrapped in each other's arms. Celina grabbed a dry paintbrush and began stroking it back and forth across Darius' chest.

"How long did you send the crew away for?" she asked.

"About an hour," he replied, grabbing her hand and placing it on his chest. Celina stroked his chest and leaned against his shoulder.

"I never knew I could feel this way," she whispered.

Darius glanced down at her. "And how is that?"

"Loved. Totally and completely loved. You wrapped your love around me when I really didn't want you to. I came here angry with my father, sure that every man in the world was out to hurt the woman he professed to love. But you," she said, pressing her palm against his cheek. "You proved me wrong. Thank you."

Darius kissed her hand. "I didn't know I had that effect on you, and you changed my life, too. I've never had a woman that I could relax and be myself around or know that the only thing you want from me is my love. I've met so many women who wanted what they thought I represented. You love me because of me, not my money or anything else."

Celina squeezed Darius tightly. "So, what are we waiting for? Let's get married so that we can start on our happily ever after," she whispered.

"What are you saying?"

"We have about a week left to finish this place. I want to get married here. This is our place, a place of love."

Darius kissed Celina gently on the lips. "As you wish, my dear. We'll get married right before the grand opening."

She wrapped her arms around his neck and squeezed him tightly and then climbed on top of him and ran her fingers down his wrists. She felt him throb against her, then he pressed into her and captured her lips, savoring her sweetness. A soft moan escaped her throat as his tongue danced in her mouth. She rocked her body back and forth against him, drawing him inside her. Then, as if he wanted to send her over the edge, he reached up and teased her nipples with the tip of his tongue, sending a shock through her system. Darius pressed his pelvis into hers and when she tightened her love walls around him, he released himself with a satisfied groan. Darius grabbed her waist, pulling her against his chest, and she fell against him and sighed. He clutched her, following a bead of sweat down the small of her back with his fingertip. They rocked back and forth, basking in the afterglow of their lovemaking.

"We'd better get dressed," Celina whispered. "I would be so embarrassed if the crew came back and found out what kind of work we've been doing."

Darius kissed her collarbone and smiled. "If this is work, then how are we going to follow it up with some fun and games?" She turned around and smiled at him.

"I can think of a few ways . . . later tonight, I might even show you," she replied.

When the crew returned, Darius and Celina were sure they could tell what had transpired while they were gone. As Celina tried to focus on her painting, her mind drifted back to Darius and the way he made her feel. Her wanton thoughts of ripping his clothes off in the middle of the gallery in front of the workers made her cheeks warm. Celina dropped her brush and headed outside. She needed some fresh air to clear her head so that she could get back to work. Just as she expected, Darius walked out behind her.

"Are you all right?" he asked.

"I just needed some air," she said. "It was getting a little stuffy in there." He stroked her shoulder. She turned around and smiled at him. "You think they know?" she whispered.

Darius shrugged his shoulders. "Who cares? You're the woman I love and if all of those people in there know we made love, I don't care."

She kissed him on the nose. "I agree. I've got to get back to work," she said as she turned toward the door.

Darius and Celina toiled in the gallery for the rest of the day. Celina finished the water scene on the walls just as the sun began to set. Darius walked the crew outside. Celina stood in the middle of the space and closed her eyes. She envisioned the walls filled with her work and the work of local artists. Her picture, *H2Love*, along with a portrait of Thomas, would anchor the center of the gallery. Celina smiled and rocked back and forth. In her mind's eye she saw patrons walking into the gallery, oohing and ahing over the art.

"I hope that smile is for me," Darius said, breaking into her thoughts. Celina opened her eyes, still smiling.

"I was just daydreaming about our grand opening."

Darius pulled Celina into his arms and gently kissed her nose.

"I love that sparkle in your eyes. I've missed that," he said.

"We've had so much craziness going on in our lives. I just can't wait for normal."

"It's coming," he replied.

"She's still out there, watching us, waiting to hurt us again," Celina whispered.

"Tiffany can't hurt us," he said as he gently stroked her back. "We have each other and nothing is going to come between us. We can take whatever she throws at us."

From the rear of the gallery in the woods, deep enough not to be seen, but close enough to hear everything that was going on around her, Tiffany steamed as she listened to Darius and Celina talk about what she couldn't do.

You think so, she thought. *You're not going to have a day of happiness. If she wants to be Mrs. Darius McRae, then she's going to suffer right along with him. No one chooses someone else over me and embarrasses me the way Darius has since that tramp wiggled her way into his life.*

If Tiffany had been honest with herself, she would've taken stock of all that she'd lost. Her business had closed down because she spent so much time following Darius, and then there was the talk of the police watching her. No one in Elmore wanted anything to do with her. Squaring her shoulders, Tiffany thought that if she was going out, she'd do it with a bang.

CHAPTER 30

The smell of gas was faint, but it had been spread throughout the building. Tiffany, who didn't smoke, pulled out a cigarette and put it between her lips. The nicotine tingled against her mouth. It didn't matter, though. Tiffany wasn't going to smoke; she just wanted to make sure the gallery went up in smoke. She was certain no one had seen her break in and by the time they figured out that she did it, she would be in Mexico. She patted her hip pocket where her ticket to San Pedro was. Just as she was about to strike the match, floodlights flashed on, shining on her. Tiffany was trapped like a deer in the crosshairs of a hunter's gun.

"All right, Tiffany, come out with your hands up," Chief Wayman exclaimed. "The game is over." Three officers burst into the gallery before Tiffany could run out.

"Put the matches down," an officer said, pointing his gun at her. Tiffany did as she was told. Another officer moved in quickly and handcuffed her. The chief walked in and looked at her and shook his head in disgust.

"Was it worth it? You threw your life away over a man who doesn't love you," he said.

Tiffany dropped her head, unable to respond.

"Get her out of here." Wayman pulled out his cell phone and called Darius.

Darius took the plate of fried chicken from Rena's hands and placed it in the middle of the table. "This looks good, Mrs. Malcolm," he said, inhaling deeply.

"Boy, if you don't start calling me Rena or Mom, I'm going to hit you," she said as she set a bowl of potato salad on the table. "Celina," she called out. "How much longer are you going to be in the bathroom?"

John laughed as he placed Rena's freshly baked rolls on the table beside the chicken. "You know that girl was covered in paint, just like she used to be when she was a child."

Rena rolled her eyes and sucked her teeth. "Darius, I hope you are ready to have paint specks in every corner of your house. I knew that girl had to be successful because she owes me for years of replacing furniture."

Celina walked into the kitchen, dressed in a white T-shirt dress. "Talking about me again?" she asked as she twisted one of her ponytails. Before Rena could respond, Darius's cell phone rang.

"Turn that thing off," Rena said. "I absolutely hate cell phones at the dinner table."

He was about to follow her instructions and shut the phone off, until he saw the number displayed on the phone. "I'll turn it off after I take this call. It's the police chief." Darius put the phone to his ear. "Yeah? What? Where? Gasoline, but there was no fire, right?"

Celina focused her concerned stare on Darius, especially when she heard the words gasoline. Had any of her paintings been damaged by the gas? "What's going on?" she mouthed. Darius held up his index finger, telling her to hold on.

"So, she's in custody," Darius said. "Thank goodness. It's finally over. We can check on the place in the morning, I just want to see her in handcuffs. No, chief, I am going to the detention center. After the hell she put us through, I want to see her." Darius snapped the phone shut and turned to Celina. "They caught Tiffany tonight."

"Thank God," Rena exclaimed. "Where was she? How did she hide for so long?"

Darius reached over and picked up a roll and broke it apart. "I don't know, but she was in the gallery again."

"What?" Celina exclaimed. "Did she mess with anything? Is everything all right there?"

"Well," Darius said as he popped a piece of bread into his mouth. "Chief said he thinks she was going to burn the place down."

Celina ran her hand over her face and mumbled a string of profanities that made her mother flinch. "Where is she?" Celina demanded.

"At the Elmore City Jail," Darius said.

Celina took off like a shot of lightning, leaving her fiancé in her wake. By the time he made it outside, Celina was backing out of the driveway. Not knowing what she was going to do, Darius headed next door and grabbed his car. He tried to catch up with Celina, who was doing a great impression of Jeff Gordon as she tore through the city streets. Deciding that she was going to the jail, Darius slowed his car and prayed that she didn't crash or get pulled over as she headed there.

Celina wanted to see Tiffany in handcuffs and she wanted to slap her until her cheeks turned beet red, but she knew she wouldn't be able to do that. She pulled into the jail's parking lot, stretching her car over two spots. Celina ran inside, looking like a Flo Jo clone.

"Where is she?" she demanded when she approached the sergeant's desk.

"Lady, what are you talking about?" The man asked in between bites of his sandwich.

"Tiffany Martin," she snapped. "She was arrested and I want to see her."

"Are you her lawyer?" the man asked, setting his sandwich on the desk and wiping a glob of mustard from his chin.

Celina rolled her eyes and placed her hands on her hips. "No, I'm her victim."

Darius burst through the doors and knew that look he saw on Celina's face.

"Celina, calm down," he said, walking up behind her and slipping his arms around her waist to stop her from leaping over the desk. "Where is the chief?"

"He ain't here. Now, I don't have time to babysit the two of you," the sergeant snapped.

"Yeah, your sandwich might get lonely," Celina retorted.

Darius whispered in her ear for her to calm down as he called Chief Wayman.

Celina folded her arms and looked at him. "Darius, I just want to see her," she said. "I want to find out why she did this to us."

"Baby, she's in jail, let's just let the police handle it. Tiffany isn't going to tell us anything. I just want to make sure she is in custody so that we can continue with our lives. She can't and won't hurt us again."

His words calmed her because she knew he was right. Tugging at her ponytails, she exhaled loudly and said, "This is over. You promise me that this is over because I don't know how much more of this I can take."

Chief Wayman walked into the detention center. "I

knew when you called me that you two were here," he said. "I can't let you see Tiffany, but here's her arrest report. It's public record and proof that we have her in custody." Celina took the papers from his hands and read the list of charges against her. Tiffany was charged with aggravated assault, breaking and entering, and attempted arson. Satisfied, and sure that Tiffany would spend a lot of time in jail, Celina wanted to go home. Before she and Darius left, she turned to Chief Wayman, "Keep her away from me and my gallery. And, Chief Wayman, thanks."

He tipped his hat to Celina. "You're welcome," he said then waved good-bye to the couple.

ONE YEAR LATER

Celina stood at the door of the gallery, eyes closed, holding her breath. She placed her hand on the knob. "That door isn't going to open itself, Mrs. McRae," Darius said as he held her from behind.

"I'm nervous," she said.

"Why? Half the town saw the gallery when we got married three months ago," he said. "And they loved it then." Darius ran his hand across her belly. Celina leaned her head on his shoulder.

"But this is my first showing of new work that captures how I see Elmore. What if they don't like it?" she said as she placed her hand on top of his. "I hope you're not getting used to this flat tummy, because if I'm anything like my mother, I'm going to blow up in my sixth month," she said.

Darius continued to rub his pregnant wife's stomach. "I can't wait," he said, kissing her on the neck. "Now open this door."

Celina turned the key in the lock and opened the door. She inhaled deeply before she pushed the door open. Inside, there were paintings that spanned Celina's career. She had just finished an oil painting of Thomas.

He was standing with his arms folded, wearing a charcoal suit and matching bowler hat. He had a big smile on his face. Celina felt that smile was for her, Darius, and their unborn child. On the day of the grand opening of the Thomas Hart Memorial Art Gallery, she knew her father had been smiling down on her. She turned to Darius and watched him as he flipped the lights on.

"Darius," she said.

He looked up at his wife and smiled. "Yes, ma'am?"

Celina walked over to him and kissed his lips gently. "I love you," she said. "I love you so much."

Darius caressed her cheek. "Tell me something I don't already know," he said, then picked her up and twirled her around. Celina basked in the glow of his love, his touch, and his warmth, happy that she had opened her heart to his love. She knew as long as she had Darius's love on her side, anything was possible.